# Rendezvous
# on the
# Opal Fields

Helen van Rooijen

Other Books by this Author

Rendezvous at Lock 6

ISBN-13: 978-0-6487261-4-2

# DEDICATION

To Martin...always

.

# ACKNOWLEDGMENTS

As always I have been assisted in this book by many wonderful people.

Editing my dyslexic efforts has fallen to Martin, my husband, and Penny, who did not want to be acknowledged, but who was a fabulous help. Thank you.

As before Martin van Rooijen designed the front cover after much discussion and proof examples. He also took the photo of Port Lincoln on the back cover.

Derek Hayman, with years of experience in light planes, seemed to take delight in discussing plane types with me. I hadn't told him the complete truth about how I wanted to use this information or rather what aeroplane would allow me to use a devious idea that I harbored as a means of disposing of unwanted items. Mike, another aviation buff, discussed another area of plane construction and also answered my medical questions. He didn't want to be mentioned either. Thank you gentlemen.

After a sudden medical necessitated flight to Adelaide with the Royal Flying Doctor Service a year or so ago (thank you) I used this experience to my own novelist ends in a way that I'm sure that the RFD would not do nor approve. But a writer uses every event that comes her way! This one does anyway. I do have a little previous experience in medical aviation working as a St John Volunteer Air Attendant which, I felt, gives me a little latitude.

Mary Gudzenovs has, once again, put my manuscript into format for publishing and Eyre Writers have encouraged me, especially the fellow novelists attending retreats at Trinity Haven, north of Port Lincoln. Thank you to my writing friends, Diane, Alison, Aileen, Kathy, Mary, Carol and Christine.

My family and friends have been supportive and patient with my need to write over the years. Thank you. One day my grandchildren may even be old enough to read my work. Not yet...

I wish to thank also my readers, who have been most complimentary although some look at me a bit 'sideways' these days after reading *Rendezvous at Lock 6*. This previous book was set in Port Lincoln and the Murray River, out of Renmark and I left a little story twist to write this sequel

Also as previously I have used actual places in my novel. I live in Port Lincoln; have lived in Whyalla, and have visited the fabulous Coober Pedy. Who doesn't adore opal? Any location errors and mistakes are all mine - and Mr Google's. However all my characters are just that; characters lurking from my imagination onto the computer and page, as are the events, homicidal, police procedural etc.

If I offend anyone with the names chosen for characters then I apologize in advance. The naming of a person comes from much contemplation and delving into books - fitting a name to a character, never any association to a living or deceased person.

Helen van Rooijen

Port Lincoln, South Australia

# Chapter 1

Red lipstick.

Blood red lipstick.

She wasn't used to wearing lipstick anymore, especially not red lipstick, but tonight it was essential.

There was no other way she could do what she had to do and, damn it she thought, it was a long time since Hood had seen her. Maybe he would recognize her but they'd only met once. Just briefly and it was typical of the man that he'd tried to seduce her then. Mesmerized by drugs into thinking she was in love with his brother Sean, she'd seen things; things she shouldn't have, and been appalled and afraid. After she was arrested on trumped up minor charges she co-operated with the police to appear as a witness against the brothers in an aborted pre-trial. Neither Hood nor Sean had even attended the Sydney Court that day, just sent their shonky lawyers and a hit man.

When Hood had put a kill contract on her life she was placed into the safety of the Police Protection Program in Adelaide. Someone had a sense of irony, or was it humour, and for more than a year, the teaching nun's life had been a good disguise.

People rarely look at a nun's face.

Rarely remember a nun's face.

People remembered just the plain habit or the simple clothing of the orders, and her fresh washed face wasn't quite beautiful enough to stun the world or be noticed specifically. With make up her long lashed and striking deep blue eyes, above high cheek bones, flashed into life. Without it, her pale freckled skin looked sallow and uninteresting. But tonight she wouldn't be using a disguise.

She wanted him to recognize her.

To recognize her and be afraid...

And the red lipstick was one she had confiscated from a school girl's hands and, at the time, she'd thought that the girl was a little slut. That was a laugh! How her thinking had been changed in the convent. Sluttish! There were reasons and she'd been that when she was the same age. Now the lipstick was exactly what she needed. She shook her long dark auburn curls free of the pins that held it in place all day and, turning before the small mirror, pulled stray strands down to frame each side of her face. Thank goodness, they no longer cut a nun's hair. She fluffed the remaining hair and let it fall down onto her shoulders. Not too bad, she thought.

Maybe it was still enough to interest him. Enough to get close to him. Close enough to kill...

With the scarlet lipstick.

She shrugged out the plain petticoat that she wore under her grey skirt and blue shirt, and near naked, slipped on a black silk evening slip she'd kept in a suitcase of clothes and belongings hidden under her meagre wooden wardrobe waiting for the time she could use them. The silk number slid with a whisper against her body, cool as a breeze, and she took a moment to let the feel of the exquisite material relax her nerves. The nerves tightly woven as the strands of silk, stretched fragile, thin and dark as the night outside.

As she moved towards the bed to pick up her black glow-mesh evening bag her clock ticked the midnight hour over into a new day. The innocent looking bag only just concealed a slight bulge of a loaded 'ladies' pistol. Innocent? Hardly! That pistol could prompt a laugh or a smirk if seen by people who didn't know how lethal the gun was in her hands. With the contract out on her life a police expert had taught her how to protect herself and she had been a natural. Tonight she planned to be at close enough range to make use of the gun and the training; at whatever the cost.

With regret she pulled the golden wedding ring that was part of her disguise off her finger and left it under the white cotton pillows on her bed. The ring symbolised her leap from the secular world into one where she had been safe and protected.

She twisted the red lipstick case and shuddered a shiver of sick dread as the red lozenge rose. Surely it wouldn't come to that, she thought, and applied a slick of colour.

Not enough!

She slashed the red across her mouth. If that was how the Boss expected women to look, then that's how she would appear.

Rhette Ryan wouldn't be sleeping in safety tonight.

Maybe never again.

Twelve months previously...

Kate Ryan lay amongst dry fallen leaves and twigs. She barely stirred as the sun speckled morning light through a sparse canopy of branches above onto her pale face. Her skin glowed as clear as a child's. Silver shards bounced off an evening bag that lay in the leafy debris beside her and a teasing breeze swirled to flip her blonde curls into a halo of moving hair tendrils.

The attention of a fly to a cut with dried blood above her eye irritated her. She raised an instinctive hand and flapped at it. Her own movement woke her further and she shivered and attempted to pull the skirt of an inadequate sequined disco dress down to cover her knees. Her knees stung and as she straightened her legs her joints were stiff with grazes, bruises, and skin that had been concertina-ed into ridges and hollows of dried blood.

She groaned and struggled to sit up.

The planet whirled about her as she opened her eyes. It throbbed and thudded into her head and she forgot about her knees and raised her hands to ward off the light that flooded pain into the retinas behind her eyes. A spreading pain that pinched in behind her ears like far too tight spectacle frame wings.

She flung her body sideways to hands and knees as she heaved, then cursed and gagged.

She passed out again.

Later, lying back against the roughness of tree bark, she forced open her eyes again to look around. The park, she assumed it was a park, usually she was dumped in a park, after they had finished with her drunk and drugged body, was not as usual. Sure there were trees, grass and autumnal drying. She wasn't sure why she had noticed that it was autumn, seasons mattered little any more. Something was different. She could hear birds, far off the insistence of a pair of crows cawed and moaned to each other, but something was missing.

She could hear no traffic noises.

No cars horns or the growl of buses. But she should have been able to hear traffic. Or the far off clatter of rubbish bins being emptied and thumped back down onto city footpaths.

Nothing.

It was deadly quiet.

Always there were road noises even on a Sunday morning. She thought it was Sunday as she'd been to the nightclub in Kings Cross on the Saturday night. Or had it been a Friday? She couldn't remember. Thirst dragged her tongue around her mouth searching for moisture. It was as dry as the crisp leaves under her hands. Drier.

She swore; the words explicit and repeated. The bastards had dumped her in the bush. Outside Sydney. Maybe they thought she was dead this time, dead in her attempts to escape from the world. Running from the man who had turned her young love into a drug addiction and then turfed her out onto the streets. Her run was now fuelled by alcohol and drugs. Sex was always the payment the men took, and lately she had been openly soliciting in the clubs to pay for whatever drug relief she could get her hands on.

She needed to find her way out from where ever she was; get herself cleaned up before she had to face the counsellor, her youth counsellor, on Monday morning. An appointment to try to convince a judge and the court that she was OK. She wasn't OK, but cleaned up and in her best demure dress she could charm most courts. On one occasion she'd charmed the pants off one gentleman judge and got the probation sentence she wanted. She was past that shame and the thought rattled around her head in a rare burst of irony.

She swore as another surge of nausea erupted up from her empty stomach. The acid of bile bit into her throat and pulsed the back of her tongue.

She went to hands and knees again, grabbed at the tree to steady herself, then slid down as her legs refused to hold her up. She lay there a while longer. Drifted off.

An hour later she was searching for her bag.

Maybe the bastards hadn't found it. Or had left her something.

The first john of the night had followed her from the dance floor. He'd been generous to her childlike face and body and she'd scored well before she went back to dance some more, already high enough to be able to forget him. The last one had been younger and strikingly handsome. She had an inkling she'd seen his face somewhere before. It was enough for her to go outside with him. He'd taken her hard against a rough brick wall of the club then pushed her into a car. An expensive car. He'd ignored her and she curled up into the sumptuous soft leathers. He started the engine and pulled away from the club. That was all she could remember.

It didn't matter.

It was her bag she wanted.

She grunted in triumph as she located it. Empty of everything but yes, a stash, her stash she'd been collecting all night. Use some - put some away for the morning crash and the numbing slump. She found it in the torn crevice she'd made in the lining of the once expensive bag. There was more there than she remembered but that didn't matter. A bonus.

The white crystals seemed to glow in the soft light as she poured them out onto her shaking palm. She tipped her head back and her tongue curled around the crystals, all of them. They seemed to make their own saliva and Kate swallowed. The white crystals seemed to glow in the soft light as she poured them onto her shaking palm. She tipped her head back and her tongue curled around the crystals, all of them. They seemed to make their own saliva and e

After the first glorious rush - darkness came early that day - and it was final.

The death was not unusual and hardly warranted an extensive post mortem. Another young female overdose. Testing involved blood, urine, vaginal and skin scrapings, but the DNA analysis was too complex to look for sperm and locating the partners she'd had before her death. A pity - but in the realm of young women and drug O/Ds the police and the courts were busy enough. Samples were kept as per policy. It took weeks for her to be identified and her body collected for burial. By then her case was filed and forgotten.

# Chapter 2

Present Time

Ana Foster was happy. Content probably was the better word with a smattering of lingering apprehension about her decision.

The time had come for her to make life changes after four years of marking time.

Piet was contemplating the lump his big fire truck made where he'd buried it in his sand pit. The ladder was just exposed. With toddler podgy hands he pushed another scoop of sand over the vehicle, arranged other cars and trucks around it, and sat back on his heels. It was fun to hide his truck in the sand. To play a trick on his mother. Hiding things was his delight and his favorite game was always 'hide and seek'. Ana smiled as she arched backwards to straightened her back; packing up a house was hard work and she took a moment to watch her three year old son.

'Mummy! Mummy! I've lost my fire truck,' Piet said.

She laughed and pushed a tuft of white back behind her right ear to join it up with her straight fall of dark brown, almost black, hair. 'Are you sure?' she asked.

He thought for a moment. Then he started as a swish of large wings ended with a thump. A bird landed on a contraption that resembled an out of place TV antennae on the garden lawn. 'Mummy look! The kookaburra is here,' Piet shouted. 'Can we give him his dinner?'

'I'll get the meat,' Ana said.

She went back into the house and retrieved a handful of red minced meat balls from the freezer. When she returned to the deck the single kookaburra had been joined by two more. The handsome birds sat watching Piet intently. As usual her protective instincts cut in as she looked at their size and their huge strong beaks. Beaks which could catch and smash a snake against rocks. 'Remember to stay still, now,' she said unnecessarily to her child.

She went down the steps and stood at his side. Tall, slim, in jeans and a crisp blue shirt, she was a contrast to the healthy softness of the little boy in his denim romper suit. A stray strand of hair caught a glimmer of sunlight and lit up fairer than his dark cap of hair. She resisted the urge to tease it back before he brushed it out of his face with his own sandy hands.

The kookaburras' attention was now on the meat balls. These would take only a few moments to thaw before they would throw them onto the lawn grass for the birds.

'There's Mrs Mac,' Piet said as an elderly woman came out onto her own deck next door over looking their garden. She waved. 'Will Mrs Mac remember to feed my kookaburras when we've gone?' Piet said his face solemn.

'I'm sure she will,' Ana said. 'The meat's ready. You can throw a piece for them now.'

Piet took a meat ball and squeezed it. It had thawed and soft enough to his satisfaction. With a grunt of effort he tossed it about three metres away from his feet. One huge bird swooped down, picked up the meatball and, after tapping it on the ground, flew with it back to the perch to eat it. Like a group of polite diners the birds, one after another, came down to take the meat. When they had eaten three pieces each Ana showed them her empty hands. The first bird to arrive, not quite as immaculate as the apparently younger birds, threw back its head and began the wind up to the characteristic kookaburra call.

'He's laughing for me,' Piet said in delight. One of the other birds joined in and the riotous laughter filled the garden. Ana had passed on her passion for birds to her son already and it delighted her.

'Yes, that's it. Now we'd better get back to packing your toys because this afternoon...'

'The men are coming to pack up the house. And all my toys...I'd better find my fire truck,' Piet said. He scrabbled in the sand. 'Mustn't leave that here.'

'And where are they going to?' Ana asked.

'To Darwin.'

'And why are we going to Darwin?'

'Because you've got a new job in Darwin. In the hostible.'

Ana hugged him to her with a chuckle. Most children struggled saying hospital and Pietie did too. 'Hospital,' she corrected gently.

# Chapter 3

The red brick house was in a shabby public housing estate. Two concrete strips, with dead thistles and straggling weeds between, marched down the side of the yard that formed the driveway. The scrap of uneven grass littered with broken children's toys and rusting bits of old car bodies, passed for a lawn.

There had been an attempt at gardening between the driveway and the fence where a geranium had been poked into the soil and a few pansy seeds had been sown. The flowers lifted their yellow and blue heads to the sun. Parsley stood brave and green in a cracked black plastic pot by the front door.

A twenty plus year old grey Holden, with patches of rust creeping along the back windscreen and an obvious ding on the rear right hand door, pulled into the drive. Donna Travers got out of the driver's seat. In her mid twenties she was scraggy thin and her dishwater blonde hair was scrunched back into a rubber band bound pony tail. A faded pink tee shirt left a gap above her old jeans and a similar coloured nail polish adorned her toes. Red rubber thongs slapped the ground as she slammed the door shut.

'You there Jason?' she shouted. She opened the car boot and struggled to lift out four heavy plastic bags of shopping. 'Jason? Give us a hand will you!' She yelled again. Louder. 'Jason!' She hefted the bags inside to the kitchen kicking the door shut as she went.

Donna grunted as she struggled to lift the heavy bags onto the table.

A drab cream coloured kitchen reflected the sparseness of the whole house. The red Laminex table and chairs were never a set and the chairs, cheap and plastic were from a hardware store's outdoors section. The cupboard, the glass panels showing mismatched plates, cups and glasses, belonged to the 70's - an old 70's not a stylish 'new design' 70's. The stove, part of the house, was new and bright. It looked as if it didn't want to belong there surrounded by the rest of the drab furniture.

A small toddler played noisily with saucepan lids on the grubby linoleum floor.

His face was dirty, snot nosed, but his light brown hair was shiny. His blue overalls clean that morning, advertised his breakfast of cocoa puffs cereal. He chuckled to himself as he spun the lids and watched the play of light from the window on the metal. Loud rap music, a TV and other children's voices were a cacophony of noise coming from other rooms in the house.

Donna bent to the child and gently ruffled his hair. 'Hey kiddo...' she said.

The boy responded with a toothless rubbery grin.

'That you Donna? Did yer get me beer?'

'I got some beer. You owe me for it, Jason.' Donna yelled into the other room. She turned back and muttered, 'Fat chance of getting my money.'

She picked up a can of beer and started out of the kitchen. 'You could've helped me unload the car.'

'Well I was busy, wasn't I...?'

Busy? That'll be the day, she thought.

Donna stopped abruptly at the door of the next room and waited a moment for her eyes to adjust.

The room was dim. Twin beds had been pushed into a far corner and all the other bedroom furniture, toys and clothing, were piled up on top of the beds in an untidy heap. Since she had gone out shopping heavy duty metres wide aluminium foil had been stuck to the walls and floor and over the window with industrial tape. Everything was blacked out to the outside world. Boxes of varying sizes were stacked in a corner. Metal trays and pipes glinted. Glass glittered in the available light.

'Jason! Where the hell are you?'

All she could see of Jason, her partner, was the once white T shirt he was wearing. The one with the obnoxious message on it she was always threatening to use as a dust rag. He was behind boxes in the middle of the room. The loud rap music that blared out was coming from a large radio.

Jason appeared and shuffled in rap dance steps towards her.

He sang in rap. 'Hey, Girl - you did get me beer.' He took the bottle of beer from Donna's hand. Still he danced around her; he opened it and swallowed most of the beer in one gulp.

'You owe me... ' she said.

'I'll pay you when I get my cheque. I promise.'

'Yeah! Right!' Her eyes adjusted and Donna looked around the room. 'Just what the hell do you think you are doing?'

At a glance she'd summed up the scene. Lack of light or no lack of light. It was rhetorical question. She knew exactly what he was doing.

Jason snapped on a set of very bright overhead lights. The room was blinding and completely lined with silver foil. Enthusiastically he was still made dancing moves as he tried to impress her.

'We're gonna have a new crop. Here – with hydroponics this time.' He waved in an off hand gesture. 'The kids can move into the lounge room. He responded to Donna's speechless scowl. 'C'mon luv – it'll be easy money...'

'You bastard! You're bloody not!' She shouted.

She charged across the room and punched the 'off' button of the radio.

The loud racket ceased. The room was immediately quiet, except for TV sounds leaking in from the front room.

Donna grabbed his shirt front; stopped his dancing moves and held up a fist with the first finger up into his face for emphasis.

She let fly. 'First – the kids are not sleeping in the lounge. This's their bedroom.' Her
next indignant finger was thrust upward. 'And I'm not bloody forking out money from my pension for excess water and electricity like last time!'

Jason pulled free. His face tried for an earnest expression in protest. 'But Donna love...' He reached for her grinning as he tried to plant a kiss on her neck.

Donna pushed him roughly away. Cut him off. Another finger was thrust up into his face. 'Not this time!'

'Aw Love.'

'And old Mrs Warren'll catch on again. She's always nosing over the fence. She hates you. She'll call the police again – like she did with your music blaring all night long. And she's suspicious anyway of all those people who came before at all hours. Buying your weed.'

'Forget her... I'll take care of her.  C'mon love, it'll be all right. I've got a contract this time. No selling from the house. You'll see... ' He made another physical attempt to appease her. 'It'll be OK.'

'No! You can't grow grass here. This's my bloody house and I'm not going to lose everything for you!'

'It will be different this time. Much more dough too.'

'No!'

With a vicious kick she thumped into one of the cardboard boxes in the corner. It split open. Seed in clear bank type envelopes slid out onto the floor. She turned to another box, a large one. Flipped open the lid. In black plastic tubes, just like those supplied by a nursery, were hundreds of tiny plants. Marijuana plants. Sneering she reached for the biggest box. There were half a dozen tubs like beer making barrels behind it.

'No! Not that one!' he protested.

Donna ignored him and opened a box of glass tubing and small boxes of white chemicals. She kicked into the cardboard.

Jason grabbed at the box to stop her. 'Careful with that stuff! Shit! Be careful! That's big money...'

She turned on her partner. Her face was an angry scowl. 'Bloody hell Jason! The grass is bad enough ...'

'C'mon Donna, it'll be OK.'

'But the other hard stuff.' She yelled as though he hadn't spoken. 'Mixing stuff, chemicals  here! With the kids and all... It's too dangerous. No! Never, never that! Get that shit out right now!'

'Bitch! You'll get your share.'

She circled around him. Punched his arm and chest with her fist to emphasise each word. Each yelled word was an angry accusation. 'Like hell I will! Yeah, just like last time. This time it would be worse... and who got caught then? Who got the fines? Me! Who paid the fines? Me! Where were you then? No bloody where!' She turned away. 'Shit faced and gone - as usual!'

'Yeah, well... This lot cost me a packet...'

'I've got a criminal record because of you. This time it'll be prison for me. Not bloody you!'

'You'll do it...' Jason raised his fists as though he would strike her.

She backed up a step then thrust her chin forward aggressively at him. Kept out of his range. 'Yeah ? You bastard! No way! Not that serious stuff...' She kicked out at the boxes again. 'Get it out! All of it! And you can go too! Leave us alone. Bloody get out!'

Donna glared again at him, shaking with anger, tears close.

He backed down, roughly elbowed past her and stomped out of the room.

She stood rigid. Wiped an arm across her face, shrugged and turned away to grab the long strips of aluminium foil and to pull them down from the nearest wall.

'Bastard!' she said.

# Chapter 4

In the driveway Jason slumped into the front seat of the Holden. He fisted the steering wheel then lit a cigarette and pulled the smoke hard down into his lungs. Punched the wheel again. He pulled his mobile phone from his jacket pocket. Dialed and waited. The connection was made.

'I told you she wouldn't go for it! None of it! Especially not the hard stuff,' he said.

There was a splutter of harsh words from the phone.

Jason listened with a sneer on his face. 'You've got no fucking idea. Shit! I'll pay you back... Somehow... Gimme time...'

He disconnected the call. Stared into the distance, worried. He threw the phone onto the seat beside him.

Gotta stay away from the hard drugs, the pokies and the loan sharks, he promised himself. Bastards! They've got no idea!

He leaned forward and started the engine, revved it. Revved it hard and exhaust smoke belched a dirty black cloud behind the car. Jason flicked his cigarette butt out the window and backed fast out of the driveway onto the street. Street gravel flew like hail.

Mrs Warren, the neighbour, opened the front door of her neat house. An older woman, comfortable in her blue house-dress and apron, she had normal upward age lines that now tensed downward as she frowned as she watched Jason's car leave. Although she liked Donna and the children there was always trouble when Jason was around.

From his car Jason saw Mrs Warren. He made an obscene middle finger gesture at her and roared off down the road.

Mrs Warren smiled watching as Jason drove away. She took a notepad out of her apron pocket and made a note. She turned back inside and closed the door. A front lace curtain twitched as she checked the street again.

Ten minutes later two leather and 'colours' clad bikies on huge motor bikes pulled up, one each side of Jason's car as he stopped for a red traffic light on Nicholson Avenue.

They pounded on the car roof with their fists and then one pulled a short iron bar from inside his jacket and smashed first at the driver's front windscreen, then thumped a blow into the side window. Smash! A pattern of spider webs marked each rapid swing.

Smash! The repeated violent blows finally broke through the toughened glass. The windscreen exploded inwards.

The motor cyclists roared across the empty intersection and away.

The light changed to green.

Jason stalled the Holden.

It shuddered wildly as he tried to take off. The car bucked and lurched forward when in panic he stalled it again.

There was blood on Jason's face, cuts from the flying windscreen glass. He sat wide eyed and stunned, wiping his face with his shirt, smearing the blood. He cleared away some of the glass from his lap and retried to get the car going.

In the distance the sound of a siren hit highs and lows as it came down the highway.

Someone had dialed 000 and a police car had been close by.

Jason got his car started. Tyres screeched as he hit the accelerator too hard and the car slid as he made a turn off Nicholson Avenue and sped away.

The police car raced on down Nicholson towards Westlands Shopping Centre.

With satisfaction Donna pulled down and gathered together the aluminum foil from the walls. A huge pile of it littered the room around her feet. She scrunched some, and quickly made a large silver ball of it.

The small boy appeared in the doorway.

She scooped him up and, carrying the foil ball, walked back to the kitchen with him in her arms. There she wiped the child's dirty nose on a tissue she thrust back into her bra and planted a loud raspberry kiss on his cheek. She put him down again on the floor and rolled the foil ball to the beaming child.

'Here kiddo... You have this. She laughed bitterly. 'We'll be better off without your old man around.'

She crossed to the table, uncapped a beer and took a swallow.

'C'mon on kids! Time for lunch. Who's hungry? ' She shouted through to the sitting room. 'We'll make fish fingers and chips.' Two older children, a boy and a girl, jostled each other running and laughing into the kitchen.

The tabby cat's purr deepened and its eyes opened briefly to display two golden orbs before closing into a smile of recognition. Claws that opened in cat joy as it kneaded Mrs. Harris's lap were tapped briskly to suggest to the animal to mind its manners while she read her book. It did; the paws softened and withdrew as the cat resumed purring.

The two bikers calmly put their running motor bikes on the stands and ran to Donna's front door. They kicked it open and threw something into the house.

Two somethings.

There was the sound of smashing glass and glow of flame as the projectiles erupted down the passage from the front door.

Into the kitchen.

Through a roar came the sound of screams.

Mrs Warren heaved herself to her feet. Her book dropped and the cat struggled clear and sped to the doorway where it washed itself in a disarray of fur and surprise. From the security of her window Mrs Warren screwed her hands into her freshly ironed apron as though crushing the poppies on the material. Her eyes widened and the lines on her face dragged downwards.

She telephoned 000 and her voice came in gulps and gasps as she tried to speak coherently to the operator.

# Chapter 5

Senior Detective Mark Llewellyn stood by the front gate looking at the wreckage of the burned house.

The roof had fallen into the gap where an inferno had blazed behind the blackened brick façade and empty steel window frames hung awry. Smoke still billowed skyward from the rear sections signaling the dirty signpost of disaster. He clicked shut his mobile phone after calling the information in to the station. Being the first police on the scene of an incident wasn't quite usual but it had happened before, he remembered.

A fireman, the Fire Chief by his insignia, came to stand beside him. The detective handed over a roll of 'Crime Scene' tape. 'Arson? Another deliberate one you reckon?' Mark said.

'Yeah! Definitely. We could smell the accelerant when we got here.' He held up a restraining hand as Mark started forward. 'Hang on a minute. There's broken glass by the front doors. And inside too. Typical fire bomb.'

Mark stopped. 'Proves deliberate, doesn't it?' he said.

'Yes, and there's bodies. The crew have just located them.'

'Bodies?' Mark echoed.

'Yeah! It looks like one adult and kids. Definitely more than one kid.'

'Bloody shit!' Mark swore. He looked aghast at the Chief. 'I hate these senseless killings. It's got to be drugs...and gang enforcers.' He pushed a hand through his curly tangle of too long for regulation hair. 'I've got the full team coming. My boys and I'll call in the Adelaide forensics.'

'Good. We'll be able to give you the safe all clear soon. The place is all electric so there's no problem now that it's all off. No gas cylinders to blow. That's a blessing, means you can go in as soon as we've finished.'

'Thanks. I appreciate what you boys do. Hard for you finding bodies.'

'Hard for everyone and I've been at this game for almost twenty years.' He looked Mark up and down. 'We've not met yet, I'm Paul Phillips.' The two men shook. 'Sorry about the grime.' he said looking down at his dirty hands. 'You're Mark Llewellyn, new in Whyalla aren't you? New boss of detectives? I've been on long service leave and missed your arrival introductions a couple of months back.'

'Yeah sorry I should have introduced myself.  Recent promotion. Does it show?  I was in Major Crime but needed a country posting for the next one. I like the country, well I think I do and it will be good to have it a bit quieter here in Whyalla than the Majors.'

'Quieter? You may be surprised...' The fireman lifted his helmet to scratch at his forehead leaving fingernail streaks in the sooty sweat. He grimaced. 'I can taste the bloody fuel in my mouth.'

A young fireman came out of the house. He stood by Paul and Mark, not sure of the latter, until the chief gave him a nod to go ahead. 'There's going to be a hold up. We've just found barrels and boxes of white chemicals.'

'OK, get everyone out until they can be identified and cleared by forensics.' The fireman nodded and went away and soon there was a quiet stream of men leaving the burned shell of the house. Two came up and deployed the yellow tape.

'So heavy stuff? A meths lab you reckon?' Mark said.

'Looks like it. It's only our second known one. The first one was found after an explosion about two months ago. We're still getting used to handling the more dangerous chemicals.'

'We can't do much more then until we get this safe then.' Mark queried. 'Have you seen anyone watching that you recognise? Anyone wanting to go inside?'

'Mrs Warren who called it in has been very evident. She was

hysterical about the children and worried about the fire spreading, with good reason. It's OK. She'd be the one who probably knows most about it.'

'Good and thanks. She'll be a useful interviewee when the rest of the team gets here.'

'There'll be our footage.'

'You film fires?'

'Just new. It started as a training thing, being tried out in the country. Long overdue but has been useful to you blokes too.'

'Great.'

'I'll have it for you tomorrow. Glad we can be of help.'

'Thanks.' Mark slapped the fireman's shoulder, shrugged as his hand came away dirty again and received an eyebrow raised grimace before he started back to his unmarked car. 'I'll post a guard on the house,' he said.

'We'll have one here as well for safety reasons.' The Chief's grin lasted until he turned back to the carnage behind him.

The pot of bright green parsley was overturned and, by the gate, the pansies had been trodden into the dirt by the firemen's hasty feet.

It didn't matter.

Donna's children were no longer alive to see and love their golden faces.

# Chapter 6

Rhette Ryan took another savage swipe with the red lipstick.

She remembered the very moment when her sister, Kate, was found in the bush outside Sydney and every word of the police reports. Of the pure uncut drug that her sister had been given; the pure opiate that was a death sentence. Like Rhette Kate had witnessed something she shouldn't have seen, or heard. She'd been killed for it … or was it something else. Revenge? Without family Kate had followed her older sister's path into the associations of people and drugs that had cost her life.

As "Miss M," Rhette had testified in camera, incognito, against her sister's killers. Against the bastards who'd supplied drugs to her and other young people. School children and disco dancers. Her evidence had been torn apart by their eminent defense attorney, mainly by discrediting her as a witness because of her own past police sheet. They got off, with the Magistrate's decision that there was 'not enough evidence to make a case', and even the chance to prosecute the real Boss had been frittered away in his highly paid lawyers' hands. The case lapsed into the frustrating prosecution annals of the 'might have beens'.

A trial opportunity missed.

Rhette was immediately put into the police protection orbit, away from Sydney. In the teaching convent she'd been safe and the convent had changed the track of her life.

All tracks except revenge.

And guilt.

Rhette's need for revenge slithered into every waking moment except when she was teaching and surrounded in a classroom full of children. With the children she'd found a peace and she had reveled in their innocence.

Revenge.

Tonight she'd do it. Kill the Boss. Or die in the attempt.

Carrying her shoes she tip toed down the cold stone of the quiet passages and let herself out through the locked double doors. She hailed a taxi from the adjoining private hospital grounds.

The nun Sister Bernadette, her mentor and the only person who knew the whole truth about her, had heard the soft whisper of Rhette's feet and she went to the Chapel to pray for her soul.

In the morning she'd make a phone call to her police contact.

Jessica Taylor tossed her notebook down onto the desk.

The youngest, the sole woman, of the three permanent detectives team in the Whyalla office, she was felt she needed to impress even though she had worked with Mark Llewellen previously in Renmark. It was then her noting that hair coloured, like her own, that was a potential tying together aspect of the case they were working on. This colouring; blonde or white streaks in dark hair, could have made Jessica a potential victim too. Had she been unlucky, like other serial victims and accepted a casual invitation for a drink, she would have died. That was in the past but it had given her credibility with Mark and he hadn't forgotten it or her. There were times when she thought that her observations and comments were just a fluke.

A lucky fluke and this morning's questioning of the people at the Quirke Street fire gave her less than she'd hoped for.

She wanted more lucky flukes for confidence in the world of hard crime.

Mark looked up across the squad room. He gestured and Jessica sat into the swivel chair opposite his paper strewn desk. He clicked down his computer screen and gave her his full attention. It was a natural trait that his staff appreciated.

'Anything useful? Other than the two bikies?" he said.

'Only Mrs Warren, the woman who called it in, had anything.

Everyone else arrived when the fire trucks came, or after.'

Mark grunted. 'And she said what?' It was like pulling teeth when Jessica wanted to get her verbal report right.

Mrs Warren had a lot to say about the people at 13 Quirke St. She was in an awful state and, after I spoke to her, they took her off in an ambulance to hospital.'

'Was she hurt?' Mark was still waiting for something. Anything.

'No. Smoke inhalation. And shock. But I did get that she liked the woman and the children of the household but the man was a complete and total jerk. She was referring to his past drug selling, the noise, bad language etc. She said they'd had been arguing before the fire. Then he drove off. The two bikies came and threw fire bombs, or something, into the house.'

'Did she know the Colours? Which gang?'

Jessica moved the chair closer to Mark's desk and put her note book on the edge. 'She did see colours but has no idea otherwise.'

'When she's able get her in and see if someone, one of our artists maybe, can get what she saw out of her. Then we'll have some idea of which gangs we're dealing with.'

Jessica made a note.

Mark waited. 'Did she see anything else?'

'When I spoke to her she mentioned, as an afterthought almost, that what she did see was another man on a motor bike. Dressed in black, no markings, who the others appeared to waved to as they rode off.'

'Interesting. Could be an important factor. How long did he stay?'

'She couldn't say. She was too shocked when the house went up. Called the firies, then us. She said she went to their yard but the fire was too hot and smoky to try to get inside. She said she could hear screaming...said she'd never forget it...' Jessica said.

There was a silence before Mark asked. 'So she couldn't tell how long the other man stayed around.'

'No. By the time she'd got her garden hose out and the fire truck pulled in, she saw that the man was gone.'

'No chance of a look at his face?'

'No he was wearing a full face helmet.'

Mark grunted. Of course he was.

That night Ana tucked up Piet in the Port Lincoln Hotel bed and went out into the adjoining sitting room.

She was tired. Bushed. She just wanted a shower, to wash her hair clear of the dust of packing up a house and the memories that hid in every corner. Memories of every hue and colour, some dim disappointing as in any marriage, but mostly good ones.

Ana took a deep breath and called her sister Kari and brother in law Blair, who had been staunch help over the years since the terrible time on the River Murray houseboat. They lived in Adelaide. 'We're on our way,' she said. She followed the call with another to her friends Lauren and Tom Bell-Scott of Sydney. This's the last time she'd phone from Port Lincoln she told them. There were pangs of regret. Taking herself so far away from family and friends, and Pietie too, but she had to cope and get on with her life. With luck she would never have to rely on others again.

'The furniture movers have been. Everything's packed and ready to go to Darwin. I've seen the allotted house they've assigned me by the hospital on line. It's the usual government type house but it will be great,' she said to them. 'I'll be too busy setting myself up and getting Pietie to kindy to worry about getting lonely,' she assured them.

Selling the house, she had shared with her late husband Peter, had become a necessity if ever she was going to get on with her life past the trauma of his death. He'd never seen Piet, his longed for son, and she regretted that almost as much as his murder. Peter had died saving her. His death had also saved the life of his son as she'd only found out about her pregnancy when it was all over.

The trip she planned with Piet was a repeat of the honeymoon she and Peter had shared, full of fun and adventure before they settled down. She planned to make it a slow trip as she had at least three weeks before she was to start work. Two weeks traveling then a week setting up their new home. It would be a trip of goodbyes to the past, and a slow trip so not to tax Piet. A day travelling then a day or two to look at things in different places, meeting people and having some fun.

Making new memories.

Tomorrow they were off to Darwin with the first stop in Whyalla.

# Chapter 7

'Match speed,' the Pilot ordered above the noise of ship's engines.

The helmsman turned the yellow Pilot boat into the lee of the huge freighter. Its wash swung away in a broad feather of sea foam.

'OK,' the Pilot instructed, 'Usual drill.'

He nodded to the two regular members of the crew, then caught a rope ladder swinging down the grey painted hull and climbed up to the ship's deck towering above.

The Pilot, with the Captain beside him, took control on the bridge to guide the ship through the top of the gulf shallows that guarded the mouth of the Whyalla port estuary. Two stubby harbour tugs slipped into station alongside and began manoeuvres that would bring the freighter safely to the dock.

Tyler was an extra; an unofficial member of the Pilot boat crew that morning. He watched and waited as the ship was brought closer and closer to the wharf. Trying to look a part of the working crew to any inquisitive eyes he almost missed the brief shard of light from a porthole high up on the starboard side.

'The signal! Yes! ' Tyler triumphed to himself. 'Got you!'

The wharfies trooped out to haul on heavy steel hawsers as the ship was berthed; bound in the uneasy alliance of a ship to the land. Last orders were called from the bridge. The Pilot exchanged final pleasantries with the Captain and came off just as a trio of Customs men clattered up the gangway for the ship's inspection.

The ship and its crew settled into shore duties.

The Pilot boat tied up close astern of the freighter. There were a few tourists and fishermen on the wharf observing the ship docking.

Nothing out of the ordinary, so far. Nothing to indicate that a huge illegal drug shipment was on board. One that would be smuggled ashore in the brief time it took to take on the iron ore cargo before the ship sailed again at dusk.

Just that flash of light.

Finally the customs men left.

They'd found nothing - as expected.

The ship slowly slumped lower into the water as iron ore swept along the conveyer belts and down into the cavernous holds below decks. A few empty handed crewmen went shore to shop in the harbour town. They were watched, surreptitiously, but they reboarded a couple of hours later loaded with supermarket bags and boxes of small electrical goods they'd paid for in American dollars.

Nothing suspicious.

Nothing unusual. Nothing yet.

The day stayed clear and mild and Tyler waited. Waited and watched. This was better than office duties; better than paper work or clambering on gangways into the dark, oil smelling bowels of ships. He stripped to the waist and enjoyed himself as he pretended deck maintenance jobs. He was undercover and his Customs surveillance vigil was set up after a telephone tip-off.

'Stay on deck. Maybe you'll see something,' his Custom's CO had said that morning over breakfast.

As the tedious hours wore on Tyler started a conversation with an elderly man and a kid about ten years old on the wharf. Their Border Collie dog, its silky black and white fur fluffed up by the breeze, lay in easy rest beside the boy's fishing gear.

'How's it going?' Tyler asked as the man bent and picked up two feathers. One had a purple tinge and the other a green sheen

'These aren't feral pigeon feathers,' the old man murmured. He stood and struggled to put binoculars to his eyes to search the gantry structure high above the ship. One arm obviously didn't work very well. 'Good,' the man said somewhat absently to Tyler; still intent on what he was looking for. He stopped, and his voice became animated as he spoke to the boy 'Do you know - I think I can see a *Phaps Chalcoptera* up there?' He paused. 'A bird, a native bronzewing pigeon. Most unusual around a wharf area.'

He squatted beside the boy; pointed up towards the gantry that channeled iron ore into the ships. 'Simon, there! It's a female - see the white stripe below her eye. She's got purple-pink breast feathers and a metallic sheen on her wings. Usually nests in the bush, not here above the sea. Well, I never! Must be a male about too. The male's much more colourful.' He mused. 'They don't swim... so I wonder how they'd go if they fell into the water? Drown, I suppose.'

The boy tucked his fishing rod under his arm, twisted his red cap around and peered through the glasses his grandfather passed to him. 'Yeah,' he agreed. 'It's a beauty. Are you going to photograph it for your bird book?'

'You bet,' his grandfather smiled. He turned to Tyler who was still watching them from the aft deck. 'You must get a good look at all the sea birds with your job,' he commented.

'Yeah, sometimes,' Tyler was non committal. He wasn't interested in birds. Not the feathered kind anyway.

'Hey! I've got a bite!' The boy jerked his rod and reeled in a Tommy Ruff. It flapped shiny and spotted, fins extended and mouth gasping as the boy took the hook out and dropped the squirming fish into his bucket. 'It's a good one too. Bet Grandma'll like it...'

'She sure will...' he said with a smile.

The dog stirred itself to sniff the fish as the boy rebaited the hook and cast out then it slumped down to sleep again.

The old man wandered away along the wharf with his camera and photographed the bronzewing pigeons and other birds as they flew above and about the ship. He came back after a while bringing a couple of additional bronzewing feathers with him.

By mid afternoon the boy had caught more fish and the old man was keen to get going. Time to go home.

The boy packed up his fishing gear then waved to Tyler, who was still watching, and got a grin in return. With the dog trailing behind them, its white tail a flag of farewell, the man and boy left the wharf.

The ship cast off on the high tide as the sun settled into the red earth open to the west. The sunset colours were vivid catching the ore dust and turning it to lances of flame.

Everything went smoothly, the ship was ushered safely out of the harbour and the Pilot boat returned to her berth. Her normal crew tidied ship and departed before the Custom's CO came on board with two other officers.

Tyler prepared to go ashore.

'Nothing to report,' he shrugged to his CO. 'Boring as hell! Got a bit of a tan though.' He stretched expansively, showing off broad shoulders, and grinned as he reached for his backpack of spare clothing, his diabetic medications and lunch box.

The Customs Chief moved forward and pointedly pushed the backpack out of his reach. Tyler's smile merged to a slight frown before his forehead creased into a surprised look. Eyes wide, his mouth stretched back into the wide good fellow grin his workmates knew so well.

A photograph was placed squarely on the chart table.

A large, very detailed photograph.

'This was brought in to us this afternoon by a retired copper on holidays. He was bird watching with his grandson and noticed a few things. Unusual things.'

In the photograph the customs officer was not evident on the Pilot boat's deck.

'Why aren't you in that photo?' the CO asked, eyes cold and grey hard. 'You were ordered to stay on deck.'

'Call of nature,' the officer explained. He shrugged to the other officers and attempted to laugh off his absence.

The faces around him remained impassive. Giving nothing away.

The CO ignored his response and threw down three additional prints.

'And what about these photos?'

In the first Tyler was just visible behind the wheelhouse signaling to a person on the freighter. In the next he was dragging in a heavy line and, in the third most damming, Tyler was lifting something out of the water by the ship's stern.

'Maybe I was helping a kid on the jetty,' Tyler said.

'I don't think so.' A stabbing finger pointed to the figure of the boy fishing further down the wharf. Obviously he was not being helped.

Tyler's smile and high colour faded.

The CO calmly put on evidence gloves, reached into Tyler's backpack and pulled out a bulky plastic wrapped parcel. As one officer produced a camera and filmed, the other hefted the package.

'About a kilo and a half here,' he said looking towards the CO.

'OK.' The words were tense in acknowledgement. 'Get on with it.'

The officer put on gloves and spread an evidence sheet under the package. A small flow of white powder coated his fingers as he made a tiny slit in the plastic with a knife next to what appeared to be a rent in the covering. White crystals and powder spilled out. He did a quick pocket computer chemical analysis.

There was no doubt as the digital indicator screen spiked red. The parcel contained drugs. Heroin and cocaine, plus the chemical ingredients for amphetamine cooking.

'Yeah. That's it,' the CO said. She turned to the officers. 'Take him!' Get him out of my sight.' She shrugged away in disgust.

There was a brief struggle and fluent cursing as the capture was made.

Tyler was not done. 'Della! You'd take an old man's word over mine?' he shouted at her.

The CO shook long dark hair free of her confining uniform cap and turned back to the offender. Her blue eyes reflected sadness, but her voice was grim offering no compromise to her former lover.

'Yes! The old man, as you called him, said he's an ex cop. A keen bird watcher too.  An old Dee never retires...and maybe because he's got a grandson he wants to keep the drugs out. Still wants to bang up the likes of you...'

She laughed. Not a pleasant laugh. 'Clever you! Caught by a bird watcher! Caught by an old man and feathers!' she said.

The sneer became abrupt, dismissive. You won't be home for dinner tonight.' She paused. 'Not tonight ... not ever.'

Mark Llewellyn boarded the pilot boat. 'Got your call,' he said. 'So my old mate Worm tossed you a lead.'

Della pushed the photos towards him. 'These are very impressive,' she said. 'The informant, the ex copper, will he stand up in court?'

There was a laugh in Mark's voice. 'Not a problem.' He became serious. 'Worm, Wally Tape's was one of the best ever. Worked in the Evidence Room after a piece of drugged up shit blew away his shoulder with a sawn off shotgun. He's retired now and he's been traveling with his wife and grand kids. He dropped in to see me last week just to let me know he was in town.'

'That sort?'

'Yes, old school.' Mark leaned forward and looked closely at the photos. One of them also showed the pigeon high on the gantry. 'He's a bit of a twitcher...mad keen.'

Della raised a questioning eyebrow. 'OK, tell me what a twitcher is,' she said a grin in her voice and on her face.

'They're avid bird fanciers. Usually they are only interested in the number of birds they see but Worm, he probably can't really be called a twitcher. He's not interested in the numbers he sees, rather the different bird species. He'd have been photographing anything that flew around the wharf area. When he called me the first thing he said first was that he'd seen bronze wing pigeons there...most unusual. Then he told me about getting the photos of the drug exchange.' Mark's voice reflected his amusement and respect for his old friend.

'Got his priorities right?' Della said.

'You could say that. He's laid back alright but dead against drugs. Old dees never die. Not the good ones and Worm'll give you chapter and verse about keeping drugs away from the young.'

'My lucky day.' Della said. The sadness had returned to her eyes.

Mark touched her arm. Sometimes it was better to say nothing about busted relationships. 'I'll give you an escort back to the station. We'll need to confirm this package with witnesses and get all the usual chain of evidence palaver sorted out for the courts.'

# Chapter 8

Ana had often fled to a little cove by the sea - out past the Port Lincoln Marina and the spit of land that was Billy Light's point.

After three months of compassionate leave, and with her belly already beginning to swell, she'd returned to the prison and her counseling job.

It wasn't easy.

Everyone, staff and prisoners alike, knew her story. There'd been a huge media rout of her privacy and her life. About the senior major crime detective who was a serial killer, prisoners on the run and the dead; Peter's death in a story that traveled from Port Lincoln to Lock 6 on the Murray River out of Renmark. The spectacle went on and on although the trial was short as the accused had confessed to everything. Still, she'd been called as a witness through the police internal witch hunt. She'd been protected from some of it by her family, and a young detective, but her need to escape had become a screaming necessity.

Her grief was too public.

This little cove was her haven where she could look out over the moving waters. Look out far and away, yet be cocooned by the beach curving around her like a soft golden shawl.

Safe from the menaces.

One was a menace of a murderer's body never found. Never recovered from the deep brown waters of the Murray River.

The sea fretted before her. Grey waters tangled up like sheets of wrinkled cling-wrap. Far glittered silver waves to where the sky and horizon finally merged to one thin grey line. The wind from the south pushed up ridges in the sea. Ridges in the cling film. Swept sand and weed debris into shale clouds.

Her eyes stung. Grit and salt tears. Ana stood on the beach

trying to gather and calm her feelings and the memories.

A sharp expletive burst from her lips, unbidden and unusual. Her own cry woke her in a mess of rumpled bed sheets. She looked over at the bed where Piet lay; he was quiet and still. She hadn't woken him.

Perhaps, she thought, these dreams would go when she'd laid all her ghosts to rest. How could the dreaming be always about those days when she'd been safe? Never be about the terror of what went before. It was just over four years ago, enough time to live through denial, regret and guilt. Piet deserved better. Her breathing settled and she allowed herself to remember her alternative escape when leaving the house wasn't feasible.

She'd made rock cakes.

Golden heaps of them until they became rock mountains. She gave them away in droves; sent them off to the prison, to the hospital canteens and the police station. Denial, she knew that. Eventually she stopped making rock cakes and prepared for Piet's birth. Port Lincoln gave a collective sigh of relief. So many rock cakes, good cakes but too, too many. She could laugh about it now but then the weighing and measuring of ingredients, the mixing and the baking; doing something that she had to think about had been essential to her mental survival.

She headed into the bathroom to get a wet flannel for her sweating face and had a pee. She took a movement to rally herself and to push her demons back into the dream.

The criminal was dead, for goodness sake. The trouble was – so was Peter and the life they'd planned together.

The time for mourning was over too, it had to be. She would never forget but life had to go on. Shit, she thought, I'm being so cliché, so mundane.

But there had been two turning points for her before Piet's birth that occurred when she went to her alternative place of escape. Both concerned whales and it occurred each time she went to Snapper Rock, just a few kilometres along from the main street of Port Lincoln.

The huge shelf of rock jutted out into deep Boston Bay water near the Flinders University Marine Centre. Gulls, pelicans and diving birds frequented a long expanse of flat stone. A place where families fished; where the occasional wedding took place with the bride often barefoot and dressed like a gypsy.

One day, there on the rock, Ana had seen a huge Southern Right whale breach, spin, leap and tail sail in an enormous display of splash and strength. Usually only the occasional whale came into the harbour waters, wandering from their usual migration route along the Great Southern continental shelf and open sea, but for two consecutive afternoons Ana saw whales. On the first day she was enthralled by the magnificence of the animal but felt insignificant and lost to its vast power. With such a display that day, crowds had gathered to watch and the 'Ooh's' and Ah's' around her forced her to leave as soon as she could get to her car and go.

Next day, a day when Ana was alone again on the rock, other whales came. A huge six metre female with a calf born in the sanctuary of the pod, near Ceduna further to the west at the edge of the Bight. Silently the huge body surfaced near Ana, with her calf protected by the expanse of her body on the seaward side. It stopped and just lay quietly in the water, and Ana felt she was being watched by the great eye. She hardly dared breathe as the mother turned to usher her calf closer to the rock and Ana. The calf nuzzled into its mother's side, then rolled over and looked at Ana.

Is she showing her calf to me? Ana questioned.

But in that moment of connection, when they were so close and within metres of each other, Ana lay a hand on her belly. She let herself be released.

Now remembering Ana instructed; counsellor heal yourself as she went to stand on the hotel balcony. It faced the sea but the thumbnail of moon was too dim to cast a path across Boston Bay. Good, she thought, she didn't need the remembrances of the total beauty of a full moon to cloud her decision to leave Port Lincoln.

Nor the healing magic of whales.

She needed the new start; she was ready, and tomorrow was the beginning.

'I thought you and David were well over the honeymoon stage...' Mark couldn't help himself remark as Jessica came into the squad room later than usual. She was trim and neat in civvies, a grey pencil skirt and a floral shirt tucked into a wide belt. He grinned at her. Long term friends and colleagues were permitted such comments especially when Lex was out getting himself a coffee. His South African sense of humour and proprieties weren't quite the same as those of the Australian police. He was learning though.

'I should be so lucky...No, Boss, I went to the hospital to see how Mrs Warren was. Maybe she'd remember a bit more when her head was clearer.'

'And how was she?'

'Still terribly shocked from yesterday but better. She got her hair singed when she'd tried to open a window to help them. She was beaten back by the heat and flames and she was putting water on the house when the fire trucks arrived. Not bad for an old lady.'

Mark tapped his pencil on his desk. Sometimes Jessica had a bit of the social worker in her. It suited her, but he wanted facts, especially this morning when no-one knew anything more about the fire. Knew nothing or weren't talking. Patched bikies had that effect on people.

'She said she'd come in to the station for her official interview today after she's released from hospital. Wants to get home to her cat.' Jessica paused, with a slight smile, before she reported what she knew Mark was waiting for. 'She did have one more bit of information. She said that the man in black was smoking. He raised his helmet visor and had a puff. He was Caucasian, that's all she could see.'

Now she had Mark's full attention. 'She could tell you exactly where he was? Did you ask that?' he said.

'Of course I did Boss. He was at the corner, almost across the road from her house.'

Lex came back into the pen carrying coffee. Three commercial carton cups.

'OK Lex, we're going on an emu pick.' Mark took a coffee from Lex's hands, and put another on Jessica's desk as he went past. 'Thanks for the coffee but move yourself. We're out of here.'

Lex juggled his coffee, and as he shrugged into his coat, started after Mark.

'Emu pick?' he said. His voice had the timbre of the open veldt but was clipped with sharp Cape Town accents. He was urban Zulu, black as midnight, but physically of heavier build than his tribesmen. His civies suits were immaculate in contrast to Mark's usual jeans, shirts and Doc Martins boots.

Mark had been startled when he'd first met Lex's partner, Grace, as white as he was black. The relationship hadn't been allowed within the old South Africa and they didn't fit into the new regime either. He'd never have got promotion there with a white wife and their two beautiful coloured children.

Lex never called him Boss, always Mark. An old South African thing he obviously avoided. Called him 'Sir' too until Mark had put a stop to that. The two men were on a fast learning curve working together.

# Chapter 9

An hour later Lex knew what an emu pick was.

They'd left the Whitehead Street Police Station; unaware as they passed glass on Nicholson Road from Jason's Holden smashed windscreen, and returned to Quirke Street. Mark pulled in across from the fire scene. Gloved and using tweezers, they were looking for cigarette butts amongst the incidental rubbish of the housing estate and the spread debris of a house fire.

'Just collect the butts, I don't reckon that there'd be anything else,' Mark said as he left Lex to bend his tall frame to minutely inspect the ground. He crossed the road to speak to the forensic team still working in the gutted remains of the fire.

The forensic scene was quiet and there was none of the usual banter amongst the crew who had flown up from Adelaide the night before.

'Anything new?' Mark asked the Adelaide chief, Wally Gideon. The latter, a tall heavy set man was dressed in protective garb, removed his glove to shake hands. Greying hair tufted out from under the hood and he rumpled it as he wiped his face.

'We're bloody lucky in some aspects. The drug lab was still in boxes. No chemicals mixed yet,' Wally paused, 'well the fire mixed some, you could say, when the boxes burned and glass bottle burst their guts. The place stinks of it and we'll have to take all the usual precautions.'

'The fire was started by incendiaries?'

'Definitely. They'll be imported from the black market and impossible to trace.' Wally gave a hollow laugh, 'It had all the bikie signatures though. The bastards might as well have put up a identifying sign.'

'They probably have,' Mark said. 'Other crims working for

them will do as they are told.' He waited but Wally's grim face said he wasn't in a talking mood. 'It was that bad was it?'

'Yeah, anything with kids is bad. The mother tried to protect the three kids and they were found all burned and fused together. We had to take them out as one. I don't know how the pathologist will separate the bodies. ' He didn't comment further and the two detectives stood silent for a beat. 'There was a huge amount of industrial strength silver foil and you might be able to get a buyer match on that.'

'We don't know who was setting it all up but we've got a make out on Jason Handly already. No sign of him yet.' Mark said.

'So you know who the meth chemist was going to be?'

'Hardly a chemist. More like an idiot. Who'd be foolish enough try to follow 101 of instructions.'

'He was going to do a chem lab in a house with children?'

'The bastard'll turn up. We'll get him then.'

Lex straightened to his full height.

His hand went to his the small of his back; he felt every one of his fifty-two years. He came across the street. 'I've got five butts,' he said as he stripped off his gloves and held out the individual plastic evidence bags. 'There were more but these were the only ones that were remotely recent. People must have stood smoking while they watched their neighbor's house burn. Insensitive lot. Same everywhere.'

'Yeah, that's people. But maybe the man Mrs Warren saw was the same. Another bugger enjoying the blaze,' Mark said.

'I'll get you a prelim report as soon as I can,' Wally said. 'It'll take a few weeks as usual.'

Mark made the introduction of the two men. Lex and Wally shook hands.

'You staying at the usual rabbit hole they usually book forensics into?' Mark asked.

'Yeah. Westlands Motel. Meet us in the bar for a beer later?'

'Done. Sixish?' Mark raised an eyebrow at Wally and Lex. Both nodded. There'd be much more information over a beer than in a written report. Faster too.

Lex was beginning to understand and work with the Australian way of doing things. He also liked the beer.


Ana stood opposite the house that Peter had designed and built for her above Rustler's Gully for the last time.

It was a beautiful house that commanded magnificent views over looking the vast harbour, Boston Island and the sea beyond. Even in the hard economic times the house had sold quickly for a good price and she was grateful for that. She wished the excited new owners well. She and Peter had lived, loved and often argued in there. Piet had been born from the house but she doubted that he would remember much about Port Lincoln, he was just too young.

'Are we going now Mummy?' Piet asked.

'Yes. Piet, we're going on our adventure now. Right now,' she said and checked the seat belt harness on his car chair. She got into the car and angled the mirror so that she could see the back window and his face. She could just see also the little bear wearing Crows football colours that was a vital part of his being. 'Is Bear ready too,' she asked.

He held up Bear. 'Yes, he's ready.'

'OK then, off we go.' She put the blue Mercedes in drive and pulled away from the kerb without a backward glance at her old house.

It was time.

The past had to retreat into the distant past.

# Chapter 10

Jason Hardly's body was found in the low acacia scrub off the Iron Knob Road. Four kilometers past Arthur Glennie Drive, twenty four hours later.

It was another murder.

Typical bikie execution style with bullets through both knees and one fired into the back of the scull as the victim lay face down in the dirt. The bullet cases were not at the location. They'd been collected in a professional manner. Neat. His Holden utility had been treated to another incendiary device and the smoke had drawn attention to the scene. It was another notice to police and the public that drug bikies had better be obeyed or you'd get what he did.

Lex got back with the report, delivered quickly and expertly to Mark. His years spent as a black and un-trusted cop in a white pre apartheid state, then a black experienced officer in a changed white department, had taught him to make concise statements. It was a pity that he'd had to move to Australia but his career had stagnated. His wife Grace and the kids meant more to him than the chaos of the new South Africa.

'So you've documented it all?' Mark said.

'Every bit. Chain of evidence up to and inside the mortuary door. Everything signed in correctly.' Lex did a mock salute. 'Everything by the book, Sir.'

'That's all very well,' Mark said with a grimaced laugh at the salutation. His face became grim. 'With these drug cases the legal mongrels they hire pick through every piece of paper as though their own mothers were the accused.'

'Nah Mark, some of them lawyers never had mothers,' Lex quipped.

Mark took a moment to chuckle again. Lex rarely made jokes. Then, elbows on his desk, he pushed his fingers into his scalp. He scratched the side of his neck in irritable concentration. This was the second such attack. He thought of these cases as attacks, in the two months he had been in Whyalla. There was almost nothing to go on to get an arrest although the forensic team, still in Whyalla, had collected everything they could.

Angry bile rose up from his stomach and bit into his throat. Cripes, he thought, better get something to eat before the acid tears holes in me too. It was an occupational hazard; too many long hours, eating rubbish at odd times of the day and night or not at all, drinking booze and smoking too much. He'd given up the smokes at least. But he still struggled with that and bummed one off someone now and then when the beer flowed.

'You eating lunch?' he asked.

'Grace packed me a chicken sandwich,' Lex said.

Of course she did, Mark thought. 'And I suppose there's cake?' he said. He could feel the saliva push up under his tongue.

'Of course,' was the smug reply. 'Want some?'

'No. Do me a favour and piss off to eat in the squad room. I can't stand to see a man enjoy his food as much as you do,' Mark grunted. With a grin towards Lex he reached for the phone and ordered a pizza delivered from the local pizza parlour. It would be filling, greasy and he'd have indigestion to follow. Antacids again for desert, he thought as his mind returned to the case.

There was one hope; just maybe one of Lex's emu picks would throw up a DNA something. Just maybe one of the bikies had a record. Mark wasn't holding his breath although he put a 'please rush' on it when the evidence bags were sent to Adelaide for analysis. A 'please rush' could still take days, even weeks. Money was short in all departments and Mark was no longer a Major Crime detective. They got first dibs in the labs.

Mark reviewed the drug situation and was beginning to dislike what he was seeing. Grass was always being grown, but the two fire destroyed meth labs, or potential meth labs, suggested that there was more meths in Whyalla than had been previously estimated. The fires suggested, either that there were competing gangs in the city, or that they were having problems with their contract workers. The place was too open to easily disguise the smell of speed cooking and the houses and occupants too well known. Then the disturbing import attempt of heroin, crack and amphetamine ingredients from that ship two days ago.

The interstate police reported that a different 'brand' of the drugs was coming in to Australia. With Highway One passing east-west from Sydney to Perth through Whyalla it was all too easy to move the stuff offloaded there into the Eastern states by truck, by car even.

The situation was building and he could foresee a new task force being initiated to investigate when he got his reports to headquarters in Adelaide.

The next problem was how the importers, the makers, and the overseas gangs were getting paid. Gone were the days of reputable bank transfers with the taxation introduction of questions asked over higher than moderate sums of money being sent overseas. Taking suitcases full of money didn't wash with airport security checks either. The scans picked it up visually. Or the dogs at the airport. The criminals had tried mailing out packages of money but the sniffer dogs again had detected that quickly. Paper money picked up drug residues like blotting paper. Funny that, Mark thought, traces of drugs accentuated and advertised the shipments.

Something new had to be used as payment.

Something the overseas market could sell and want. It would be interesting for the Task Force to work that one out, he thought.

By afternoon Mark and his team had settled back to review the fire case and get back to the usual doses of Brake and Enters, the stolen cars, assaults, the domestics and all that a city of twenty thousand people offered. Lately scams were another problem. Not the computer scams telling people that they'd won a lottery in Nigeria but more subtle ones that milked money from trusting retirees. Sometimes organized crime acted more softly with the same monetary results.

This was Lex's assignment as he knew most about the African political and social setups. He was less than happy with this because he felt an embarrassment for the South African government's abject denial of the AIDS epidemic and the likelihood that poverty could ground his birthplace into chaos again.   Probably now that Mandela was dead, he thought. Mandela was the glue that had held the political factions together. Politics and crime; always bedfellows within the stresses of developing nations. With Lex the most computer literate of his detective unit, Mark had added the work because of his expertise.

What Lex had never expected was that Mark had also given him a once only access to his own personal file, to read about him, to know the man who was promoted over him when Lex had rather expected that his longer experience would give him the promotion he wanted when he came to Australia. He respected that disclosure and they'd formed trust and a cohesive working relationship that was broadening into friendship. It could never have happened where he had worked before in Africa, where trust was never the norm.

Jessica came into the squad room where Mark and Lex stared into computer screens and reports. 'You'll never guess who I talked to in the mall at Westland,' she said.

'Are we talking crim or a real person?' Mark bit.

'A very real person,' she smiled.

Mark grunted, go on.

'It was Ana Foster. You remember her from Renmark, Mark?'

Something inside Mark's chest rolled and clenched. She was a witness and the victim he'd almost made a fool of himself over. 'Yes, I remember her,' he said. He turned aside to stare blankly into his computer screen while he pulled his thoughts and emotions into line.

Ana...

The tall slight frame, but still Ana was an all rounded woman. Her dark hair and the extraordinary natural white streak that swept down each side of her face. That was the one factor Jessica had brought to his attention that helped him tie all the murdered victims together in that terrible case. Tying them together before he'd realized that they'd been chasing the wrong man for the serial murders. It wasn't just the escaped convict who had been the killer but his own boss, Senior Sergeant Rick Charlton. It was the case that had cemented Mark's name and reputation in the Major Crime section.

In an instant Mark was swept back to the days that changed his life. His future. As promised Rick had confessed to all of his crimes. He'd provided the diary entries, the evidence and the horrific finger talismans he had collected, typical of serial killers. Standing in the Supreme Court, he'd seemed to shrink in physical statute before his ex- colleagues. Rick had received an automatic guilty verdict and had been sentenced to life imprisonment. Then, in the Adelaide Remand Centre awaiting transport to the secure G Section at Yatala Prison, Rick had evaded possible retribution from other prisoners by suffering a massive irreversible stroke. After lingering for weeks in the prison infirmary he'd died, saving the justice system untold future problems and expenses. Rick's funereal was a footnote to the case, ignored by the media who hadn't been informed of the occasion and the police force who, as a body, were shamed by the crimes of one of their own. Mark was a lone sad attendee; more to give a closure to the case and the mentorship, the friendship even, that had been his relationship with Rick Charlton.

Through it all, probably from unsought media attention, Mark had become an embarrassment, and the hierarchy had set his path away from the investigation special team of Major Crime to get regional experience. Hence to Whyalla and the area north to the Northern Territory border.

Now Ana... he thought.

Her husband had been killed in the showdown at Lock 6 on the Murray River. He had met Ana previously briefly when she lay in the Port Lincoln hospital bed, her head with her distinctive hair, swathed in bandages. Rick too had been there to interrogate her after an assault and had not recognised his 'Target,' his nemesis. After that, as the investigation into escaped prisoners wound to a conclusion at Lock 6 on the River Murray, Ana and Mark had often spoken on the phone as he'd tried to help her.

It was during those telephone conversations when her voice, an essence of her, had found a place within him. He cared for this woman but what he remembered most with Ana, was holding her as she screamed rocking in shock and horror as her husband Peter lay dead in a pool of blood on the houseboat deck. Stunned himself by his arrest of Rick for the murders and the filthy slimy wall of the lock towering beside them Mark had tried to keep Ana clear of that danger, so that she could not fall between the lock walls and the houseboat and be crushed there.

Later, when Rick recognised Ana at the Renmark Police Station and attacked her, Mark had thrown himself between them. In those moments he had cemented a feeling that he knew he should not be forming between himself and a witness. The feeling lingered any time he thought of Ana since those terrible days. It was almost as if he had fallen in love with a memory, but more than that he recognized the inner strength and compassion of the woman he had believed in and saved.

Jessica was waiting. He needed to respond. 'How's she doing?' he said casually as he turned back to face her.

'She seemed OK. Remembered me. That was nice. She had a little boy with her. Looks about, maybe three years old. Said his name was Piet.'

'Ana's husband was Peter,' Mark said.

Lex broke in. 'Piet's often used in South Africa as a derivative of Peter.'

'So it'll probably be her husband's child. It was about four years ago.' Jessica smiled. 'A nice woman. Despite her grief and everything else she sent me flowers when I was in hospital with the broken arm and concussion after the confrontation and job climax on the houseboat.'

'Yeah, it was about that long ago.' Mark's head was full of the jumble of events. Remembered as if it were last week especially when he'd held Ana in his arms for that brief moment in her grief.

He could still feel the fit of her body.

'She hasn't changed much at all,' Jessica said. 'Still looks the same. Some people are lucky that way... She said she was staying here for a few days.'

'She say where she was staying? Where she was going?' Mark said. His voice was casual.

'I didn't ask.'

Mark grunted. Of course you didn't, he thought.

# Chapter 11

Doug Napier raised his tin cup to the clear night sky.

'Cheers!' he saluted the yellow planet Venus that glowed low in the east; just risen above the far craggy line of inland ridges. It straggled behind Mars already riding red high above. Scattered like white ice chunks across the indigo-black puddle of night sky, the stars floated so close that he could almost grab one to put in his whisky. Doug chuckled a thought; as if a Scot, even an Aussie-born Scot, would pollute his good whisky with ice!

He gulped a swallow of the fiery liquid.

Careful, he cautioned as he came close to spilling his last few drops. Got to leave some for tomorrow night, his lips curved into the wry chuckle. 'It's my birthday tomorrow!' He announced aloud to the cold dark desert.

A lonely man talking to himself.

Doug was considered an enigma, a hermit, even by the myriad of characters and lifestyles of men who were Coober Pedy miners.

Few lived and worked this far north from the main opal fields and none shared his camp. Or shared his lifestyle, living on his mine lease. He'd quarried, first with a bull dozer making a pit, then he had dug into a side wall to both search for opal and make a room to live in. Both were successful. A bright shot of colour continued for a hundred metres, and he dug sideways parallel with the surface following the opal. His ever enlarging room was comfortable and cool. Overhead, at top ground level, he had a series of solar panels for light and power to cut his stone, and a similar system provided him with an environmentally friendly toilet. Once a month he went to Coober Pedy and booked into a motel for a decent shower. Then he'd deposit his opal in the bank, shop for stores and any mining equipment he needed, borrow as many books as the library would let him, have a restaurant meal, get thoroughly drunk at the pub and return to the motel to sleep. As the sun rose next morning he'd begin to feel the claustrophobia of town living. After another long shower, sometimes he'd check his mail box for the rubbish it usually contained, then he headed out 'home' to sleep the rest of the day off.

Around his camp and especially to the south the inland desert spread out like an empty pitted canvas – dust rumpled and mineshaft creased, way away to the horizon. Further north lay the Breakaways. Glorious low flat topped hills that lit up with colours ranging from the reds through to gold at dawn and sunset. In the valleys shadows played with the last or first rays of light.

Doug started as way off he heard the sound of a dingo howling. The Dog Fence was not far north so Doug knew this dog was most likely a dingo. A few got through or around the thousand kilometre fence stretching from Queensland to Ceduna to keep the feral dogs from the stock, especially sheep, and farmlands.

It howled as it waited for the moon!

Doug shifted in his camp chair. That dog again! His tin cup wobbled.

'Infernal animal!' he cursed aloud. 'Be bloody off with you!' His slurred shout dissipated into the darkness.

The dingo howled again. The yowl ended in a throaty cough.

Doug steadied.

This was an old animal, he knew it. Almost as old as he was; almost as old as he felt. He sensed the presence at dusk when the night sucked the desert heat away. Always the dog edged behind the ridges. Always just out of sight.

He would talk to it. Ramble on to it; and the surrounding emptiness for hours.

Once he was sure that the wild dog's sudden howling during the daylight had warned him an instant before his first mineshaft collapsed. After that he had never been sure if it was a friend, or a foe like everyone said. Dingoes were vermin, undomesticated and wild, and it unnerved him that the animal left tracks all around his campsite while he slept.

And he'd never seen the dog...

But like his conscience the enigmatic dingo was always there.

In the daylight. A yellow shadow... watching.

But as shadows lengthened and night descended its black covering blanket, everything changed.

The dingo owned the dark.

Doug resisted the impulse to turn towards the repeated howl and the insistent cough that followed the howl. It sounded like one from a man who had smoked hard tobacco all his life. If he moved he knew the animal would slip away down from the crests to meld into the star cast shadows of his bull dozer trenches and shafts. He shuddered as the feral presence sent a wave of tremor down his back. His tatty denim collar pressed stiffly into his neck. The warmth seeped from his whisky and his thoughts threaded back...back...to a time thirty years ago. He didn't want to go there but the memories always hung in the depths of his whisky cup.

Back when their chosen road had been the grey bitumen line that sang like a cello under their car's wheels.

Doug and Gina had gone north to the limitless horizon that merged ahead into an indigo sky. Past where the cultivated paddocks had petered out to the open red saltbush plains and arid sheep country. When the black bitumen had run out the old Ford had lurched and thudded into the many potholes on a track that meandered towards low rising lands beside a towering purple range. The Flinders Ranges – mountains as old as time thrust up from a long dead seafloor, encrusted with fossils. As they drove towards the ranges Gina's fringed hair had stuck in hot sweaty tendrils to her head, her scalp showed through the pale strands, pink as the baby she'd held to her breast. Her cotton dress was hiked up and the baby rocked contentedly in the striped folds with each of the car's shuddering, bucking movements.

They were happy. Planning and laughing with anticipation despite the heat.

An adventure to seek a home; a better life away from the city.

Two years after his stint in Vietnam.

They'd bought unseen a patch of dirt and stones, north of Hawker, with a slate bottomed creek that was marked on the maps. Hardly a creek, it only flowed very occasionally in winter. With it was an old wattle and daub house butted into the rising ranges shaped like sleeping dragons that breathed white dust on cool days and fearsome red swirling clouds in the heat of summer. A rusty rattling windmill pumped scant water as it turned its huge face to the winds. Eagles circled high above and black flies, hovered low, to sip moisture from their eyes and mouth.

Gina waged a continual war on the flies shooing them away from the babies. She loved the blue wrens and diamond finches that chattered out of the scrub and clustered around her tin dish birdbath. She'd planted gardens into the arid red soil and, barefooted, carried the children's bathwater out over the sharp stones. Every drop was used. But the heat and dry almost always won. If the desert didn't get them then the kangaroos, emus and wild goats did. She'd laughed, poured over the catalogues when the children were tucked up for the night, and planted more seeds.

The sheep thrived on saltbush and had done pretty well. But each year Doug was forced to drive the huge stock trucks when the money was scarce and the market price for their sheep was too meagre to send them to the slaughterhouse. He'd be away for weeks at a time but they had managed. Gina would see to the children's radio 'School of the Air' lessons and make a damper bread to eat with the eternal mutton and eggs. Fearlessly she chased away a dingo that slunk down from the ranges to attack the chooks and waited until Doug came home again.

Doug brought the whisky cup back to his lips. Cursed his impotence against this dingo nemesis as the hot spirits arched down his throat. He coughed, a sting in his mind, knowing that he had to relive everything again and again.

Every night in the dark, by himself.

Back to the drought years so long ago.

Drought and fire. The fire that sped like a black and red billowing devil across the land until the rain came in torrents and ash eddied around his feet like dirty snow. Oddly it was the rain Doug thought of tonight. Individual raindrops that hurled up ash crowns of dust.

But the rain had come too damn late to save anything; Doug swore grimly standing in the fire aftermath and turmoil. More large drops made pathways through the grey ash masking his face and barely disguised the slow tears that wound down the creases of his lean whiskered jowls. Behind him an emergency fire vehicle sped away its siren yawping into a sad note that threaded back along the homestead track and echoed away into the smoke of the scorched hills.

He'd gone out afterwards with his rifle to slaughter the last of the burned sheep as they stood or lay still in clumps like blackened clay. Stinking of burned wool, burned flesh and pain. Killed them all. One at a time from his single shot .22 rifle. Shoot, reload; shoot until his arms ached and his hands were sore from pulling the bolt back. Tried not to look into their eyes – just put them out of their misery. The whole flock, all damaged, all gone.

He looked up as the lone dingo slid away, a survivor on the burned landscape. It would be back to feed on the carcasses. He fired off a quick shot at it in useless retaliation.

He already hated the inevitability of wild fire. It was the beginning of his hatred of dingoes.

The house was a wreck. Almost gone...

But Gina... she'd coped.

Doug's eyes glowed in memory in the dark lonely campsite and a half smile twitched and softened his features.

Gina hadn't just sat and looked. When he came back to take her into his arms to comfort her she'd shouldered him aside. She had beaten him into the twisted corrugated iron and smoldering timber stumps that was once their house. Into the mess. She'd found a string shopping bag in the car boot and poked about until she'd found things worth saving.

Anything. Anything to put into her string bag.

A blue and white plate, four mismatched cups that she'd bought in an op shop on the journey north. A scorched metal picture frame and one of Rhette's red shoes she'd danced in to the tunes from the old wind up gramophone player. The player was burned but the lone shoe glowed ruby red still and unmarked in the ashes.

She collected anything she could tell a story about. Everything had a meaning to Gina.

Always her meanings and his promises.

His smile broadened as he remembered that Gina had framed the single child's shoe in the dented frame and hung it triumphantly in their borrowed caravan. Her survival trophy...

# Chapter 12

Rhette clung onto a basin in the hotel ladies rest room.

Someone had spilled perfume, a sharp exotic spicy fragrance into the basin and that, with the fear that welled up from her stomach, made her gag. If her fingernails could have dug holes through the fancy porcelain basin they would have. So bloody much for giving evidence in camera, her thoughts tumbled and raged.

He bloody well recognized me! She thought. He knew it was me who testified against them.

The taxi had stopped in front of the South Australian Hotel.

'That'll be $25,' the driver said looking her up and down. The meter read $20 but she looked classy enough to pay the extra. She gave him $20 with a sneer, still too street wise for his game. She dropped then stepped into her red high heeled stilettos as she got out of the cab.

Before he could take off she leaned back into the car. Handed over an extra fifty. 'You going to be here all night? Rostered here?'

'Yeah.'

'I've got a bit of business to finalize,' she said. 'I might have to leave in a hurry.'

'So?' The extra tip hadn't been that good. She could've fooled him but she still didn't look like a pro. Didn't sound like a prostitute either.

The red slash of her mouth widened enough into a smile to show a set of good white teeth. Chanel No 5 perfume wafted. 'I'd make it worth your time to keep a look out. Be ready to jump the queue for me.'

He handed over a card with his number on it. 'It'll cost you.'

'Yeah, I don't doubt that,' she said.

Inside the night function was well under way. The reception desk was deserted and no-one was checking invitations anymore. The older patrons of the benefit dinner had departed when the South Australian Symphony Orchestra had finished its required repertoire of light classical music and had packed up its instruments and left. The echelons of high mighty and wealthy society had left too after they had been contacted and charmed by Dieter Hood. He made arrangements for business meetings in the following days in organized crime business so blatant he could converse and do his deals in a public place. They, the needy unknowing charities, wanted his dollars very badly. He was invited as a successful interstate businessman and entrepreneur to these events. To them, he looked and acted like a benefactor, a slickly styled operator from before the credit slump. Silver hair and expensive hand stitched suits, covering a still good body, could do that.

A DJ was besieging the eardrums of those who'd stayed on with heavy rap and rock.

Dieter Hood had stayed on too.

He watched as the lesser people, many who had fast money to burn and who frequented the celebrity pages of newspapers, stayed on too. He could fleece these idiots, make instant cash and get whatever he wanted from them for the night. Sometimes there were interesting pickings amongst the younger women.

Rhette swung her hips as she sauntered into the centre of the crowd who were shuffling the latest dance moves. Dancing without messing up their hair or their designer rags. The new day was young but the enhancements of copious spirits and drugs would well change that pseudo dignity before dawn. She carefully passed the bar. Her whole being craved a drink, but after six months with only the occasional glass of convent sherry, she knew she would buckle under a swallow of the real alcohol, real spirits.

She looked up.

Looked quickly down.

Damn!

Hood was on the second level, where tables of people sat watching the scene below and enjoying last quiet drinks. But Hood was surrounded by his entourage and a gaggle of underage looking girls. There'd been a brief time when I was going to be one of his women, Rhette thought. Before she'd met his brother. Hood liked them ripe, and preferably a little dependent on the drugs he could supply. She looked up again. His bloody tastes had changed. Getting to be a dirty old man now. The girls look younger than ever. Or maybe I've been away too long to know, she thought.

A large hand reached out and cupped her breast. Easy to do on in the mix of a crowded dance floor.

She pushed the hand away. Jabbed a sharp elbow into a man's chest.

'You going for Assault and Battery now Ms Ryan?' a deep voice said. 'You can't do that to an officer on duty.' The voice was friendly, and she recognized him.

She was busted.

'Bugger off Harry! Get your filthy hands off me,' she said.

'Who me? I never touched you...'

Harrison Shaw was Major Crime. 'I'll bloody Assault and Battery you.' She looked him up and down. Smiled into the handsome, yet ugly, bulldog face of the man she'd known in Sydney. A cop who'd rescued her on more than one occasion, and there had always been an attraction between them. Tonight Harry, a big man, was impressive in his formal black suit, teamed with a deep maroon coloured tie.

'You don't scrub up too badly. Even managed to tie your own bow tie,' she said.

'Yeah, and I just love wearing a monkey suit.'

Rhette moved in closer. 'You transferred here or just on loan?' she said.

'On loan, and they don't mind my ties.'

Rhette smiled up into his face. 'All their taste must be in their mouths. You have the worst collection of gaudy neck ties I've ever seen.' She slipped closer. Almost into his arms. He didn't seem to mind. 'Dance with me, Harry. I want to look a bit more.'

'Well, don't look too hard. You're totally out numbered tonight.' Harry kept one elbow in against his side as he moved; kept his piece out of sight.

'It's that bad is it?' she said. 'You all carrying? Expecting trouble?'

'No, just being prepared. The gentleman you're looking at is moving into Adelaide big time. We want to keep a track on who he meets. Even here tonight.'

'Good luck on that bastard.' He gyrated with her. She grinned up into his wide open face again. 'You never could dance,' she said.

'Dancing's not part of my job description but keeping innocent bystanders from getting involved is.' Hardly innocent, he thought and the smile he gave her was warm and very real.

'I've always liked you, Harry, it's a pity...' she said still moving beside him.

Rhette had been a police informant for years, on the edge of things as she fought her own drug addiction devils. She was Harry's contact and a relationship of trust had grown between them. Maybe it had a chance of more. Then the death of her sister Kate had changed her perspectives and she'd vanished from the Sydney scene.

He'd missed her but people went missing all the time, especially after a court case where someone connected to big time crooks was in the dock. Someone who'd got off and whose associates were not happy about being hauled into court. Then witnesses sometimes went missing...

Harry felt a surge of relief as he watched her. It was a year or more since that court appearance and he'd kept an eye out in case she turned up again. At least tonight he knew she wasn't dead. Now as he towered over her on the dance floor he was appreciative too of what he saw.

Rhette looked hot tonight and he was sure she wasn't concealing anything under the black silky thing she was wearing. He eyed her red shoes then her black bag slung casually over her arm. It looked a little too heavy to just contain a lipstick and a change purse. It was big enough for a knife. Or a gun. 'You've haven't come out to do anything silly?' he said. 'Come on, hand it over or I'll have to take it.'

'Obviously I'm not doing anything now with you here.' There was an edge of annoyance, replacing the banter in her voice as she slid closer to him and her fingers opened her purse. With almost a conjurer's speed the pistol disappeared into Harry's pocket. Rhette pushed away from Harry's broad chest then glanced past him and up again.

Dieter Hood was looking directly down at her as he stood by the top level rails. As one of the young pussies came to him, Rhette noticed a tall slim shadow who stood just behind the Boss. Hood stared down at her and shifted a perfectly tuxedoed arm to encircle the younger woman's waist, obviously for Rhette's benefit. The man loved playing the elegant gangster.

He raised an eyebrow.

Rhette pushed a hand through her tangle of auburn hair, lowered her eyes then raised them to look directly at Hood.

The look he was now giving her was cold and hard.

Her application was refused.

Hood reached back and slid his hand up and down the hip of the girl who pouted prettily beside him then turned and said something to the shadowy figure.

'Shit! I'd better get out of here,' Rhette said.

'Get to the ladies loo,' Harry said. He stooped down to break the line of vision of those above. 'We'll head them off and I'll have someone meet you there.'

'Don't bother. Give me a few minutes. I've got an escape in place. Just please make sure I get out of the door OK.' Rhette turned back to him standing tall on her stilettos, almost as tall as he was, and brushed her lips against his. 'Thanks for your help,' she said.

The flippant had given way to fear.

She's need to get out of Adelaide.

But going east to Sydney or Melbourne wasn't going to be an option.

The shadow smelled her waft of perfume and fear. He listened as the red stilettos click- clacked in haste down the hall from the ladies room and heard her intake of breath as she struggled with the handle to open the EXIT door to the outside lane. There was a final rustle of silk before the door shut behind her.

He returned to his post on the balcony.

He shrugged, missed her, to Hood.

# Chapter 13

Ana had booked into the older style four star Whyalla Foreshore Motel, on Watson Terrace, where, she thought, she could take Piet for walks on the beach after the day's drive.

She stood and looked out their unit's window towards the beach. The brochure had promised an absolute beach frontage but the beach was nothing like the beaches they knew in Port Lincoln. At the top of Spencer Gulf the tides were slow, weak, and there was going to be a long walk across the sand flats to reach the shallow water's edge. Pietie could fossick in the pools and there might be shells to find and soldier crabs to chase, she thought, now as a grin spread across her face. He was good at collecting crabs, tiny ones, to put in his bucket to let loose again in the sea.

Always fun...and running on the beach was a good way to take out the kinks from being in the car for four or more hours.

Their room had sea views and her car was not visible from the street. She had decided that she'd get rid of the older blue Mercedes, Peter's much loved Mercedes, when she got to Darwin. Until then it was comfortable and dependable for the trip. Parking it off the street usually meant that it stayed safe from the temptation of potential thieves. Or vandals.

That morning they had seen the 'Loaded Dog' sculpture based on Henry Lawson's famous bush tale at the Mount Laura Homestead Museum. Ana told Piet of the playful dog, Tommy, who'd make off with a stick of dynamite in its mouth, dragging the fuse through a campfire and creating mayhem in the chase that followed.

He listened with rapt attention, laughed and then asked. 'Mummy, can I have a dog when we get to Darwin?'

'We'll see,' Ana said.

After lunch they drove north on the road to Port Augusta to the maritime museum and the land locked corvette 'HMAS Whyalla' which nosed out onto the Lincoln Highway.

That was when Demetrius Quinn roared past the Mercedes on his Harley heading for Port Augusta and the long haul to the state capital city of Adelaide. Glancing sideways, he saw the woman driving. The heavy bike wobbled on the road as his hands jolted the handlebar in shock. He corrected the machine to recover quickly.

Ana Foster!

He knew her instantly.

Without any doubt. When a person had been close enough to try to strangle someone in broad day light then they remembered the face. And her hair.

He'd looked for that face wherever he was in Australia. Her face, and the face of his son.   That whore had still to answer the questions he had for her.

He continued on past her and waited out of sight near the Maritime Museum. When her car pulled into that car park he decided that she was probably staying in Whyalla. He pulled back into the trees before kicking his huge bike into life and continuing on the hours ride to Port Augusta. From there he made a phone call back to Whyalla before he did the extra business the Boss wanted in the regional city.

Just a hint, he thought, of what was in store for her. He wasn't sure what yet but he'd plan something. Something that got what he wanted without the pigs knowing he was alive.

So far he'd stayed under the police radar.

As Piet sat in his car seat, his little legs were tired after climbing up and down the steep steel ladder-ways on the Whyalla corvette, Ana got out her lap top and calculated on her petrol needs for the next days. The Merc slurped up the petrol and she wanted to make sure she had sufficient for the next part of the journey. Yes, she'd need to tank up before they left. They would stay another day in Whyalla, there was plenty to see yet and they'd been assured that they could stay in their motel for another night. She sent a text to the motel to confirm the booking before glancing back at Pietie. He'd nodded off, his head drooping with Bear clutched to his chest.

She put the computer onto the seat next to her and started the car. It was warm inside and automatically she pressed the window controls and put both front side windows down. Better air than air conditioning.

With thoughts of Pietie waking hungry when they got back to the motel, she turned back onto the Lincoln Highway. A ripe banana, yes and maybe a chocolate Fredo Frog as a treat, to curb his hunger until dinner. She'd be able to have a few minutes to herself to read a bit then while he played with his Lego. As she drove back to Whyalla the acrid smell from the BHP iron foundry made her press the controls to close all the car windows again.

That action to close the windows saved their lives.

As Ana moved away from the traffic lights and crossed McBride Terrace, two motor bikes pulled in behind her.

They loomed dark in her rear vision mirror.

One passed on her driver's side and twice swung a metal bar against the window and door frame of the heavy vehicle. The strong Mercedes structure held. Startled, she saw only a full face helmet and black leather as he changed gear and the motor bike sped away.

Instinctively she'd dragged at the steering wheel and the car bucked towards the left. It spun the rear tyres and she fought to control the skid into the road side gravel. The other biker swung hard to avoid the slewing car and flying stones. Despite the speed he was traveling he managed to get a foot on the ground to steady himself.

He threw something. It flicked past the window and thumped onto the front engine bonnet. It bounced off and it flew high in an arch behind the car.

The bikie roared away ahead.

Ana's car was ten meters on, still ploughing through the verge when the incendiary petrol bomb exploded. It took out a bus stop and the boom was heard as far away as the city centre and police station. She pulled over to the side of the road and threw herself over the front seat to clutch Piet to her body, to protect him from the inferno behind the car.

'What's happening?' Piet's eyes were bleary with sleep. The blue eyes cleared. 'Look a fire...'

Ana fought to keep the shaking out of her voice. 'Is Bear alright?' she asked.

'Yes, Bear's good,' the little boy said.

'We're OK then...'

Ana got out of her car, moved away and was standing holding her son tightly when the fire trucks, an ambulance, Mark and the police arrived.

# Chapter 14

'Mark ... Mark Llewellen?' Ana said.

Surprise swept across her face followed by a hesitant quivery smile. She stood up from her protective crouch over Piet and, still holding her son's hand, she just moved into Mark's arms. It felt the most natural thing in the world as he wrapped her into a close embrace. It was brief and both stepped back, flustered by their own actions.

There was a beat.

Piet clung to her clutching Bear. Ana's fingers cradled the boys head against her thigh.

'Are you OK? Not hurt?' Jessica gave them the interruption they needed.

'Yes! Yes. They attacked me?' Ana said. 'Why me?'

'It was random,' Jessica was quick to suggest. She was getting experienced and knew that police gave that excuse before any investigations were done. Somehow she already doubted the attack was random.

Ana let her question hang as the fire engines poured water on her car. The paint was blistered from the inferno. Uniformed police pushed at the crowd then put up the inevitable yellow tape around the scene. Bystanders shuffled back and gawked. Many lit cigarettes.

'Do an emu pick on the butts,' Lex said to a uniformed officer, 'after the scene clears.' The man nodded. Lex walked back to Mark. Got that expression right, he thought, but he wasn't expecting any spectacular DNA results. The men, reported to be on the big Harleys, had left the scene.

Lex watched as Mark, still with a hand just touching the woman and child, scanned the crowd of onlookers to spot anyone suspicious. Both men didn't miss much.

An hour later Ana and Piet were seated near Mark's desk in the police station.

Jessica had gone out and bought sandwiches for them all, and chips and chicken nuggets for the child. With that Jessica had become Piet's number one friend, after Bear that is. Piet sat eating and watching Lex as he swiveled in his chair. He knew Aboriginal people but this huge ink black man was different. Lex pulled a friendly face and winked, and Piet laughed. Another friend.

'The first thing you'll have to do is get rid of the car,' Mark said. 'It's damaged anyway. Ana had blurted out her destination. 'And maybe you should fly to Darwin...'

'I don't want to do either.' Ana said her voice had become flat and withdrawn. She hadn't touched her sandwich but had drunk the coffee from the commercial cardboard cup.

'It's essential that you do both, Ana. I don't know why you were attacked but indications are that they were bikies. It's just not safe when they are involved.' He was more insistent than Jessica had ever heard him speak to a victim. She looked at him. She saw the spark that was more than of concern. Mark continued. 'Your car's material evidence anyway. There'll be evidence of the incendiary they used. I'll have to impound it.' Mark exchanged glances with Lex, and the latter turned away and opened his mobile to call the Forensics Branch again.

Ana watched the exchange. 'I'll agree about the car. But surely it was a random attack, as Jessica said.'

'I'm sure. And flying's the safest way. Though you'd have to go back to Adelaide to get a flight. I can arrange that.'

'No, I'm still going to drive to Darwin. I've promised Pietie. If I change my plans now he'll be disappointed,' Ana said. Her hands were stubbornly flat on the table. 'I can buy a new car.'

Jessica noted the look of almost defiance as Ana's dark eyes flashed at Mark. Like there were already covert messages between them.

Don't push me.

I want you safe. I'm more than concerned.

Lex waded into the covert fray. 'How about I take Mrs Foster to look at cars.'

'Ana please,' Ana said as she smiled at Lex and the diversion he'd provided. The tension between herself and Mark was almost palpable.

Lex's returning grin was open and frank. His reading of this fascinating woman with the unusual hair was that he recognised her as like him, a bit alien, and exotic even in this fascinating land of Australia. From Mark's file he knew the story, and said. 'Ana, then. Thank you. I'd suggest a four by four as the safest vehicle for driving to Darwin. I know it's all on the bitumen but you'll need something strong.' He didn't add that a four wheel drive would be a common vehicle on the Stuart Highway and wouldn't stand out like an invitation for trouble as the midnight blue Mercedes did.

'I can afford something new, as long as it's not too pricey. Or big.' Ana appeared relieved with an alternative outlet.

'OK then. But first I'd like Jessica to take you back to the motel and we'll move you to a safe Bed & Breakfast we've used here before,' Mark said. 'Then you can go car shopping with Lex.'

'Will you stay with me until Mummy gets back?' Lex asked Piet. The child shook his head and went to Ana. He clung to her hand. Ana smiled a thanks but she needed her son with her. To feel his presence. Lex flashed a big wide smile and said, 'Well, I'll see you later then.'

Ana sat at the dining table of the B&B.

She was exhausted but had ravenously devoured the chicken casserole that her hosts, Janet and Charlie Ross, had provided her for dinner. She tasted the bottle of white wine served with it. Delicious and she'd drunk a glass. Her hosts were kind, unobtrusive and had accents that flowed over her like sun warmed Scottish heather reminiscent of Gus McMahon her old friend from the Port Lincoln Prison. She clung to the remembered comfort.

Being put into safe quarters after a crime was not new and Ana shuddered. This time she had her son to care for.

Now Pietie was fed she read 'Cat in the Hat' yet again to him, letting her tongue slide around the rhymes and rhythms of the words. She cuddled him and sat on the side of his bed until he slept.

She felt like a shuttle-cock. Hit back and forth over a net of trouble. So much had happened since they'd left the ship "Whyalla" museum in the early afternoon. Her car had been attacked. The Police, the fire engines, then seeing Mark and Jessica again, followed by the necessity to move out of the motel for her safety. To replace the damaged and heat warped Mercedes which was a write off, the big black policeman had gently led her to buy the new four wheel drive car that Mark had insisted had to be bought immediately. It was garaged in the B&B she was now in. The registration, insurance and all the rest of the buying was handled easily and with little fuss.

At first she was sure she didn't need all the Outback gear, as the salesman called it, things like extra mechanical bits for the car, a winch and ropes. A first Aid kit. Lex in his quiet way had suggested that she was traveling a huge distance, like across Africa, and she could never know what could happen or what she might need. These were all bought and put in a special box on the luggage rack, also recommended. A large jerry type can of water, another of petrol, were put into the vehicle.

She was again prepared for the trip to Darwin, better even than before leaving Port Lincoln and she realized that she had been a bit *lasse faire* about it all. When she and Peter had honeymooned across this huge land they had though little of what they'd need. Young and inviolate, they had been safe.

It was different now travelling with a child. Pietie was so precious.

But now Mark...

Out of nowhere Mark was here – again when she needed him.

She was aware that it wasn't just gratitude she felt for the detective who had been so kind in Port Lincoln and Renmark. Who had taken her calls when she was pursued by an escaped prisoner, had believed her and in her. Who for brief moments had held her, protected her, when her world was imploding around her.

Not once but twice now.

He had made an impression she had never forgotten.

Ana folded the linen napkin and placed it beside her plate. She went in to check on Pietie. He was so beautiful in sleep, a thumb in his mouth and Bear held at his chest. She gently took the thumb out of his mouth as a discrete knock came at the door. 'A moment,' she said, and bent to kiss her son's cheek. She moved on quiet bare feet back to the sitting room. 'Come in.'

Janet bustled in. She brought a finger to her lips. 'Is the wee lamb asleep?' she said. 'I've come for your tray.' She looked at the empty plate with a warm expression of approval.

'My meal was wonderful. Just what I needed.' Ana said to confirm the woman's good cooking.

'Stay as long as you want,' Janet stated as a figure appeared behind her. She turned and smiled at Mark. 'I'll leave the wine. There are more glasses cooling in the little friggie. There's beer there too.'

'Thanks Janet,' Ana said.

'Thanks,' Mark said almost in unison with Ana as Janet left. She flushed yet it broke the ice yet again. 'I'll get myself a beer then.' He raised an enquiring eyebrow at her and went to the fridge. He chose a small beer and opened it. He turned back to Ana.

'I'll have a little more of the wine. I'll get it,' she said. 'Please, sit,' she gestured towards where two separate chairs and a matching velvet covered settee waited in the lounge area.

He chose a chair and put the bottle onto the floor beside him. She poured her wine and sat opposite. 'How's Piet...?' he asked. He seemed unsure of how to finish the question.

'Pietie's doing fine. He's asleep. Tired out. It's been an exciting day for him although he doesn't seem at all fazed by it.'

'Children are pretty adaptable,' Mark said. With a laugh he

added, 'not that I know much about kids...'

Ana smiled in return as Mark faltered. 'He's Peter's son. I didn't know I was pregnant...until after he died.'

After he died helped. It cleared a space in the air between them.

Mark was relieved that she could speak of his death. It made the guilt he was feeling about the resurgence of feeling he had for her allowable. Permitted the slow pulse that had flowed through him when he saw her again to quicken; and the moment when he had held her again. And found she fitted, as before.

Ana leaned forward. Her hair fell forward over her face and he marveled again at the broad natural white strands. With her hands she parted the hair back behind her ears and he saw that she had aged just a little since he saw her last. Four plus years, grief and a baby on her own must have done that. But she was still lovely.

'He's a beautiful boy,' Mark said. The term beautiful came very easily.

'Yes, he is.'

There was a beat. 'But you have to think carefully about what you are going to do next. I know you've bought the new car...but that can be changed. You should fly to Darwin – get there quickly and safely. Get out of the area. I think this was a random attack but you never can tell.'

'Are you making a bogey man for me from this bikie attack?' Ana said. There was a look of annoyance in the dark eyes. 'They missed me. I don't think they'll try again.'

'You could go on the Ghan. It stops at Port Augusta...put your new car on the train.'

'Well, I'm not changing my plans. I've got the car as you suggested and I'm going on to drive to Darwin as soon as I can,' Ana said. 'For goodness sake – Lex and the dealer set me up with everything for outback travel. An extra fuel container, tools... heaps of stuff I'll never use but have in case I do need them. Pietie and I'll be fine.' She looked at him with both defiance and a look that insisted that she made her own decision. The look hid the fact that amongst the things that had happened today she was very confused by the presence of Mark.

She felt the attraction between them and that was not what she was expecting.

It could ruin her plans and Mark was a part of the past she was moving away from.

'I don't like it but...' he frowned. He wanted to reach to take her hand. To say – no don't go – but caution held him back. She was a victim again and his professionalism held him in check. He took a swallow of his beer, then decided that he should go and put the bottle on the occasional table. 'You must be exhausted,' he said formally. 'I'll get Jessica to pick you up when you're ready in the morning and we'll get a statement done then.'

They both rose from their chairs and Ana followed him to the door. 'Goodnight,' she said, 'And thank you.'

They stood another beat.

Bloody hell, Mark thought. If she hadn't said thank you like that he might have touched her, given her a hug, something. Now that thank you sounded like it was to the detective copper, not the man. He let the brief moment pass and went out.

Ana closed the door quietly and slumped against it. She was torn between the past and what might so nearly have been.

# Chapter 15

Sister Bernadette frowned.

'For goodness sake Rhette,' she said. 'I know you went out last night. Going out and after Dieter Hood. I feared you would one day and I heard you come back after we'd finished First Prayers. Don't treat me like a fool.'

Rhette held her coffee cup tightly as they sat at the heavy rectory table. 'I know you're not that... but I do have to get away.'

'No you don't. You can be safe here. I'll call the Protection Unit again and make sure that they know you're back.'

'You told them I was out?' Rhette's voice took on an edge she usually didn't display with the nuns. 'Major Crime know I'm in Adelaide but the Protection guys think I'm lying low. Not being seen. Well that's it then. I have to go.'

'Rhette, listen to yourself. You're being irrational. You can settle back into the life here and go on as before.'

'The bastard saw me...' she flicked a brief sorry look at Bernadette. 'He knew who I was.'

'You're still here this morning aren't you? Back safe.'

'Yes, but I don't know if I was followed. He could have got to the cab driver. I paid him plenty but Hood could have paid him more.'

Sister Bernadette walked around the table and seemed to put a blessing on the distraught woman as she touched her shoulder. 'You have to learn to trust. What you did last night was against all we've talked about.'

'Yes, I know but...'

'And I thought you'd made the transition to a more useful life. Not gone chasing a ghost.'

'I didn't drink or do drugs. I didn't kill although that was my aim last night if I got the chance.'

'My child, you did it all in your mind. You planned to do it.' She sighed. 'I don't know how you found out that Mr Hood would be there last night. You did, and I hope that you don't pay the price for it.'

'Or I make you all pay the price. This place's busted. Hood could finish it and everyone here. Have it fired bombed and everyone'd think it was an accident. He's a total bastard...sorry...but no Sister, I have to go.'

'You can't just go. You'll need a plan. Maybe the Major Crime people could help...'

Sister Bernadette changed the subject. 'Has this anything to do with the letter you sent a month ago? When you asked me for the postcode for Coober Pedy?'

'A little, maybe. I found out that Hood was going to be in Adelaide and thought that I'd better finish some business just in case.'

'In case of what, Rhette?'

'Alright, my father should be told of his younger daughter's death. About Kate. Even if he probably wouldn't care...if something happened to me too.'

'So you sent a letter...'

'No... just the death announcement.' Rhette's teeth gripped her lower lips like a petulant child's as her mentor looked up as though seeking guidance.

'So, what will you do now if you are so sure that you can't stay here ?

Rhette pushed the barely touched remains of her breakfast away. 'I'll get in touch with Harry. See if he has any ideas...'


'There's a message for you,' Lex put his head around Mark's door. 'Came through on the land line. Harry from Major Crime said you weren't answering your phone last night.'

Mark raised a hand in acknowledgement and leaned back in his chair. 'Did he say what it was about?'

'No but I got the idea he was calling in a favour. He made some lurid comments about your phone being off...'

Mark chuckled. 'He would. We've worked together. A good bloke. I'll introduce you to him when we get to Adelaide next.'

An hour later Mark knocked on Ana's door.

'Got a favour to ask,' he said without preamble when she came to answer it. After last night's visit he was careful this morning.

As she let him into the room the butterflies in his stomach were wearing football boots and his professional veneer was buffeted as he saw her face was pale. The skin of her cheeks was stretched tight and half moons of shadow lay below her dark, dark eyes. 'Are you OK?' his question was spontaneous.

'I'm just a bit tired,' she smiled. 'Things got much too scary yesterday, especially with Pietie there. We've lead a quiet life...' she intimated now...'and the trip north is going to be adventure enough.'

Piet came into the room clutching Bear. He wrapped an arm about Ana's leg, hefting up the blue skirt she wore. Mark willed his gaze to remain on her face, or on the child's face, and to ignore the expanse of slim bare leg that Piet had disturbed. Ana's colour rose as she pulled her skirt down and lifted the child to her hip. 'You said a favour...?'

# Chapter 16

Mark's whole being wanted to tell Ana of his renewed feelings for her, but it wasn't the time or the place. One didn't romance a woman with a child on her hip even if, he suspected, her rush of colour said 'maybe.'  His professionalism, with reluctance, kicked in again.

'You've had time to think. Are you still determined to go on to Darwin?' he said.

'Yes. As soon as I can.'

'Would you consider taking a passenger with you?'

'What, as an escort? Surely I don't need that,' she said. Again the flush as a thought occurred. 'You don't mean...?'

I wish, he thought. 'No, it's a woman we need to assist to get to the Northern Territory.' Her eyes widened. Registered doubt. 'She's OK. I know her and she's near your age. Currently she lives in an Adelaide convent,' he said.

Ana's eyebrow rose.

Here Mark hesitated. He didn't know enough about Ana to guess what her views were on that. 'She's not a nun... She's in Witness Protection.' Damn, he thought, I probably shouldn't have said that... 'I also think that two women, with a child, travelling up through the Centre together would be less noticeable than you on your own.'

Ana's mouth twitched in doubt.

'Maybe she could help with the driving. Give you a break...'

'She can't fly? Or go by bus?' She asked.

'We'd prefer to keep her out of the public travel system at this time,' Mark said aware that he was talking in police jargon. 'It would be better if she was moved in a private capacity.' That sounded so official he almost flinched at his own words.

Ana paused in thought. 'There's no way she'd put us in danger, is there? Sounds more and more mysterious to me.'

'I don't think so. I could arrange a phone call between the two of you to see if you could get on. It's a long way to go with a stranger.'

'That would probably help. Can I think about it and get back to you...this evening?'

'Sure,' Mark's voice was casual but there was a leap of blood inside him. A different time of meeting and then it would be goodbye again...it was urgent that he try to at least say something. Not leave things as they stood as contact had been made again.

Mark reflected as he started his car to go back to the station to arrange the telephone call through Harry. He didn't have a good record with long term relationships...could he do better now? If...and his thoughts stopped...if...they could do a long distance one...? His thoughts raced back to the final meeting with his ex-fiancée Erica.

It was 3 am, more than a year and a half ago, when he was still working with Major Crime, when Mark switched on the light. His pager had just gone off.

He headed out of bed and down the hall to the toilet. Gotta have a piss, he thought, and find a wearable shirt and get to the station. He saw the huge pile of ironing waiting in the basket on a table. Hmm, not there.

Life was easier when his 'on again off again' fiancée, Erica Marryat, was still with him. Washing and ironing done, meals and everything else, even if they paid for a woman who came in twice a week to do it. But the everything else bit was probably the best ...brought a wry smile.  Erica worked in the same professional area, sort of, as an up and coming criminal defence lawyer.

Still, he thought, his smile vanishing into the muddle of clothing in the basket, she wasn't called back at all hours of the sodding night to question an arrested suspect. A very rich and influential man he'd been investigating for weeks. Normally when Major Crime ordered – don't leave the state without telling us – people didn't. The suspect was alleged of trying to leave and was arrested and brought in for it. He'd have a gaggle of attending lawyers with him.

Mark cautioned himself to hurry up.

Erica was probably still tucked up in her bed asleep. Somewhere. Not in his bed. When they were together she would have opened one eye at least to acknowledge that he was going out on business.

'Bloody Shit!' he spat the oath aloud as he fossicked in the basket. This basket wasn't even clean clothing. He hadn't done the washing. He stormed back to the bedroom past the kitchen with his dishes in the sink and the take-away noodle box pulsing a miasma of stale smells above the table.

Got to find a shirt somewhere.

The wardrobe. He grabbed the first shirt his hand hit.

He'd been away on one of many country cases and, even if he was slack at home since he was on his own, he thought that the interview needed a clean shirt. Not a T shirt, this time. A clean shirt to face the barrage of lawyers. Even at this time of night they'd be suited up. He thrust his legs into his good black trousers. Small change and his car keys spilt out onto the floor. He ignored the shrapnel coins, scrabbled for the keys and found one shoe. "Where the hell is the other bastard!" he muttered, aware that he was taking too much time to get going. The bloody lawyers could have sprung his suspect by the time he got there. He found the other shoe and headed out the door.

In the car he calmed down.

It wasn't Erica's fault that home things had got into the muddle. I'm a selfish bastard! He remonstrated as he pushed a red light on King William Street. I'll have to get my act together. Send Erica some flowers, anything, promise her the earth and try to keep the promises to get her back. It had worked before...

He pulled into the Adelaide Police Station and pushed his card through security, sped into the lift and arrived a trace out of breath at the Interview Room 2 door.

To his surprise Erica was there.

She looked him up and down.

Erica raised a perfectly arched eyebrow.

'My client isn't happy,' she said as she walked ahead of him into the room and sat beside her client. Two stern faced junior lawyers frowned in unison from additional chairs.

Mark pulled a chair that was usually used by an assisting officer from against a wall and sat opposite them at the interview table.

Erica continued her indignant spiel. 'Mr Hood's been arrested like a common criminal and hauled in here. At this time of night! He's got a heart condition and needs his rest. Couldn't you people have waited until the morning?'

Dieter Hood looked in robust health; of an athletic build in an expensive suit and a tie that was perfectly matched. Mark noted that he, and his attending lawyers, were all attired as though it was 9 am and they were well rested. Ready for an important meeting perhaps but Hood also looked like a person with an early plane to catch. Mark let that observation stand. And the heart condition comment? With the man's perchance for multiple women followers he wasn't obviously a critical heart attack candidate. OK, he thought, I'm not a doctor so I can only go on the man's observed and reportedly Viagra assisted activities.

As if on cue Hood placed a manicured hand against his chest in the vicinity of his heart. Erica and the secondment of lawyers managed concerned looks.

'No it couldn't have waited until the morning... and your client didn't appear to be waiting either ...other than in an airport motel with checkout booked at 6am.' Mark snapped.

Mark sat back and looked at them for an answer. A pause. It was obvious that none of the four chose to comment.

Erica placed the arrest papers down onto the desk, all with professional distain.

A whiff of her spicy perfume riveted Mark's attention back to her. At her yards of long legs topped by a grey business suit and a whisper of lace showed where usually a woman wore a shirt. Above that her striking and intelligent face. Her fair hair was pulled back into an immaculate chignon. God she was beautiful. And sexy. But he'd had no idea she was representing Hood. The man was bad news and a person of interest in crimes originating in the New South Wales murder and drug scenes. Lately he'd been seen in Adelaide which was why he was under surveillance. His professional detachment took the second hit.

Erica replayed her up and down look at Mark. She focused on the white dress shirt. 'I don't know why you are grumbling now. You've obviously been out on the town tonight. Hope we didn't interrupt anything...' Erica's immaculate eyebrow rose again and her voice was over-loaded with amused dismissal. 'Or maybe you've been moonlighting as a waiter.'

The spare lawyers gave a titter of appreciation.

Dieter Hood didn't laugh but there was a flicker back to Erica and a look passed between them.

Mark knew the engagement was totally finished and flowers and chocolates weren't ever going to do anything again either.

From that moment he realised he didn't give a shit about her anymore.

# Chapter 17

Demetrius Quinn paced his motel room in Port Augusta.

When he had got into the room he had slung his black leather jacket onto the bed and the sweaty white tee shirt he wore showed off a magnificent physique. Prison years had started that and he kept up the exercise regime needed to keep in shape since he'd escaped. Tall and long legged, he quickly had to turn to continue his pacing in the small room. He sat on the bed and pushed off the boots that went with his Harley. It was too bloody hot for them too.

Like the town of Port Augusta the motel room wasn't the most glamorous of places. Utilitarian, slightly reminiscent of the prison cell that he had spent ten years in, but that was the least of his thoughts.

First he had to do the Boss's work.

He'd confirmed the contacts for transporting another parcel of chemicals to Whyalla and also to Port Augusta. It helped that there was a prison at Port Augusta. He had links there with prisoners and some of the wardens. After they were out the former made good money cooking drugs. He smiled; parole boards and counselors thought themselves shit clever setting parolees up with menial fuckwit jobs after release. He could and did promise more lucrative work. Much better paying work.

Whyalla and Port Augusta, he thought. Part of the Iron Triangle of industrial towns. In Whyalla the steel works spewed red stinking dust to the winds and at Port Augusta the burning of dirty brown coal in the power station gave the same camouflage to the drug lab smells. At least that's what he promised the contract workers. Many times it was correct and the heat endured by both towns kept many people off the neighborhood streets in the daylight hours.

Enough business, he thought and his handsome face screwed into a scowl.

But that bitch Ana Foster!

He'd suspected that she'd returned to Port Lincoln after their last meeting and his life, working in the gangs out of Sydney, kept him away from his pursuit of her. He had never believed that she didn't know where his son, Clinton, was living. He hated counsellors, always hated the bitches. She knew where the whore of a mother had spirited the boy away to when he was arrested in Port Lincoln. Probably with Ana Foster's assistance. He didn't doubt it. Not for a moment.

He'd just had to shelve it in his new life of survival and getting near the top of Dieter Hood's dung heap of associates.

Now he'd seen the whore.

One hell of a coincidence, he conceded.

First time since he'd tried to kill her in the prison, and then again on the houseboat on the Murray River.

Giving her the fright in Whyalla was out of pure vengeance. That felt good. He was contemplating what the next action against her would be when his mobile rang.

The ID was Johnny Fox, his immediate boss. As usual he didn't mince words although they were guarded. You could never tell who might link into mobile phones.

'Find the bastard who ratted on the import ship cargo. Or get the other one who messed up before he gets to court.' The voice was a million cigarette and drug hits husky. Quinn had no idea how the man still functioned with throat and nasal passages a mess. 'There's more coming so get that fixed and the labs set up. Bloody immediately. If not sooner. You're way behind with the fucking quotas. You'll also need to go and sort out the idiot up north. He's behind with supplies too.'

Quinn's report regarding the fire bombing of the labs in Whyalla didn't go well. Johnny was OK with his retaliation against Jason Hardy. An example was always a good idea. There was a pause. 'What was the idea about ordering the bombing of the

Merc?'

'Needed a random act to confuse the cops...' Quinn said.

'That's not what I heard, you dip shit! It was personal...'

'There's no way it could be traced to me. Remember I'm dead.'

'You fucking will be of you try something like that again. You put the bikies in the gun and you know that never works. They get annoyed. You also almost took out a kid.'

Quinn took a sharp breath. 'A kid? A bystander?' It was OK to kill kids if the parents were at fault. Often it was more effective than targeting the parents.

'No, you idiot! A kid, a little boy, was in the Merc. With the bloody woman.' There was a grunt at the other end of the phone followed by a hacking cough cut short abruptly as Johnny clicked off.

Quinn sat on the bed to digest that piece of information. A kid. The whore had a kid. There had to be an angle he could use sometime, someplace.

And he'd get the fuckwit bikie who'd ratted on him to Johnny Fox about the Foster bitch...

Mark fronted to the door of B&B flat.

His heart was pounding. I'm like a stupid teenager, he thought. He raised his hand to knock as Ana opened the door.

'I saw your car pull up,' she said.

He hoped her smile was not just because she'd noticed his flustered face. He ran a hand though the tangles of his hair. Was reminded that, as usual, his hair was too long.

'Thanks,' he said as he passed in front of her into the lounge room. Her fresh floral perfume sent his senses onto alert. When she indicated for him to sit tonight he chose the settee rather than the single chairs. He told himself that the light was brighter there. He could see her face better. The space next to him yawned empty and she sat down beside him.

'I spoke to Rita...' she corrected herself, 'Rhette isn't it? Pietie said hello too.' She smiled always at the mention of her son. 'He liked her...and I've decided to offer her the trip north with us. It sounds a good idea.'

'Good. I'll arrange for her to come to Whyalla straight away. It might take a day or so.' The day or so would also give him more time to see her... 'You're OK with the slight delay?'

Mark's blue eyes met Ana's brown ones and he wanted to swim in the dark chocolate depths.

'Yes,' she said.

She smiled a meaning and he looked down to find that he'd taken her hand. Her fingers curved to interlace with his.

'Ana...' he said and without any effort she was in his arms. As natural as each other time he'd held her. Their first kiss was warm and awkward. Then her lips held back a laugh against his and he let her go.

'It's alright,' she said. 'It's been a long time and... I didn't know where to put my arms...my hands.' She flushed scarlet.

He was very sure where he'd like her to put them.

He drew her to her feet and the kiss that followed, with bodies pressed together, held the sweetness of a slow mounting passion. Mark felt a groan start in his throat as his body responded to his longing for this woman who was more than he remembered. Their kisses continued the exploration of their mutual wanting and desire.

Ana pulled away. Her face was flushed 'I'm sorry,' she said. 'I'm not being a tease but this is happening too fast.'

'But...' Mark started. He felt the beginnings of foolishness. He held her still but felt the world and the moment dropping away...

Ana leaned back in his embrace. 'Mark, I want you right now...God I want you ...' a gleam turned to fire in her eyes. 'From the moment I saw you again yesterday...the need was there. It brought back the last time we were together. Then when we held each other. That was difficult... terrible...and now this has happened I need a little time to sort out my feelings.'

She moved away, still holding his hand, far away enough to look into his eyes.

'I think I understand but you haven't ever been out of my consciousness. You've always been there...since...always.' Mark said.

She pursed her lips and her eyes were large. 'But you were engaged...?'

'Erica? That ended in a whimper...not a bang,' he corrected himself. 'It just ran it's course and both of us knew that it was going to. I don't think I ever loved her not...'

She put her fingers against his lips. 'No, Mark...don't say that. Love takes time and we haven't had time yet. Whatever happens has to be thought through. I'm not the same person I was before. I loved Peter and I'm a mother now. Things are different.' She saw him wince. 'That doesn't mean that I won't love again.' She leaned forward and kissed him, a quick enticing kiss.

'Now you're teasing me...' he said.

'Not tonight,' she said and the gleam was back in her eyes. 'And not for long...'

# Chapter 18

The green and yellow St John's Ambulance pulled into the bay at the side of the Royal Adelaide Hospital. A female patient was wheeled out on a stretcher and her luggage was loaded aboard the vehicle.

'Transfer to the Whyalla Hospital?' the attendant asked as a burly man patted the woman's hand in goodbye. 'You coming too?'

'No she's on her own. Look after her.' Harry grinned. Just as they started to close the back doors he passed a small package, wrapped as a present, to her. 'See you,' he said and leaned over the stretcher and planted a kiss on her lips. A kiss that was warm and so fleeting that Rhette only had time to register that Harry's lips were soft and the pressure may have been more than just friendly.

'Not before…' The doors closed on her reply. Rhette's eyes widened and her tongue flicked along her lips as though tasting the memory. She slipped the parcel under the blanket covering her and smiled.

The attendant, sitting beside her, flicked though papers and called through to the driver as he made a radio transmission and started the engine. 'No orders, just a straight Royal Flying Doctor transfer. Typical sometimes the RAH tell us nothing.' Nothing also meant that she'd probably had surgery and needed more hospital time; cheaper time in the country hospital. Also the incident of post operative infection was less away from the major city hospitals. He turned to speak to his patient.

Rhette closed her eyes, yawned and pretended to be sleepy. Without makeup and her auburn hair scrunched back with a rubber band she looked like any other sick patient. Days of worry and tension had helped. The purple shadows that lurked under her eyes were all hers.

The attendant returned to his papers to leave his patient in peace. Hospitals are not places for rest and sleep, he thought. Too many footsteps and noise during the day and night. He preferred the intermittent drama and excitement of ambulance work.

Over the next four hours, Rhette was taken through the Royal Flying Doctor security doors at the Adelaide Airport terminal, loaded on to a RFD Pilatus PC – 12 aircraft and flown to Whyalla. The female air attendant, who introduced herself as Sally, was kind and considerate and, as the patient was apparently sleeping, she spent the flying hour with her medical checks kept to a minimum. She took the opportunity to document her reports and logs for the past flying days.

The plane buzzed over the inter-tidal mangrove marshes at the top of Gulf St Vincent out of Adelaide and over and near a vee formation of a dozen pied cormorants below that cast shadows over the shallow waters. They crossed the thigh part of the leg shape that was York Peninsula to Spencer Gulf. As the sun set the aircraft landed in a cloud of red dust. An ambulance was waiting and Rhette watched as a man who looked very ill was quickly transferred to the aircraft from it. Thank goodness, she thought. The RFD hadn't made the trip just for her; they'd been scheduled for Whyalla anyway on what looked like a priority case. No wonder Harry had arrived at the convent and hustled her to the hospital and the flight from Adelaide.

The plane took to the sky and the local ambulance crew took Rhette to the currently being updated and rebuilt Whyalla Hospital. They unloaded her from the stretcher into a private room with 'Infection Control' notices on the door and a cheerful nurse, in mask and gown, brought her a cup of tea. In her other hand she balanced another tray.

'Why am I in a room with the special notices on the door?' Rhette asked.

'Different hospitals have different infection bugs and we have to check that you are not introducing anything new to our hospital,' she said, and proceeded to take a blood sample from Rhette's arm. 'This will go to the lab straight immediately.'

After an hour, Jessica arrived at the door. Rhette carefully checked Jessica's credentials and, satisfied, allowed herself to be discharged into the policewoman's care.

'That was interesting,' Rhette said as she shed the hospital gown and changed into the street clothes from her suitcase.

'A rare happening,' Jessica said. 'Major Crime has some contacts in the RAH and I think that they used up all their brownie points on this transfer. A useful donation was made to the RFD too and they'll never know why.'

'Well, I'm grateful.' Rhette said. She changed the subject. 'Where to from here?'

'We've got you booked into a Bed & Breakfast. You'll have a chance to meet your contact Ana and the boy, Piet, tomorrow morning.'

Out in the Coober Pedy opal minefields Doug Napier slumped into his chair. He took a deep breath and, as though he needed pain to confirm his existence, he reached dirt- caked fingernails into his breast pocket to touch the sheet of paper. After fifteen years the paper was so old it no longer rustled. His elder daughter's words had faded but they were black-acid etched into his mind.

'By the time you get this...' the teenager Rhette had written...

He stopped his mental recitation as the dingo howled. Was the blasted thing listening to his thoughts?

'Mum will have gone for good. She said she was going and she's done it this time. We're staying with Gran. Don't come home. No one will be here. Stay with your stupid opal. Your dreams never included us – except for the promises. No one believes in them any more, anyway. If you die down in those deep holes of yours, no-one would know – or care!'

His mind stalled. He knew he deserved it. Maybe it was a legacy of Vietnam that he'd chased dreams; always after the elusive something. His menial jobs ended and the opal dreams, the self-imposed demands, started. He was lured north again to make his fortune – others had – and his stubborn black Scot's pride had got involved. He couldn't return until he had struck pay opal colour. Lots of it. Until he'd kept his promise of riches and a good life for his family. A man always had to prove himself even if it took years, especially after what he'd done to Gina and his family.

Now he had nearly enough opal. He'd been mining it for years then taking it to Coober Pedy for cutting. That had cost him a packet but now, as much of it resided in a bank deposit box; he had enough to justify his absence. That was always his excuse. Enough, always the amount to gratify this need grew. It was a denial, he knew, not to have said enough years ago. Now he had enough, nearly was getting close, especially as he had another load of opals in the uncut form. Good stone, he knew it was; good stone.

The dingo moved restlessly still awaiting the moon and a stone slid beneath its paws and rattled down the slope. Distracted Doug instinctively turned his ear to the sound and all movement stopped.

The letter had finished relentlessly. 'Stay away!'

He shivered as he felt into his inner pocket again. Another harder envelope was there, so new it had not had time to conform to the shape of his body.

He could feel every insistent corner of it.

It was like Rhette's second card that had found him almost six birthdays ago; the one that told him she was getting married and hinted forgiveness in a brutal offhand way. He wasn't invited to the wedding and there had been no birthday cards waiting at the Coober Pedy post office since.

Doug was sure that he had not been pardoned.

But last month, when he went into town for supplies, he found the new crisp envelope waiting. He had not yet opened it, expecting it to be for his birthday, and it festered with hope and dread in his imagination.

The air was chill now, the sun long gone.

A full moon edged white and cold above the ridges.

His camp fire flung red and yellow lights into the night, and it was one of his few luxuries in an area scant with trees that he'd bought in wood from outside. Luxury, his whisky he thought of as a necessity against the cold of the empty nights... the wood was for special occasions.

The dingo circled silently around him and suddenly slunk in front to where Doug could see it. He started in shock as green-yellow eyes reflected briefly in the fire's glow. He yelled and the shape scuttled away. Holding his breath he could just hear the soft wash of displaced tailings above the clamour of his thumping heartbeat.

Then he was alone. As alone as he had ever been in his life.

The sky crouched lower pressing silence into the desert rocks and sands.

He shuffled his feet disturbing the fire and the smell of the stringy bark stumps was there for his nose, but the embers slumped softly refusing to reassure his ears. Around him he imagined the dunes moving in and suddenly he was claustrophobic with loneliness. Pulling his jacket around his head he cocooned himself.

Against the night.

Against memory, guilt and place.

Skewer points of the new envelope pricked into his huddled chest and the moon sloped higher flooding a pale light.

Doug straightened. He had seen his nemesis dingo and survived. Now for better or worse it was suddenly imperative on this birthday eve to open the envelope and face the inevitable. He dumped another stump on the fire and as sparks flew he pulled the envelope free. Smoothing the face of it, his rough fingers felt the stamp. Fumbled as he tore the paper open.

As the wood caught and the flame flared and caught he saw the card showed a face. His face twisted into the beginnings of new hopeful, yet wry, smile. Trust Rhette. Maybe she remembered when they had each flown red kites on the beach with the waves and wind flicking salt spray at them...

He fumbled for his lantern, flicked the switch and his campsite lit up. His drab grey tent was zippered up against the night's desert dew and his filthy work pants were slung over a camp chair. His opal sorting table held his teapot and cup. An outside lean-to he'd made held mining and digging equipment. Away from the underground trenches where he'd dug for opal or slept cooler on the hot nights. Everything there was neatly utilitarian.

The photograph lay face up and he grabbed it.

It showed his second daughter.

O God no! It was a funereal memento card. Edged in black. His daughter Kate!

She was breathtaking in her fair beauty.

He felt he had been punched hard in the chest and he keened to the sky as he rocked back and forth.

There was no accompanying letter and the lack of it was worse than a curse.

Slowly he got to his feet. Feet that moved into a shambling trancelike shuffle. He held aloft the photo.

'Come out! Come out, wherever you are,' he shouted to the dingo. 'Come and take me...'

The dingo coughed, still nearby, but did not show itself.


Next morning the sun poured heat and black bush flies over the opal fields.

The dingo sat high on a tailings heap.

Doug thumped the steering wheel of his old Land Rover. He'd left everything in his camp intact. His bull dozer, his Caldwell mine head, his tractor, everything. Just taken his clothes and the opal.

The dingo scratched then lifted its hind leg in a rude farewell. As it loped away, Doug confirmed his reasoning that it too was an old male.

'Go home! Home to your bairns,' he screamed as he let out the clutch and the vehicle lurched forward heading south on the rutted desert track.

A lifetime of hot opal colour bulged in his pockets and a huge jot of fear was in his being as, in the clear light of day, he left to answer the call of the funereal card.

Going to find a home somewhere, perhaps in Coober Pedy.

There was no where else that would welcome him.

# Chapter 19

Black and red the solitaire patience cards lay before Lex on the computer screen. He swirled the mouse in irritation on his desk pad then diminished the card game to the lower tool bar. With a frown he maximized the screen that was the real reason for his conjecture. He stared into the screen for another minute then flicked back to the card game. His hand automatically clicked the cards as his mind went elsewhere.

Black on red. Red on black.

Sometimes he played Spider. Red on red. Black on black.

Playing computer card games was Lex's work idiosyncrasy, and despite his detective rank, he was teased about it by just about everyone on the station. But he got results and they'd learned to accept his methods.

Mark put his head around the doorway and saw the card game. 'Got a problem, Lex,' he questioned with a broad smile.

The detective returned a chuckle. 'Yeah! I've been looking at some Parole Board stats...'

'And...' Mark waited.

Lex rubbed his left hand over the black shaven head that resembled a polished bowling ball. He extended the movement down to his shoulder to ease the tension there as he flicked back to the police screens.

'Yeah, I know. Maybe my way isn't the accepted way to solve crime. Sometimes it helps.' He smiled, 'Lets the subconscious run free.'

His senior officer kept a straight face, almost. 'Yeah, sure...'

Lex let the comment pass. 'The parole stats for the Port Augusta and the Port Lincoln Prisons have just come out. Six months behind as usual. Many more released crims are coming to Whyalla. These increases could have skewed our crime figures,' he said. He moved his shoulder to let Mark have a clear view of his screens.

'OK...' Mark was always interested in reasons for changes in crime rates. Part of his new responsibilities. He leaned in to look at Lex's screen. 'Got comparisons?'

'Sure.' Lex brought up another screen from the lower toolbar. He pointed out the movement increase from Port Lincoln that was almost four percent higher over the past six months. 'I think that's significant. These have come to Whyalla and a further ten percent have come here from the Port Augusta releases.'

Mark raised an eyebrow. 'Could be...'

'And,' Lex continued. 'The Augusta parole stats show more crims staying there too. Crims who were paroled to return to Adelaide have gone back to Port Augusta or Whyalla after a week or so in the city. That's a lot and no one can tell me that the two towns have suddenly become that enticing. These are crims who should have returned to Adelaide according to release procedures and haven't stayed there. A fourteen percent increase? That's a hell of a jump in numbers. There's not much work here. Nothing extra in the steel works, nothing in industries connected with it and the ship building I've heard about is a thing of the past. Even in Port Augusta the power plant is being phased out.'

'Could Roxby Downs mining be the reason for parolees to come back?' Mark asked.

'I'll check with the local parole boys and see if they have anything on the ex cons working in the mine. Possible but I reckon it's unlikely.'

'OK.' Mark grinned and reached for the inevitable cup of cold coffee that did little more than decorate his desk. 'I'll lay you odds that no ex crim has the trade qualifications to work in the mining industry.'

'The money's very good.'

'Yeah, but they'd have to work too bloody hard for it.'

Lex flicked his mouse and the solitaire game he was playing came up. Mark stood up as Lex tapped the screen. 'That subconscious running free I was telling you about...it hit. I'm becoming convinced that the meth labs are being set up from within the correction systems. Sure, someone's financing them from outside but they're getting their labour from the released prisoners. The parolees. There's also an increase in bikie activity here and in Port Augusta.'

There was a pause as Mark went with Lex's jump in conclusions. 'The correlations are there,' he said. 'Go with it. I'll decrease your normal work load and give you the time to get into it. Give me anything you get as you get it. OK?'

'So I can play patience and leave the emu picks for Jessica?' Lex quipped.

In a move totally uncharacteristic of Mark, he aimed a playful tap at Lex's shoulder. He laughed. 'Sure, and you can explain why to Jessica. She'll be enthused...'

Ana met Rhette with some reservations but as Piet seemed comfortable about her, and as Mark also knew the woman, she just went with the plan that they would travel together to Darwin.

Ana's car was new and just getting used to driving the 4x4 after the Mercedes kept her involved as they left Whyalla. Mark had come to see them off with a small police car toy for Piet. With Rhette standing by, and Jessica fussing with Piet and his new toy, Ana wasn't able to say more than a quick goodbye. She hoped that her eyes said a bit more than that and she'd promised to text and phone him each night.

Rhette saw, heard and raised an eyebrow.

'It's OK,' Mark said with a broad grin. 'Just keeping tabs for her reassurance.'

Jessica didn't miss much either. She wasn't a detective to make up department numbers.

A juicy titbit to tell her husband David, a traffic cop also working out of Whyalla. They'd keep it confidential between themselves but Jessica was pleased that Mark was starting a relationship with a woman she remembered from before at Renmark. It was about time he had someone in his life again. She'd never liked the snooty Erica.

# Chapter 20

'So Rhette?' Ana said. 'That's an unusual name?' They had left Port Augusta after only a petrol and comfort stop with Woomera the planned overnight destination.

'Ever heard of "Gone with the Wind"?' There was a laugh in Rhette's voice as she pushed her sunglasses up through her loose mop of red hair.

Ana flicked a look at her and back to the Stuart Highway as it stretched endlessly in a straight line to the horizon ahead. 'Yes?' she said.

'My mother saw that film a dozen times when she was pregnant with me and was smitten by Clark Gable as Rhett Butler.'

Ana gave an involuntary chuckle. 'You're kidding...'

'No. She was convinced that she was going have a boy and she'd call him Rhett. When I turned up she made up the name and here I am, Rhette.'

'What did your father say to that?'

'It wasn't an issue. He was just back from Vietnam and whatever she wanted he'd agree to.'

'Well, it's different...quite distinctive too.'

'I've learned to live with it.' Rhette turned to look at Piet who was strapped into his back seat chair and sleeping Bear and his police car clutched in soft hands. She reached over and adjusted the window shade to keep the sun off him. 'I gather that Piet is for Peter. They've told me a bit about you and your past history. The Whyalla thing now must have been bad.'

'Yes, and I've no idea why that happened. They've tried to convince me that it was a random attack but...'

'Yeah, they do that. So we're two women on the run from things...' Rhette stretched her arms and legs out before relaxing back into the seat. 'Pity about the Mercedes, lovely comfortable thing for a long trip. This's OK but it's not a Merc.'

'Yes,' Ana agreed. 'We do seem to have a common element for this trip.'

Looking straight ahead Rhette said, 'But I fancy that you have something back in Whyalla?' There was a knowing woman thing, a smile in her voice. The sunglasses came down onto her nose again and she shut her eyes. 'I might take a nap until you're ready for a change in drivers if that's OK with you?'

'Yes.' Ana said, but thought. Something...someone...

Doug Napier fronted Frank Mason in his shop with the biggest private parcel of quality cut opals the dealer had seen in many years. He'd added the recent stones to those he'd retrieved from the bank vault. Even to his eyes the quantity and quality was impressive.

The miner waited patiently as Frank looked at them after wetting them with water, and immediately the thickness of black opal, red fire and harlequin opal had been clear. It was a fabulous parcel in quality, brilliance, variety and the sale added up to be a very valuable amount. Much more than a couple of million dollars. Now there was a shimmer of shaking in his hands as Frank spread the gems out on white paper on the glass counter. He looked intently at Doug.

'These from the northern fields?' he asked. 'Out past the Dog Fence?'

Doug stood straight and looked coldly at the dealer. With an estimated million plus holes dug for opal in the surrounding desert a miner didn't reveal his exact mine location. Huge areas were mined out and he knew he had good stone from a good mine. A lifetime worth of stone and there was still more out there with a pipe that seemed to go on and on. 'Yeah, something like that...' he said a frown creasing his forehead.

Frank needed the opals package to be sent on immediately, but there was a difference about these gem stones. 'These aren't fossil opal are they? Ichthyosaur bones opalised.'

Doug's face stayed still. He knew they were opalised fossils and also that there was another opalised specimen lying next to the one he had excavated. Sometime in the far distant past two great creatures had died together and their bodies sunk to the bottom of the seas that covered the inland. Sometimes he fantasized that they were a coupling pair who died, other times a larger carnivore had eaten another and then somehow they'd both died. All he knew was he'd unearthed two great fossils and the one remaining he would give to science one day. A promise he'd made to himself. 'Maybe...' he said. 'It would need to be tested to prove it...'

Frank straightened to look closely at the slim man standing across the counter, dollar signs multiplying in his head. A word there at next point of sale and the market would pay more for opalised fossils.

'I can only pay for what I see as you've cut most of the stones.'

'Yeah, I'm expecting that but I want your best price,' Doug said.

Although he'd had a good reputation in Coober Pedy as a buyer for twenty, thirty years Frank Mason had always suffered from a little gambling habit. He'd become a serious gambler for only the past two years. Computer gambling had done it. Got him in with the eastern state loan gangs in a big way and now he was forced to buy for them. Lately there weren't many opals that weren't tied up with mining companies and the private parcels coming in to him had been uninspiring. What he'd supplied were of meagre quality stones and deliveries were few and far between. Not enough to satisfy his creditors. This parcel was a godsend and would take some if not all the pressure off him.

'Don't get your shirt in a knot...I'll weigh these up again now; you can have them back. We'll meet tonight. Tom and Mary's Greek Restaurant, OK? We'll fix a price then. How does that sound?'

'Name the time and I'll be there,' Doug said. At least he'd picked a good restaurant, he thought. Best food in town, always was. 'I'll want cash, a bank transfer or a banker's cheque at the very least.' The days of swindles were not long past and Doug trusted few men, not even Frank Mason whose reputation remained good. He'd been mostly out of town for six months except to pick up supplies and hadn't heard any adverse gossip. Word traveled fast on the fields. Especially the bad.

'This parcel is worth more cash than I can lay my hands on...I'll bring an open bank cheque. That's the way I prefer to do business.'

The two men shook hands and Doug went back to his underground hotel room to arrange to lock up the opal he was offering, and his uncut stash, in the secure safe. It wasn't an unusual request and the hotel manager, an ex copper, could only imagine the millions of dollars of opal, and cash that had resided in that safe over the years. It was all normal and the fleeting notion went through his head that one day someone would rob one of the hotel safes. He checked his keys and double locked the safe, then put the keys in another safe in his personal office. A robbery wasn't going to happen in his establishment in this sometimes wild town, he thought. Not on my watch.

Unaware of the care being taken with his opal, Doug set out to check for mail at the post office and look into the local real estate market. Frank made a phone call to organize a money transfer and went to his bank to fix the cheque.

After a good meal the two men parted company, stinking of garlic and good wine, paid for by Frank, and each were satisfied they had each made a good deal. One to keep his skin intact and the other to drink himself into oblivion for the night before paying cash to rent a dugout home next day. He could now easily afford it.

# Chapter 21

After hours of driving through the desert of treeless plains, by the mid afternoon Ana, Rhette and Piet drove into Woomera, the town that serviced the Rocket Range. They booked into a motel, sharing a family room, before going out to explore the facilities and exhibitions.

They were impressed with the history of rocket launches that were still carried out as, on occasion, international companies and governments sent their communication and scientific satellites into orbit. The clear skies and vast deserts were ideal for the enterprises.

The fact that Woomera was a base for the British atomic bomb tests wasn't advertised greatly anymore as it was a political hot potato with on going public repercussions. The Aboriginal people, who were badly affected by the fall out so long ago, were one of them.

Piet's eyes resembled moon orbs as he led the women from one huge rocket, to aircrafts, to the next shining object in the exhibitions they visited. His squeals of discovery brought smiles to the attendants' faces.

Next morning, as they passed a widening of the highway after Glendambo, Rhette smiled. Painted on the road was an emergency airstrip with Royal Flying Doctor markings.

Ana pulled the car to the verge to look at the area and the long black tyre markings where planes had landed. 'Look Piet, this is where aeroplanes come to take people to hospital,' she said.

'Why do they have to take people to hostible, Mummy?' Piet's questions started.

'Sometimes people get sick. Or have an accident,' Ana

replied.

The little boy's face became concerned. 'Are they taking them to your hostible in Darwin?'

'No Darwin's too far away. They will go to closer hospitals. In Port Augusta or Woomera. That's where we slept last night.'

'How far is Darwin? How many sleeps to get there?'

Rhette listened to the piping voice and the quiet patient replies with amusement. Looking at the RFD airstrip she remembered her flight with them and was grateful to realise that the inland outback of Australia was covered by this amazing organisation.

She spread out one of their detailed maps of the long road north. She looked up and stared into the distance. Yes, she wondered. How many sleeps before they got to Darwin? She felt safe away from a city but this dry red land with ridges of sand hills and low spinifex scrub was so very different from Adelaide. A realm, far away from the harbour and the multi-cultural millions of Sydney. She felt a tingling as the hairs rose on the back of her neck as the skin contracted. Cities gave you some where to hide. The open spaces and the heat suddenly weren't so comforting. Not when there was one road and then nothing on every side.

Rhette pulled her sunglasses down and settled for a nap before she would take the wheel to relieve Ana.

Half an hour later Ana stopped the car.

'What's up?' Rhette said, coming out of her dreamless sleep.

Piet sat up tall in his car-seat. 'Ohhh…' he said as he peered to the side of the road.

Two huge, black and brown wedge tailed eagles hunched over the carcase of a road kill kangaroo on the verge of the road. They tore into the flesh ignoring both the car and the gauntlet of other smaller predator birds; another wedge tail and a crowd of hopping crows. High above circling whistling kites flitted shadows as threats to the feast below. For an instant one of the gorging wedgies lifted a bloody head from inside the belly of the body to view the car. It plunged back with a shift in its threatening protective wing spread stance.

They watched in silence, the scene quietened even Piet. 'What about we change drivers for a while?' Ana said. She knew that Pietie would find a range of unending questions soon and it could take half an hour of explanation, with a look in their bird book, to satisfy his curiosity. The women exchanged a glance and left unsaid that they felt too close to get out of the car without feeling daunted by the size of the wedge tailed eagles perched on top of the downed roo to exchange seats. Ana backed up twenty metres. Rhette grunted an agreement, glad that Ana had moved the car away from the scavenging birds.

As Rhette stood to make the change she realised that she was about the same height as them. She shuddered then stretched her arms high and looked around the unending landscape. It went on and on forever. Again the feeling of almost a phobia returned as her need for the closeness of a city closed in. Where could she ever feel safe again? Here she was exposed, naked almost to the primal expanses. She moved quickly into the driver's seat and her grip on the steering wheel gave her comfort.

An hour later they'd changed drivers again and Rhette read aloud from a brochure. 'Coober Pedy named from the Australian Aboriginal words "kupa piti" commonly assumed to mean "white man in a hole" is a unique town like nowhere else in the world. It produced eighty five percent of the world's quality opal and is surrounded by a moon like landscape cratered with shafts and mullock heaps extending out about 40 kilometers in all directions.'

Ana interrupted. 'I love opal. Peter bought me a few little bits when we were on our honeymoon.' She laughed. 'We were dirt poor. We'd both just finished at University and not employed yet. Maybe I'll indulge in an opal pendant.'

'Not me!' Rhette's voice was insistent. 'It's beautiful but...' she gazed hard at the road ahead before she seemed to shake herself and picked up the booklet and started to read aloud again. 'Listen to this bit,' she said. 'You'd better keep a strong grip on young Pietie while you're here.

'Tourists are warned not to step backwards when

photographing or they could drop down one of the thousands of disused narrow mine shafts. From a fall down a 30 metres shaft there's about a fifty-fifty chance of being retrieved alive by the trained group of volunteer miners who've become experts in such rescues. These miners, many migrating from southern and Eastern Europe after the Second World War and from an estimated 45 nationalities, give the town a distinctive and strong ethnic flair.'

'Maybe there's a gorgeous rich miner for you,' Ana cast a sideways look before concentrating on the turn off road into Coober Pedy. 'From what you've said you've led a pretty quiet life these last few months. No men at all?'

'Hardly.' Rhette said as she put away the map she'd barely needed. With the one road north only the information on the RAA maps was interesting. 'It's been a long haul,' she looked over at the trip meter...'we've done 536 kms since Port Augusta.'

More than 600 from Whyalla... and Mark, Ana thought.

'Thank goodness we're travelling with good air conditioning,' Ana said as they got out of the car outside the Visitor Information Centre. 'It's hot here.' She shaded Piet's face against the blast of summer sun that hit them as they scurried into the cooler building.

Inside, Ana decided that as they were staying for a few days to soak up the atmosphere, they should stay somewhere special and cool and she booked a family rooms suite at the Desert Cave Hotel. It was four star and had rooms above and below ground. She smiled. Her friend Lauren would approve of her choice. She looked over where Rhette was frowning at the accommodation poster on the wall.

'You're joking.' Rhette said. 'I can't afford this!'

'Nope, I'm paying. I've sold my house for a good price, downsized my car, and I'm going to a good job in Darwin. We deserve this...and it will be cooler for Pietie too. We should try the underground section for the experience.'

'I see you're playing the kid card, OK then... so I'll get dinner.' She went over and chatted quickly with an attendant. 'They say that Tom and Mary's Greek place has the best squid anywhere. Bit of a joke to eat seafood this far from the sea.'

Ana looked at the town map on the wall. 'Sounds good. I love calamari. It's almost next door to the hotel too.'

'I'll book it for six o'clock so that Piet can have his dinner at a reasonable hour for him to go to bed. Then you can phone Mark...perhaps...' Rhette said with a grin as Ana felt a flush of pink spreading to her hairline.

Rhette just missed seeing her father as he arrived at the restaurant half an hour after they left to go back to the hotel.

Doug was celebrating his renting an underground furnished house. Somewhere to live while he made up his mind about staying on and resuming mining or leaving the opal fields for good. He'd have to return to his camp anyway soon to secure his mine shaft and collect his belongings that he'd left there on the morning of his birthday.

# Chapter 22

'That bastard Quinn's alive!' Mark exclaimed. His hands formed fists beside his computer before clasping into his hair.

Lex looked up. 'Who's Quinn?' He typed the name into the computer. 'Many Quinn's are listed. Which one? You're not telling me...?'

'Demetrius Quinn,' Mark cut in, his voice still incredulous. 'Look him up while I get my thoughts in order.' He left the room to get a cup of the terrible station coffee that was only drunk in emergencies. This was a mental emergency.

Lex opened the file. One eyebrow rose as he read further and further into the record. 'Shit!' he muttered as he correlated this file with Mark's personal file in his mind.

Mark came back with another cup for Lex. He stood behind Lex as the two men drank and both grunted, almost in unison, as the poor coffee taste brought pulled-in faces.

'Shit Mark,' Lex said. 'The bastard's worse than this coffee...' He gestured to the screen. 'Everyone thought he was dead at Renmark four years ago. Now he'll be back at the top of the Most Wanted lists.' Lex screened into the Major Crime pages. He watched the dossier on Demetrius Quinn went up with a 'Most Urgent' note. 'There he is up. 'Wanted for the Murders of Peter Foster and...'

'Yeah! Yeah!' Mark cut in. He dragged a hand through his hair as he turned and paced the squad room. 'After he'd killed her husband I told Ana that he was yabby meat. I convinced her that he was dead. He was shot. I saw him shot, and he fell into the Murray River. Shit! And when he hit the water the bastard had a great hole in his guts. We saw the blood on the lock. Never found a body so how did he stay alive?

'It was right thinking at the time...you can't be blamed for that. Everyone thought the same.'

'Now I'm sure that the attack on Ana wasn't random.' He thought for a moment. 'I'll have to tell her.'

'Yes, I think you will. But she's as safe as she can be going north to Darwin and Rhette's a resourceful woman to travel with.' Lex said.

'I'll get the word up the Highway for the local coppers to keep an eye out for her and to act immediately if anything unusual happens. On the Murray I did that and...'

'It worked then,' Lex interrupted. 'This time hopefully belief that Ana could be in danger won't be needed.'


'No!' Ana staggered to her feet from the bed she'd been sitting on that evening ready for a long and intimate phone call with Mark. 'No!' she repeated. 'Quinn can't be alive!' A cold draft seemed to permeate the warmth of the room and Ana felt a drawing in of cold to the back of her head and neck as if she would faint. She sat down. 'How can he be alive, Mark?' she managed to say as nausea swamped her.

'I'm shocked too but a DNA sample from his prison days has proved it. He was here in Whyalla...recently.'

There was a pause. Ana's voice faltered to a whisper as she struggled with the fears that whirled about in her brain. 'So that bomb attack against my car ... could it have been him?'

'I won't lie to you Ana, it could have been Quinn who ordered the attack on you. I don't think it was him personally though, I think he is involved with bigger activities here.'

'Is he still there?'

'No, probably not. We've got immediate arrest warrants out on him now – since we've got the DNA evidence. We think he's gone back to the eastern states, Sydney probably.' Mark kept his voice as quiet and reassuring as possible. He hoped that Quinn had gone and the danger was over for her.

Ana's fingers pushed the mobile phone hard against her head as she grappled with the thought that the man who murdered her husband Peter, the man who took his life even before he knew he was going to be a father, was still alive. She gulped air past her teeth but the air around her didn't seem to be entering her lungs.

Mark could hear her ragged breathing with the knowledge that he couldn't change the past for her. 'Ana are you alright?' he said.

'O Mark, I feel sick with regret, with hatred too. I can't forgive him...Is that bad?'

'No it's not...and I just wish I could be there to hold you. To feel you safe in my arms.'

'Yes, I want that too.' There was a pause. 'I think I've got to go and look in on Pietie. Maybe I'll have a talk with Rhette too in the morning. I'll call you tomorrow after I've had time to think about this.' She attempted a laugh. 'I'm not going to thank you for telling me about Quinn, I had to know, but I'm glad it was you who told me. Now I know I have to be more careful.'

'Yes Ana, take care of yourself, for Pietie, and me too.' Mark said.

There was a pause before the call clicked off.

In that telephone call they knew their commitment had become real.

That night Ana dreamed her dream of the wild beach and was shaken awake, as she threshed and called out, by a concerned Rhette.

'It's alright,' Rhette said. 'I'm here...' She stroked Ana's hand until her breathing quietened.

'Pietie? Did I wake Piet?'

'No he's sleeping. Probably dreaming of his car...'

'And Bear. Thank you.' Ana said. 'I think I should tell you a little more of Quinn. What happened and why I feel so vulnerable.'

'Yes, maybe it's time...'

The two women talked and drew closer for it.

Rhette wondered if the person she only knew of as Mr Hood's man, was the person Quinn, described by Ana. The possibility was there. Both were psychopaths, and feared by all those who had ever come into contact with them. Their only comfort was that they were going further away from both Whyalla and the Eastern States and away out of danger. They would stay on in Coober Pedy for a day or so to give Piet a rest and to have a look around. Maybe to buy the bit of opal that Ana sought as a distraction.

# Chapter 23

'OK then, get your gear off,' Quinn said to the woman standing before him in the Coober Pedy hotel suite. A bikie woman. Young. He had the position in the Australian crime hierarchy to ask for a woman to service him. Anywhere. Anytime.

'My name is Lucy,' she said looking him up and down.

Not bad, she thought, at least he had a good physique and stunning good looks. His scalp shadow promised a full head of hair cut to stubble length, like his cheeks. Blue eyes so deep you could sink into the depths. Ah, she thought as she noticed the scars on the backs of his hands. They looked as though he'd had rough tattoos removed. Surgically removed. She'd seen that before. L.O.V.E and H.A.T.E punched into the knuckles of men's hands.

Prison tatts; so he'd been a con.

Now he was hiding the fact.

It made her more cautious.

This was the first time she had been 'given' by the bikie gang as a sexual partner to satisfy a senior man. The 'given' was a requirement and she'd hoped that the encounter would be better than rape. Slowly she dropped the spaghetti straps from her shoulders and her green silky shift fell to the floor. Naked and still in matching Jimmy Choo stilettos, she stepped out of the dress. She bent looking up at Quinn, before she carefully folded the garment and placed it over a chair.

In turn Quinn looked her up and down. He grinned. She was slim yet had a voluptuous figure and this was OK. He didn't like thin women and her blonde hair and pixie face suited him. He didn't like brunettes either.

'You clean?' he said.

Her temper almost showed. 'Of course I'm bloody clean.' She

said, but didn't dare ask him the same question in return.

'I want a shower. Get in there and turn it on for me.' She made to step out of her shoes. 'Leave them on,' he said.

The first sex was rough, urgent against the tiled wall as the hot water played over their bodies. He hadn't had a woman for a few weeks and he needed the relief. The second on the bed was more leisurely. He took time too with it. To kiss her breasts and neck, to push her downwards for himself, then to enter her and to take them both to orgasm.

Afterwards he went back to the shower.

Lucy lay spent on the bed. She leaned over the bed and ruefully checked her wet shoes lying where they had fallen off her feet. They cost me a packet, she muttered. But he went twice, she thought. Not bad. Probably Viagra, a common usage with bikies. His body was excellent, a few scars but that was usual with them. Made them more interesting. He wasn't heavily tattooed, but he had a massive scar on his stomach. She stretched. Flexing her toned body. Maybe he'll think of me when he leaves this god forsaken town and take me with him. She curled up into a position that she knew she looked good in for whatever he wanted when he came back from his shower.

Quinn came back. He slapped Lucy's bare bottom with a hand that left a bright pink mark, a playful tap as far as she was concerned given her protector's usual handling. 'Get up, woman, get yourself showered and dressed. I've got an opal deal to set up.'

A woman could be a convenience and a disguise for a man acting alone.

'My name is Lucy,' she said.

'Yeah, I know...'

'What's that Mummy?' Piet pointed at a huge conglomeration of rusted metal, rubber and faded painted pieces that appeared to be a vehicle of some sort. It lay in a yard in front of an Opal shop.

'I know what it is,' said Rhette with a chuckle. 'It's from the film "Mad Max" made here ages ago. It's listed in the hotel brochures of places to see. Out at the 'Breakaways' they did "Beyond Thunderdome." We'll pass those hills when we go on north to Alice Springs.'

It was already getting hot and they'd been in the car driving around to look at some of the many attractions the town offered. To the Big Winch Lookout to see over the town, the explorer John McDouall Stuart Monument, then out to Potch Gully Road to see the Wind Turbine Generator and after that they'd found themselves at the Boot Hill Cemetery. Ana and Rhette exchanged a laugh as they stood beside the grave of a man, Karl Bratz, who had designed the cemetery. His coffin was apparently made of corrugated iron because everywhere he'd lived it was the usual building material. His beer keg headstone seemed appropriate for the characters and stories of the outback town.

They went back to the hotel for a rest and lunch before setting out to explore the opal shops.

Piet liked the potato chips and the chicken he was served and picked at the salad of green lettuce that Ana put in front of him. The best bit of eating chips was that he could dip them in mayonnaise or tomato sauce as he ate them. It wasn't necessarily a pretty sight as the yellow mayo and the red sauce played for space around his mouth. Ana rolled her eyes in small embarrassment and Rhette chuckled as the glop was cleared away with a serviette before he started the painting of his face again with a bowl of vanilla icecream. The three year old, miraculously, still had a cleanish shirt after lunch when they started their quest for opals.

In the afternoon heat they wandered from one air conditioned opal shop to the next. All along Hutchinson Street, the shops offered fantastic displays and welcomed customers proudly displaying every facet of the industry. As Ana and Rhette entered one shop they paused beside a wall chart of information and an older woman salesperson approached them.

She smiled. 'Are you interested in the geological story?' When Ana and Rhette nodded, she said. 'I love to tell people about opal and I've lived here almost all of my life so I've learned a bit.' Her hand pointed to a map of Australia and pictures beside it. 'A hundred and fifty million years ago, and more, this was part of an enormous inland sea. When the sea retreated silica formed into opal and much of the opal contains fossils. Opal shells, ancient squid, and sea sponge fossils are common, and during the age of dinosaurs mighty marine reptiles roamed the seas. These too became fossils.' She led them towards a huge display case. 'See here. We have a replica of the opalised back bone and snout section of an ichthyosaur. It's worth a huge amount to paleontology research. That's now in the South Australian Museum and they have the only examples of opalised worms found anywhere in the world.'

The information was fascinating and Ana squatted to show Piet the drawings of the ichthyosaur. "Like the dolphins you've seen in the Port Lincoln.' She shrugged grinning to Rhette and the sales woman as Piet's face lit up and his excited voice told her of the dolphins he remembered. 'Shall we buy a little plastic ichthyosaur model with the lovely opal colours?'

'Yes, please.' His toy car went into Ana's handbag as he clutched the new treat with Bear.

With Pietie happy they looked at the jewellery displays. Rhette, caught up in the beauty of a green opal ring, a doublet, bought it and Ana purchased her self promised pendant and matching solids earrings displaying red fire.

As they went back out into the heat to go to the car and to return to the hotel, Ana stopped. She stood staring back at a nearby shop doorway. She grabbed Piet's hand. Her legs just wouldn't move.

Rhette was a step behind her. She almost bumped into Ana's rigid figure. 'What's up?' she said.

There was a gasp from Ana. Her face in the heat went as white as her hair swatches. She swayed then pulled Piet behind her. 'It's him! Quinn!' she said. She stared back towards the door.

'You're kidding...' Rhette started to turn to where Ana was looking then saw again Ana's face. 'You're sure?'

'He's with a woman! I know it's him! Don't look yet... he might not have seen us.'

Rhette looked anyway at the figures now moving into the street fifty metres away. A tall dark haired man in black and a small woman in a slip of a green dress. They looked a handsome couple, but ordinary. 'Come on then! Move!' she said as Ana still did little else but shuffle her feet. 'Back to the hotel. I'll help with Pietie.'

Ana grabbed her son and hoisted him into her arms as Rhette hustled and pushed them into the car. She pulled his face into her shoulder and turned her body away from Quinn and the woman.

Rhette started the car and drove down the street to the back carpark of the hotel. 'Stay here a minute,' she said. 'I'll have a look and see if they have followed us.'

Rhette was back in five minutes to say that she couldn't see any sign of them being followed.

Quinn had seen Ana.

He had recognized her again immediately.

Staying at a lesser hotel, Quinn ordered room service, ate sparingly, and told Lucy to go to bed. She heard him leave the room and later return. When she tried to entice and seduce him he turned his back to her, not interested, and he lay awake in the early hours smoking cigarette after cigarette.

Quinn had seen the boy. So she bloody well had a son while he was still looking for Clinton, his own son. His anger brought bile up from his stomach that burned into his throat.

In the night Lucy woke as Quinn ground his teeth. He flailed and threw punches and swore over and over in his sleep. She moved as far away as the bed would allow fearing the dark intensity of the man beside her and wondered whether the possibility of going away with him would be as good as she had previously hoped.

# Chapter 24

'I've seen him! Quinn! He's here in Coober Pedy...' Ana said, in an urgent phone call to Mark. Her voice was husky with fear.

'You're back at the hotel?' Mark asked. At her intake of a ragged breath he said. 'Stay there. Stay out of sight.'

'He's got dark hair now. Very short...almost shaved right through to the scalp. He must be colouring it as he's naturally got blond hair. Well he did before in the prison...' Ana said. She could feel and hear she was babbling, trying to get her voice calmer. To give Mark the best information she could.

'You're sure it's him?'

Her calm voice raised a pitch. 'Yes! I'm sure. It's him. I'll never forget his face. Never, ever!' Her mobile was pressed so tightly into her ear she could hear the echo of her own heartbeats.

'Darling...just stay there, you, Piet and Rhette. Leave Quinn to us.' Mark said.

'What in the bloody hell is Quinn doing in Coober Pedy?' Mark said aloud to his empty Whyalla office.

After he clicked the phone off from Ana, Mark immediately alerted the Adelaide hierarchy of the appearance of one of the state's most wanted man. A murderer who had been written off as dead as his body had not been found in the deep water of the Murray River.

The Whyalla police region went as far as the Northern Territory Border, and as the senior detective, he assisted his IOC to quickly set up the plans for capture. Quinn could be cornered in the town that had few road exits except by going out into the desert. The latter was unlikely as Quinn was a city man. Not trained by experience to cope and survive in the relentless

Outback. Mark stopped that thought. Quinn had coped, been resourceful, in the Murray Valley region. He'd lived off the land and used the river to his advantage. The desert around Coober Pedy offered no quarter and, Mark knew that he himself would be looking to use the experience of the local police, the Aboriginal people and bushmen.

Unable to stand still, Mark paced the detective's room again as he talked to Lex and Jessica. He was expecting the order to fly, probably in the police plane, to co-ordinate and lead the local experienced Coober Pedy police staff, including the State Emergency Service of volunteer miners, and the men who knew the area.

'Why would he be there?' Mark repeated the question he'd asked Lex. 'He's not still chasing Ana... surely not?'

'No, but I'd put some protection around her, if they have the staff.' Lex suggested.

The idea was awful but unlikely, even to Mark's state of mind about Ana.

Mark grunted an agreement as Lex cut back into his thoughts. 'Putting two and two together, could make five, but maybe he's buying opal to pay for drugs.'

Mark stopped his pacing. 'Lex, you could be right. Brilliant deduction. That'd be how they are paying for the drug and chemical imports. Makes sense. No one would suspect that opals were this currency. I'll bet shipments go overseas all the time. Legitimate parcels. Follow that lead up as priority. Finally a meat and potatoes possibility, hopefully a probability.'

Jessica raised an eyebrow. 'Meat and potatoes?' she said.

Mark cast an amused glance to Lex. 'The meat is the idea and the potatoes the proof. Like a good meal.' He said to her.

Jessica paused. 'I had an uncle once, who commented "all that meat and no potatoes" when he saw a well stacked woman...'

Mark kept his gaze at Jessica's face level. Away from her nicely filled blouse. 'Well, maybe it started like that but that's what we call an idea and the needed proof.' He turned back to Lex who was trying to hide a grin, 'Anyway get your ass ready to join me in Coober Pedy on the next commercial flight.'

The grin disappeared and Lex frowned. He didn't like flying in the 'small birds' as he called them. 'Can't I drive...?'

Mark knew about Lex's pedantic assumptions regarding small planes. "Shit Lex, Rex has thirty seaters. I'm putting you on a commercial plane...' his lips twitched at the Lex Rex repetition of words, 'not with the small police stunt jockeys. Our flight'll be full already as I expect they'll have a couple of the Major Crime boys coming as well.' He shook off the levity as the weight of responsibility descended again on to his shoulders. 'Jessica, sorry but you'll have to stay here to sort any local stuff. There'll be more than enough to keep you busy.'

'Sure Boss,' Jessica said. Her desk was already covered in files.

Mark turned again to Lex. 'I need you – your big black head of ideas is handy sometimes.'

'Sure, I'll let Grace know and get myself packed,' he said. 'I'll get her holding thumbs too.'

Mark wrinkled his brow in puzzlement. 'Holding thumbs?' he said.

Jessica cut in a laugh in her voice. 'He means he'll get Grace to cross her fingers for luck, when he flies...it's one of those South African sayings.'

'New one on me, and tell her "Hi" from me, and that I can't promise when you'll be back...' Mark said. His grin extended to his eyes as he turned away.

The possibility went through Mark's mind that maybe he'd have a problem finding clothes for his bag. As usual he'd washed but had put off the ironing. Never mind, packing always rumpled things...

The OIC's secretary put her head into the detective's room. 'Mark,' she said, 'the Boss wants you to be in on the video meeting this morning with Adelaide.' Her eyes flicked up and down inspecting Mark's usual dress of neat jeans, tie less shirt and Doc Martins boots. 'You'd better suit up first though. It's formal.'

Mark went to his locker and changed into his suit and tie he kept there for just these and other, including media, occasions.

Before going to the conference room and the camera, he went back to speak to Lex.

Jessica looked him up and down. She nodded in approval.

Why do women always give me that up and down look about clothing? The thought was pushed aside as Mark said, 'Lex I'm going to put that opal for drugs idea you came up with to them. It could be a factor that they can act on, with the Federal Police and customs. I'll put your tag on it...'

Already the morning dragged as the women stayed confined in their room and Piet was getting restless and even cranky. Rhette had been quiet, thoughtful, and suddenly she said to Ana. 'Why don't you take Piet to the hotel interpretive cave area again, you should be alright there. I'm going to follow up on something...a hunch...'

Rhette's first stop was the Post Office in the Miners Store.

'Yes, they collected mail for Doug Napier.'

The woman at the counter had regarded Rhette with some mistrust at first. People had been known to come looking for miners for all sorts of reasons. People like deserted wives, private detectives, and debt collectors. The first rule of Coober Pedy was that you didn't ask questions nor give out information on the approximate 3500 inhabitants scattered over the mining area. But Doug had been into the post office this week looking for his mail, so she knew he was probably still in town. He'd seemed upset and worried. Commented that he was looking for accommodation.

'Are you a relative?' the woman asked.

'I'm his daughter and probably the only one who'd send him mail,' Rhette said. She smiled her easy smile; open and level.

The woman took a chance. 'He's in town. Looking for somewhere to live...' That didn't tell much just a little bit. The woman smiled at Rhette. She would have to go and find him herself. No real break of confidentiality there.

'Thank you. You've been most helpful.'

Rhette left checking her town map next for a land agent. Here she immediately struck pay dirt. She'd gone into the cool office and, as she was greeted by a very over made up woman at the desk, she could see the name 'Doug Napier' on a buff coloured folder on the desk.

'I see Dad's been here,' she said. 'So he was successful in finding something...?'

The dark pink mouth stretched with apparent reluctance into a smile of greeting. A smile that didn't crinkle the eyes where a woman of her age should have crinkled. Botox even out here, Rhette thought.

'You'll have to see Richard,' the woman said. 'If you wait I'll tell my husband you're here.' She rose and went unannounced, down a passage and through a doorway. As the door opened Rhette could see a younger woman there. A dark mess of casual hair dragged into a wispy chignon, an alive face and a glimpse of legs in killer stilettos was the competition sitting beside a desk and laughing towards an out of sight hearty male voice.

The male voice belonged to a tall dark haired man who carried his few extra kilos of weight seemingly effortlessly as he followed his wife back down to the reception area. Now Rhette could see why the woman wore so much make up, and the reason for the botox. Always the relationship triangle.

'I'm Richard Netherby,' he said and extended his hand. The handshake and enterprising look was that of a flirtatious man. 'Mira said you're looking for Doug Napier. He'll be here any minute to sign the papers for the house he's buying. He was just going to rent it and today he's changed his mind and he's bought it.' The standard 'rules' of Coober Pedy didn't seem to extend to him in his satisfaction of a sale in the still less than buoyant local real estate market.

'Can I wait?' Rhette asked. She was provided with a glass of iced water as she sat and browsed through the Coober Pedy 'Houses for Sale' brochure. Richard went back into his office and Mira, the wife receptionist, thumped computer keys harder than was necessary when the younger sales woman waved keys and fingers to them as she left the building.

Rhette's eyes registered nothing as her mind whirled and seethed.

# Chapter 25

'Rhette! Good God girl, is it you?' Doug came though the door of the land agent's office. He started, paled and hung onto the inside door knob as though it was the only thing holding him upright. 'Rhette!' he repeated.

'Dad! Are you alright?' she said and rushed to his side. His arms went around her and they moved back to the seats. Damn, she thought. Her daughter reaction overrode her long held irritation, her anger, with her father. This wasn't how this meeting was meant to go. Still, seeing him she instinctively reached to take his hand as she saw how old, wizen and sun-browned he looked. 'Dad?'

Richard Netherby opened the office door to come back into the reception area. He saw the apparent reunion and halted. 'Mr Napier do you need more time? Or would you both like to come to my office now?' he offered. They followed him to his office and both sat barely hearing him as they looked the twenty years away.

The house sale file lay open on the desk.

'I'm buying a house. An underground one. I saw it yesterday, rented it and today I'm buying it...' Doug stated and his words ran together as he pulled the house photo across the desk towards them. He stopped. 'Maybe I should wait...we should talk. See what you want this time...'

Richard broke in. 'You just need to sign the papers...' He could see a sale slipping away. His glance to Rhette was less agreeable than before.

'I need to talk to my daughter,' Doug said. He seemed to relish saying daughter. He took a slow inward breath, breathed out. 'I'll just rent for a bit longer...need time to think. That should be OK shouldn't it?' he said to Richard.

The land agent looked even less happy. 'The seller may be willing to drop the price further,' he said. 'But there aren't many houses for sale at this time. Don't want to miss out on this one...'

Rhette had been unusually silent, but now as she looked at the rows of pictures of houses for sale, she stood and looked towards Richard. 'We should go now. Talk over a drink... I could do with a real drink.'

'Yes lets.' For a reason that he could not explain as he'd never served in the navy, Doug said, 'the sun's over the yardarm I want a drink now too.'

An hour later they'd drunk two beers, appropriate to the weather if not the occasion, apologies and explanations made, Rhette and Doug were silent. The talking wasn't over but it was enough for now. The conversation got to the here and now.

'Doug,' she said. Her voice was flat, hesitant. 'I'm not in Coober Pedy by choice...I'm really on the run.' Somehow in the past hours the Dad was gone. This older man, wrinkled and skin sun damaged was Doug. It fitted. Dad had been lost in time and the relationship was subtly altered.

'Are you?' He'd noticed that Rhette's eyes followed the passage of anyone who came into the bar area where they sat. He leaned forward and clasped her hand on the bar; worry furrowed his forehead lines. 'From the coppers?'

'No, I'm good with them. It's a Sydney based gang. It's part of the long story of Kate. For me it will never be over and there's been a contact again.'

'Are you in danger?'

'No...I'm not sure. Come on, there's someone I want you to meet. You may be able to help us?'

'Us...?'

'Yes, I think she's the one in real danger.'

Ana's eyes widened as she opened the hotel room door to Rhette and Doug.

'Meet my father, Doug Napier,' Rhette said.

Ana looked between the two faces; yes there was a resemblance, around the eyes especially. Their carriage was similar, tall and long boned. Piet came running out from where he was watching cartoons and took to Doug immediately. He showed him Bear, which was always an indication of his acceptance. While Ana raised enquiring eyebrows at Rhette, Piet brought his toy ichthyosaur for inspection and was soon engrossed as Doug pulled a piece of opal, he'd kept from selling, from his pocket and they compared the colours.

The child held the opal tightly, clutching it back into his chest, to keep it. He thrust his lower lip out... 'Pietie' Ana said scandalized.

The boy handed back the opal.

Doug laughed. 'Not this piece, little man, but you can ask me and I'll show it to you anytime you want.'

A great deal can happen in a short time when the discussions met an urgent situation.

'Stay here with me in Coober Pedy,' Doug said immediately. 'There's plenty of room in my new house.'

They checked out of the Desert Cave Hotel, a bit reluctant to leave its attractions, but sure that they could have a better chance of disappearing from enquiring eyes. Quinn's eyes. They left no forwarding address to give the assumption to the hotel reception staff that they were leaving Coober Pedy. Going north to Darwin as planned.

Doug's house had six rooms. The back four bedrooms were totally underground, a kitchen and sitting room at the front with also two bathrooms. The temperature in the underground rooms was naturally at a pleasant 23 degrees due to the tunneled out stone. Air-conditioning kept the front rooms the same.

'Why's the house so big? So many rooms?' Rhette asked.

'They must have found good opal as they dug out the house. Probably just kept digging new rooms until the opal ran out. There could be more still.' He pointed out a line of podge with colour near a doorway. 'See here.' Doug swung Piet up on his shoulders to look and the boy tapped at the fragment with interest.

'Like your opal?' Piet asked and peered again into Doug's shirt pocket. 'Pretty.'

'I'll have to get you your own little pick and you can explore for opal,' he said. 'Would you like that?' He swung the child back to the floor.

'Yes, please.' Pietie turned to Ana. 'Can I look for opal too, Mummy?'

'That would be fun,' Ana said. 'Maybe later.'

'I think your mummy's a bit busy now,' Doug said to Piet. 'Let's go play while they sort things out.'

Piet was immediately interested. 'Can we play Hide and Seek?' he said. 'I play that with Mummy. Sometimes I trick her...' His little boy's laugh echoed through the rooms.

'Sure we can, let's go,' the tall wiry man held a hand out to the little boy. 'We can play and explore as well.'

Later Ana and Rhette drew up a shopping list and sent Doug shopping to the Miners Store and the IGA supermarket. To his mind, a man who'd lived frugally with almost no luxuries; it was amazing what was required. Although the house was 'so called' furnished, they needed bedding, linen, crockery, another frying pan, cutlery and food all at the exorbitant outback prices that covered the transport of all things from Adelaide or the eastern states. After chuckling at the fresh vegetable and fruit on the list he said he'd do his best. He made a mental note to buy beer and a drop of whisky or two. Doug added a car tarpaulin to try to keep Ana's car away from prying eyes, and to cover it as he said, 'A car so new its paintwork is bloody blinding! If you'll pardon me ladies?'

Doug suggested that he should shop alone as Quinn might have seen all of them, he set off. Rhette and Ana got to work to make the house livable.

The house was fascinating to them. From the front, where a façade was made by cementing gibbers, or the indigenous rocks, together into a wall face that included a wooden and glass front door and a large double glazed window to the street, the rest of the house was underground. The colours blended the house completely into the surroundings. There was a veranda giving shade to the front of the south facing house. Inside all the rooms were gouged out through the siltstone rock and, as Doug said, apparently the house like most others was mined for opal as it was excavated. The ceilings were smoothed and left bare. Divisions between the huge bedrooms were a mixture of rock and wood, although the latter was expensive to transport to the treeless town. In two rooms tall wardrobes and storage cupboards were fitted in as walls and the space above left clear for air circulation. Otherwise air circulation and cooking exhaust fumes came and went through air-vents with systems to keep out the heat, the rare occasional rain, foreign objects and insects. With the temperature so stable inside, there was no need for air conditioning at all and the women commented that privacy in some rooms could be interesting.

Like all of inland Australia the flies were eternal and the locals called the flies 'friendly.' The women exchanged glances, sprayed each room with low irritant fly spray they found and put insect repellent in the bathroom ready for use when anyone went outside.

The one decent picture in the house was in the second bedroom and they brought that into the main living room. It was a landscape of gum trees reminiscent of a Hans Heyson and a very different view from the Coober Pedy surrounding pitted area of a million abandoned Calweld shafts.

There was almost an air of festivity when Doug returned. They made up beds, surprisingly sufficient for all, even if Piet would be sleeping in a single bed rather than his cot for the first time. He had tried this at home before they left Port Lincoln and he was excited about being a big boy and doing it again. Ana eyed the straight backed chairs in the kitchen-lounge area and decided she could make up a makeshift barrier to stop him falling out of bed in the night. Everything to the boy was fun and he was an infectious spirit to them all. As they worked he had fun playing hide and seek and 'surprising' them from his new adventurous surroundings.

At six, Doug looked at his watch. I've just got time, he thought, to nip back to the pub and get a bottle of bubbly. To toast the new house, the reunion and new friends. A drop also to drink a farewell to Kate, with his older daughter.

'I'll be back in a moment,' he said.

'Can I come too?' Rhette asked caught up in the spirit of the moment. 'It's almost dark. Everyone will be away to their evening meal.' Ana was making a roast pork dinner and she had set the table. It was fun cooking for a family and she was a little bit nervous about the amounts she had prepared.

The spectre of Quinn was pushed aside in the activity of the evening.

Rhette and Doug set off for the nearest pub.


Quinn had set his Bikie minions to scour the town's accommodations to find Ana and the boy.

Her son, he knew it was hers. He'd guessed, correctly, that this child was the son of the idiot that he's killed with his arrow on the houseboat. He had no idea what he would do if he found them, only the endless notion that she, the whore, would know where his own son Clinton was. Maybe even after all this time. The boy would be about twelve now and probably with his mother Faye Bishop. His ex. That bitch had taken off; with Ana's help he knew It, when he was arrested in Port Lincoln for murders he didn't commit. Sure he'd killed when he'd escaped, but his pursuit of Ana at that time brought him no closer to finding his son.

The son who was his only reason for living.

And why, he thought, should she have a bloody son when Clinton was lost to him? Revenge was an active thought.

He eyed Lucy. If he decided to take her with him; and she wasn't bad, she wouldn't be allowed the pill or any other sort of pregnancy protection.

None of his women had ever been allowed that.

He wanted another son.

Rhette went with Doug to the pub.

There she was seen by Lucy. Normally Lucy would have kept her eyes on Quinn at dinner, enticing him as was her assignment, plus maybe as an out for her from this town. But, instead her attention had been diverted by a squalling overtired child heaving about in a car seat as its parents pulled into the drive-through bottle shop. Rhette had glanced towards the child as she carried her bottle of bubbly to the car. Her eyes had met Lucy's through the dining room window for a fraction of a moment. She had quickly looked away but Lucy had spotted her.

Later as Quinn ranted about no-one seeing Ana, the boy or their car, Lucy said. 'What about the other woman with them outside the opal shop? I saw her tonight...'

# Chapter 26

'I'm sorry Mark...'Ana said. 'I was so ripe...it's been four years, more...' Her embarrassment made him gently laugh as she buried her face into the hollow of his neck. Their lovemaking had been urgent just happening after they closed the door of his room. Their clothes were gone in seconds and they'd just made it to the bed. Ana had gasped and gone wild as he'd entered her. She'd flashed off like a firecracker and taken him with her.

The police plane had landed at the Coober Pedy airstrip just after dark that evening. A 4 x 4 Land Rover was waiting for his personal use and he followed the other officers to the police station for a briefing and a meal of sandwiches. Then at nine o'clock he went to his hotel and phoned Ana. Given the address, he'd set the GPS, followed the voice instructions, and quickly pulled up at Doug's house.

Piet was asleep, snug behind the barricade of chairs, and Rhette had introduced her father before she shooed them out the door into the night. She and Doug would babysit as they still had lots to talk about. 'Go. Come back when you're ready...' she'd almost said 'done,' she thought and by all accounts it was about time. In rueful mind Rhette thought – it's about time for me too.

Mark ran gentle fingers across Ana's right breast and down to the scar below it as he raised himself up onto one elbow to look at her. He traced the other wound on her thigh, the only imperfections. Even stretch marks from having her baby were minimal. He looked into her deep brown eyes as she flushed again under his gaze, 'You're beautiful,' he said. 'Every bit of you. Just as I knew you were...'

'I'm a woman with baggage,' she said not realizing the depth of his appraisal. Nor quite where she'd fitted into his thoughts over the years.

'Baggage is OK,' the grin spread across his face and she reached up to touch his hair. 'It will be interesting to investigate everything about you.'

'That's the detective in you talking isn't it? Will it be a long investigation?' She glanced down at his apparent new erection.

He gave a chuckle at her flirtation. 'O yes, woman, and it's going to take years and years.'

She stretched up and clasped both arms around his neck. 'Well,' she said her voice husky, 'where and when do you intend to start...'

He lifted her gently and she could feel his fullness again. His lips went to her breast...

'Here...and now,' he murmured.

# Chapter 27

Small boys have a tendency to wander.

Especially inquisitive little boys and Piet was one of those.

After breakfast when Ana went to the front room to tidy the kitchen area she found the front door open and Piet gone. 'Pietie, where are you hiding?' she called as she looked in the bedrooms inside before going outside to the barren yard. Only her car was there under its tarpaulin. Doug had gone to replenish the bottled gas earlier. She played 'Where are you?' around the covered vehicle for a moment.

No Piet.

It was now ten o'clock, Australian Central daylight saving time, and the day was already starting to get hot after the cold of the desert night. He doesn't even have his hat, she thought as she called again. Now louder.

Rhette came to the door. 'What's up?' she said.

'Pietie's wandered off. It's not like him to do that.'

'He didn't go with Doug?'

'No, he doesn't have a car seat. Pietie always travels everywhere in his car seat,' Ana said.

The two women scouted the area, the surrounding houses and gibber stone yards. A short distance away there were Calweld shafts, other holes and mullock heaps from the mining and housing excavations even in the town area.

Rhette raced towards the nearest rough ground. 'Careful,' she said as Ana ran to her side.

'Piet! Answer me!' Ana yelled into the heat.

'Let's listen a minute. If he's close he should hear us.'

They listened, their heart beats thudding into their ears. Nothing except the whistle of the wind through the electricity wires and far away a crow cawed. The mournful sound lingered and was repeated before the bird flew and they saw the black light reflect off its wings.

'Ana, you go, check the house again, and then call Mark. I'll stay here and keep looking.' Rhette ordered. 'We'll find him.' She didn't add don't worry nor voice the suspicion that both of them denied, that Piet he could have fallen down one of the open shafts, or worse.

'A child's gone missing!'

The call went from the police station to the Coober Pedy Hospital from where the State Emergency Service operated the Mine Rescue group.

A collective shudder went through the town.

A few years back a deranged man had thrown his son alive down a shaft in a tragic case of custody abduction. The man would spend the rest of his life in psychiatric custody and the wife had committed suicide after the child's broken body was eventually found.

The swarm of men and women, most dressed in the SES orange overalls or the police inland rig, spread out from Doug's house, and the house itself was minutely searched again.

Ana was frantic.

Almost incoherent in her worry.

'I latched the front door,' she said to Mark who arrived with the police contingent. 'I know I did. Pietie was looking out. Playing with his toys. I was just in the kitchen. I was only a few metres away from him.'

Mark checked the height of the door latch. 'Could Piet have opened it?'

'He might just reach it, he's bright enough...but I've told him he's not to go outside without me. At home ... he could play in the back yard...' Ana stopped. She was babbling. She clung to Mark regardless of who was there with them. 'All I can think of is the 'Danger' posters around the town. People falling down shafts.' Her hands went to her ears in emphasis as she shuddered at the sound of a crow's cawing moan. 'I can hear him scream…'

Mark took her face in his hands. 'Wait,' he said. 'I'll need a photo of Piet, to show around to the search crews. Have you got a recent one?'

Ana grabbed at her mobile phone and her hands trembled as she opened it. She flashed photo after photo images of the boy at Mark. Her voice and face crumpled. 'Which one do you want?' she said. She pulled the phone back against her throat. 'You can't take this…I have to have every one of them.'

'I'm just going to email one to the station then it's yours again. OK?'

'Of course…O Mark, I'm sorry. I can't think. Take what you need just find him…'

On a situation such as this search for a child, the police manhunt for Demetrius Quinn was put on hold; for the moment.

Mark, after his night with Ana, had begun the investigation ordering questions everywhere. The known bikies, when questioned, had shrugged in their usual silence but others indicated that there was no one new in town. If there were, he or they had gone. Their response was a typical shut out non-speak, giving nothing away.

Two hours later the police and mine rescue people regrouped at the front of the house where a Salvation Army trailer was dispensing cold water and cheese sandwiches. One of the Mine Rescue Team had a huge shepherd dog that was renowned as a search and rescue animal. With Pietie's pillow as a smell target the man and dog searched the house, checking every possible nook and cranny, every cupboard, anywhere a small child could hide, and places where it would be impossible. Nothing. It went outside and nose to the earth it traced circles about the front of the house and minimal yard. Nothing.

Heads were shaken. 'We'll start again but we've already searched for more than a kilometer in all directions,' the Chief said. He divided the groups into two, some to start again from the house and some to continue fanning the search out further. An experienced bushman had walked the area and reported that he thought that no child had walked away from the house. They would get an indigenous tracker to confirm his assessment.

It was a pity that the bikie gang had found Ana and Pietie...

In a bikie dugout a short distance out of town Lucy found herself looking after a beautiful, trusting little boy. She wasn't happy with the situation but knew that she had to do as she was told.

The usual. 'Shut up! Ask no questions.'

But Lucy had been lucky in her first interaction with the child as, when she'd wiped his teary face; she'd admired his special little bear.

# Chapter 28

It seemed that every man and woman in Coober Pedy, every shop and business was closed or staffed with minimal personnel as the determined search went on and outwards for Piet. The first hours of any search were vital.

Tourists, their cars and caravans, were checked. They were warned not to go looking for him on their own or they could become the next casualties in the area of open mineshafts. The signs against falling down disused mine shafts was real. Add the desert heat and no water available outside the town, as dangers too.

The professional search personnel didn't need more casualties.

By the end of the first day the Adelaide media caught on and flew their TV and print representatives to Coober Pedy next morning. They caused chaos as they took over the town's hotels and motels; in rooms that the miners usually took when they came to town. These men, back in town to be in the search, had to make camp in the Serbian Orthodox, the Catacomb Church or the more usual above ground churches, or at the Drive in Theatre. Accidents, heat exhaustion cases and there was a rise in suspected heart attacks with so many people out searching. The twenty bed hospital was almost full. The RFD took three heart attack victims and two miners to Port Augusta or on to Adelaide for treatment. The latter affected by drink and good intentions, had crashed their ute into a stobie pole.

Ana was frantic.

Frantic, in a calm wide eyed, locked in way. She barely spoke, barely ate and even in the hours since Piet was gone she appeared to have lost weight and seemed shrivelled into herself. She saw

Mark, who was overseeing the search with the local experts, only on the evening of the second day when he came again to see her. She melted into him then pushed him out.

'Go back. Find him,' she said, her voice flat, her eyes wet with brimming tears.

Mark was shocked as she had the unseeing look he had seen in the eyes of people in distress and initial grief, as if she were looking kilometres away into the distance looking, searching...past everything except the image of her son.

Rhette became her carer, staying with her just in case the boy somehow came home, or he was brought home.

Mark called a conference at the thirty hour mark of the search. It was six o'clock, very hot, and darkness would fall in a couple of hours. They were all exhausted. Lex, who'd arrived from Whyalla that morning, also had lost his usual vigour when he'd seen the open spaces they had as a search area.

'We'll stop tonight,' Mark said, 'but give it until dark.' He raised an eyebrow at the senior SES and Miners Rescue men, 'Yes?' There was nothing more they could do after daylight went and the surrounding desert became a dark void. 'Thank you,' he said. Everyone knew now of his relationship with Ana. It was just accepted. There were glances and pats on his shoulders as the men and women filed out of the room. He knew that a few local men would walk the streets they knew well listening for sounds in the quiet of the night.

'We'll be back in the morning...if we haven't heard anything before that...'

Mark dropped into a chair. He looked up at Lex. 'If he's in a mine shaft the poor little fellow is gone. I see it in the faces of the miners and the rescue mob. Gone...'

Lex said, 'Kids are resilient. I've heard of them lasting longer...in South Africa...'

'Or he's been taken.' Mark raised his face to look squarely at the tall black man standing beside his chair. 'Quinn...' he said. 'Quinn.'

Lex's lips whitened into a hard line.

'In the morning I'm going to get a squad together and we'll rip this town to pieces! Every Bikie, every one who is suspected with the gang links, we'll take them apart!' Mark's voice was edged in steel.

Lex was the total detective. 'Yes, in finding Quinn and the little boy, and with luck we may find the links with opals and drugs. That would be the lesser coup,' he said as he watched Mark's face, 'but worth it.'


'If I hear any word that you have spoken to the cops I'll come back and fucking do you,' Quinn kept his motorbike visor down but Frank Mason knew this was the man he had to pass on the parcel of opal he'd bought from Doug Napier.

'I'm not talking to anyone,' Frank said trying to keep the tremor he felt from his voice. 'Just tell your boss that I don't owe him anything any more.'

Quinn's hand clamped down on Frank's arm. 'Don't you presume to think that this is over, you little weasel! We'll tell you when your debt is paid off.'

'But...' the tremor was back, 'you said that this was a bloody one off. I was to buy one big parcel and that was it.'

The pressure on his arm increased. Quinn leaned forward and the black helmet bashed into Frank's face and he grabbed the tightly packaged parcel of opal from the dealer's hands. 'Don't count on it. And this lot had better be as good as you said. Worth every dollar you say. One bit of lesser opal equals your guts splattered when you hit the bottom of a shaft.' There was a quiet chuckle from behind the visor, 'I'd like to do that...' Quinn released the arm with a sharp twist to the shoulder.

The air in the dusty side alley of the shopfront was suddenly cold for Frank Mason as he watched the tall black clad figure of his contact put the parcel worth millions into the pannier of the motor bike. Quinn kicked the Harley into life and the thump of power filled the space.

It took a long time for the air and Frank's heart rate to settle as this man in black leather; a man who'd never given his name to Frank, spun the bike in a tight circle and took off.

The phone buzzed inside Quinn's jeans pocket.

'The Boss suggests that we terminate the opal connection as soon as practicable.' Fox's rasp was brisk.

'Is this fucking necessary? He didn't see me.' Quinn asked.

'So now you question the Boss's orders? That's not your call, you stupid bastard.'

'Listen, Fox, I'm still trying to stay out of sight. It's bad enough being back in South Australia, especially in this stinking shit of an oven here, without doing some bastard.'

'That's the order. Do it. Like I said it's not your fucking call. The Boss wants no loose ends. And let's face it Frank Mason's seen you. He's a gambler and he could be made to talk. He talks, you talk and the Boss's in shit again.'

'So that's the level I'm at is it?' Quinn said as he gripped the phone hard. 'I'll bet it's you, you bastard, who keep the itch up his butt that I could talk if I'm caught.'

'Just cementing my place,' Fox coughed as he attempted a laugh.

'I'll cement you one day...'

Quinn was cut off. 'Just do as you're told without a bloody argument for once.' Fox said.

The call ended and Quinn threw the phone onto the bed. It slid across the bed and onto the floor with Quinn's boot lashing out at the steel bed leg. 'Bugger!' he said.

# Chapter 29

The old fashioned bell on the door clanged as Quinn stepped into the air conditioned sanctuary of Mason's opal show rooms. The afternoon heat was just past its forty degree height for the day. Frank had almost decided to close the shop after his fearful interaction with the man in black leathers. Now, as he looked up and saw that his visitor had returned, he wished he had.

'You're back,' he stammered. He glanced up at the cameras that he had been assured by the slick sellers would protect him from problems and hoped that these would be enough.

Quinn didn't raise his dark helmet visor. He strode directly to Mason and delivered a killer punch to the point of his jaw. A punch, that given the latest criminal charges, would ensure the assailant an immediate eight year sentence in any Australian court. Frank Mason was thrown backwards by the force of the blow; he hit a counter and his body slewed sideways and slid down to the floor. Quinn pulled off a leather glove and deftly felt for the carotid artery in Mason's neck. It was still throbbing with the downed man's heart beats.

'Bugger,' he said aloud as he replaced his glove. He reached for a plastic bag intended as a customer carry bag from beside the counter. It was a handsome bag with the Coober Pedy logo emblazoned in bright colours. 'Help you with a bag for your purchases, sir?' he quipped to the empty shop and the body at his feet. He pulled the bag over Frank's head and tied it around the neck. With the man unconscious there was no immediate struggle as the air was depleted in the confining bag with each halting breath. With his hands on his hips Quinn watched for a moment then slammed his fist through a glass display cabinet. From the enticingly collection of gold pendants with good sized opal stones, he chose one that caught his eye and put it onto an adjacent counter.

Quinn turned again to Frank Mason as the man's heels thrummed on the wooden floor. The plastic bag clung tightly to the dying man's face; pulled in by his final breaths. His hands made a floppy automatic attempt to pull at the empty bag before all movement ceased. The killer pulled the bag off the victim noting that there was now no attempt from the body to breathe. He checked the pulse again. Nothing. 'About bloody time,' he said. He placed his selected opal gift into the plastic bag and slipped it inside his leathers.

After a shrewd visual search of the shop, Quinn, still helmeted and gloved, flicked a salute at the cameras he had spotted. He picked up a stool, one that Frank often used to rest on as he worked on the beautiful opal stones, and reaching up, he smashed them. Glass and exposed wires tinkled down and the little red light that had been an assurance of confidence to the client, dimmed out.

Demetrius Quinn flipped the welcoming sign to 'Closed', locked the door and strode to his Harley. A glance around, all clear, before he kicked the bike to life and roared off.

Quinn headed north with the intention of making a wide circle of the town as a reconnoitre before he went to the bikies stronghold on the outskirts of Coober Pedy. He'd slip past Mason's shop to see if there was any police activity on the way back. He questioned, then dismissed an idea, that he could commit a little arson to destroy the premises then decided against it.

A risk without benefit, he thought.


In Doug's house, with the very air closing in on her, Ana had come to a conclusion.

Quinn! It had to be Quinn!

He had taken Piet.

It was logical otherwise her baby would be dead, or found already.

She got to her feet and collected her car keys. As Rhette looked up Ana said, 'I'm just going out for a minute. I can't just sit here...'

'I'll come too.'

'No need. I'll only be a while,' Ana said. Her voice was flat. Calm.

'Well I'm coming...' Rhette said.

The two women went out of the house into the heat and pulled the covers off the 4 x 4 vehicle. Ana took the wheel. She drove apparently aimlessly around the deserted streets.

'Leave the searching to the police.' Rhette said. 'They...' she shut up as Ana scowled wordlessly in her direction. Suddenly Ana swung the wheel and began to follow a man in black leathers riding a huge Harley Davidson motor bike. He was going north.

Rhette looked at Ana a frown on her face. 'You must be kidding? That's just a man on a motor bike.'

'Well, he's all in black, no colours or insignias. It could be Quinn.' There the name was spoken out loud. Like an evil mantra. 'Quinn. Quinn,' she repeated. She pulled a straining hand off the steering wheel to push the long strand of white hair behind her ear. 'He was after me, to kill me, before on the Murray River. We've seen him here. He's got Pietie.'

'You don't know that...' Rhette said.

'I do know. I feel it...'

The motor bike went off the bitumen strip of road and on to an unsealed track much like the majority of Coober Pedy's roads. It was still going north, heading out of town.

Ana followed.

Rhette looked between the motor bike ahead of her and Ana's set jaw determined face. She clicked open her mobile phone.

'No!' Ana said. 'Don't...'

'Why in the hell not?'

'This is between me and him,' the nod was towards the bike ahead. The rider was swerving his bike between the ruts of twin car tracks searching for the smoother ride. 'I can drop you off if you want.'

'Of course not! Are you mad, Ana?'

'Well, shut up then and let me concentrate.'

Ana floored the accelerator and the car jumped forward.

They drew nearer the bike ahead.

There was a wobble as the rider fought to keep upright at speed on the uneven track. After righting the bike the man's blank black visor turned towards the car bearing down on it. He thrust a fist of menace into the air before crouching down over the petrol tank and putting on speed. Ana pushed harder on the 4 x 4's accelerator, gaining a fraction more out of the car. The bike ahead had the capacity to pull away but not on this track. Her car was more stable in the stones and sand ruts.

The accident was over in a heart beat.

At a bend the bike's front wheel hit a rock, a slightly bigger gibber than usual, and the wheel slewed sideways. The bike followed the path of the front wheel and stayed upright for a few metres before it lurched and fell over. The engine continued to roar. The rider flew over the handlebars and cart-wheeled forward.

The man's body came to rest beside the track and lay still.

'Bloody hell!' burst from Rhette's lips as she looked back. 'Now look ...!'

Ana jammed on the brakes, stopped then backed and pulled up beside the figure. A cloud of red dust hung above them encasing the scene into one of disbelief. She turned off the engine and slumped over the steering wheel. Her face, flushed with the adrenalin of her intent, slowly went ashen. 'What the hell have I done?' she said.

Rhette took control. She got out of the car and opened Ana's door and pulled her out. She knelt by the still figure lying virtually on his back, but twisted and partly faced up. The leather clad chest was rising and falling. He seemed to be breathing. Just. 'You'd better have a look at his face. You've done this and now here's the result.' Rhette's voice was accusing.

Ana fumbled with the black mask.

Rhette leaned down and with a, for goodness sake sound, she pulled the face mask open.

Ana gasped and sat back on her heals.

A shudder ran through her frame.

'It's Quinn!' she said.

# Chapter 30

Quinn opened his eyes and stared up at Ana.

Recognition of her flared into his eyes. He struggled to sit up then fell back. His eyes glazed in pain and his right hand grabbed at his left shoulder.

'You bitch!' he mouthed. His voice strengthened. 'You fucking whore! I'll kill you...this time.'

Ana sat still back on her haunches.

Her world spiraled in onto Quinn's face. Blood was slowly seeping from a forehead cut where his face mask had jagged the skin off. He tried to move. He looked past Ana to Rhette as he realised that she now had her foot solidly on his right arm, closest to Ana. He tried to pull free and she pressed harder.

Rhette patted Quinn's pockets through his leathers, frisked him looking for a gun or knife. 'He's not armed,' she said as she watched Ana sway as she stared into Quinn's face. 'Ana! You've got to help me here. Get a rope from the back of the car; we'll need to tie him up.'

With a shake to clear her head Ana struggled to her feet, opened the tail gate of the car and got the rope. A thick long tow rope. Part of the desert survival kit Lex had put together for them.

Rhette dragged Quinn's legs together and took a tight loop of rope around them. His eyes darkened in pain as the movement pulled at his whole body. It gave Rhette enough time to lay the rope up across his body to his throat. She roughly lifted his helmeted head and looped the rope around his neck and pulled it firm.

With little effort she could choke him.

'I don't think I like you,' Rhette said in a conversational tone as his gaze flattened on her face.

'You're a dead woman,' he sneered at her. 'I remember your ugly face bitch and you're dead. Like your sister, you're dead meat.'

'What...?' Rhette started as he looked away towards his bike.

But Ana squatted again next to Quinn cutting off Rhette's question. She pulled his face towards herself. 'Have you taken my son?' She said in a husky voice that was as though she was being choked again. Her hand went to her throat and her voice was a thread. 'Pietie. Where is he?'

Quinn's mouth pinched into a straight line. 'The kid's that missing? I might have him. You'll never know.' His face screwed up and he coughed as Rhette gave a hard pull on the rope.

'You'd better answer nicer than that,' she said, 'or I'll test the rope again.' The roar of the motor bike engine threatened to swamp their voices. 'Do you know how to turn that bloody thing off?' she said to Ana.

Ana shook her head, 'No.'

Rhette thrust the rope into Ana's hands. 'I'll do it. Keep him under control otherwise...' Obviously she hadn't though through the otherwise. She ran the twenty metres to the Harley and tugged out a key. In the heat of the afternoon the abrupt silence was a blast of relief and the echo seemed to seep away over the gibber plains and the moonscape of crater shafts. Rhette came back with heat sweat pouring down her face and neck. A rivulet of perspiration had made a shadow at the back of Ana's shirt.

'Getting a bit hot?' She asked Quinn. 'I'm a red head. I don't like being out in the sun. I think Ana and I'll get into the shade of the car.' She said and motioned Ana back.

Quinn lay out in the full sun. He was in full leathers, black leathers and they knew he'd be feeling the heat as the sun poured into the black. The driver's door was left open and the rope swung from Quinn's body to Ana's hands.

Quinn grabbed at the rope with his right hand.

'No!' Ana shouted. Her face hardened into clenched lines as her teeth snapped shut after her yell. It was as though something clicked inside her. She hauled hard on the rope pulling it away from his grasp. It was a thing of vengeance in her hands.

Maybe he had Pietie.

This man had killed her husband and he had almost strangled her at the prison.

She held the rope tight.

Quinn gagged.

Rhette gasped. 'Stop it, you'll kill him.'

'So?' Ana said. 'He deserves it!'

'You won't get an answer if you kill him. It'd be murder...'

Ana's hands released the tension of the rope as Quinn fought to get breath back into his lungs. His body heaved with effort.

'How does that feel?' Ana shouted at him. She yanked the rope again.

In that instant she wanted to punish him, choke him, to claw at his face until he told her where Pietie was. Again Quinn's body heaved upwards. He got his right hand up, grabbed the rope and stopped the continued pull. He couldn't release the thick rope that encircled his neck. The only thing that stopped the rope going into his flesh was the Bikies leathers. They acted as her shirt did when Quinn was strangling Ana...as part of the pressure on his throat.

Ana stepped out of the car and kicked Quinn's hand away from the rope. 'Tell me where Pietie is?' Ana screamed down at him again.

Quinn's arm flopped down.

He was beginning to look bad. Mottled and purple in the face from the throttling rope and his face glistened as sweat poured off him. He was dying of it. Dehydration and shock of the accident would kill him.

'No! I have him alright...you bitch.' His voice was a ragged scrape in sand.

Quinn's energy gave out and he stopped struggling against the rope. 'You'll never find him if you kill me.' He choked out. 'And if the fucking pigs get me I'll tell them nothing. Nothing!' He was silent for a moment then his face twisted into a mask of spite. 'The only way is for you to get my boy Clinton back. Then I'll tell you...maybe I'll tell you ...'

Far off there was a flutter of sound on the wind.

A deep throb of an engine quickly grew and grew to announce that there was another motor bike on the track.

'Ana...' Rhette said. 'We've got to go...now!'

Ana gave the rope another hard pull before she dropped it and she started the vehicle's engine. She shut the door and, as she spun the wheel to go, rocks cluttered over the figure lying still behind them.

Within a kilometer they passed another black leather clad rider on a Harley boring down the track towards the scene of their confrontation.

Ana gave a howl of anguish. Tears of frustration joined the sweat on her face as she drove the car back to Coober Pedy.

With an absolute clarity of mind Ana could see the parallels of the scenes.

Quinn had tried to choke her before; now she'd almost choked him.

Both times it was over a child. She couldn't tell Quinn then because she didn't know where his son, Clinton, was and now she was trying to force him to tell her where her own son was.

A probable dead end.

Assault and stalemate.

The sun set on Coober Pedy and that day of searching was over.

# Chapter 31

'You should have phoned! You should have phoned me when you thought you saw Quinn. Nothing else.' Mark's voice was angry. His face was drawn, white except for two red splodges of colour high on his cheekbones as he confronted Ana and Rhette.

He paced the front room of the Police Station where they had come to report what had happened. Mark's hands went through his hair as he stopped, then paced again. He turned again to the women. 'Just phoned! We'd have had him in custody. Then we could have found out where he was holding Pietie.'

'He said he'd never tell if the police had him...' Rhette said. She looked for some comment from Lex who was seated in the interview room with them. The big man raised eyebrows and drew in breath. He agreed with Mark.

Ana sat hunched. Her hands hung; then clenched and unclenched as the words were thrown at her. Her face fallen, dragged down in defeat.

Paralyzed by delayed shock.

What she had almost done?

She'd wanted to kill him and she knew that if they'd been able to stay there much longer Quinn would have died from the rope choking him. Or from the accident.

Maybe he was dead now.

Quinn couldn't be taken to hospital, Mark had said that.

Since the women confessed to their action with Quinn Mark had ordered a policeman to act an orderly in the out patients area. It was an unlikely occurrence that Quinn would turn up for treatment even if he attempted to demand it at the point of a gun. The Miners Rescue team worked out of the hospital making the chance of Quinn going there even less possible. Already the message had gone out of the injured man to hospitals across the state, including into the Northern Territory. The airport was being watched.

The police had talked to a doctor who said that Quinn's injuries, as the women described them, sounded like a broken or dislocated left arm, possible internal injuries, concussion and certainly shock. With luck and crude bikie attention he could be patched up, depending on if he had internal injuries.

'I should arrest you on any number of charges over this. Both of you!' Mark threatened. His voice was sharp; louder than anyone in the room had ever heard from him before. He paced the floor in front of them; footsteps long and stiff legged as if he had a need to stride out to shake off the enormity of their actions. He couldn't remain still let alone be seated.

Rhette raised her eyebrows in question at him. 'Surely not? We were just...'

'Any number,' Mark interrupted. 'You've described assault. Attempted murder. Causing an accident. Leaving the scene of an accident just for starters.' His face was hard, resigned with confusion.

Lex avoided looking at Mark. These were serious charges that could be laid but he doubted that Mark would do it.

'That other bike came too soon,' Ana looked up and snapped. 'Otherwise I'd have got where Pietie is from Quinn. I'd have killed him if I had to...' Her hands were clenched into fists.

'That's enough! I should bang you into the station lockup for all this but finding Piet is still my first consideration. I don't think this attack on Quinn incident has helped us at all.' Mark glared at Ana and swept his look on to Rhette's strained face.

There was a sharp exhaling of breath from Ana; her body seemed to sway and crumple in her chair and her hands spread. Her fingernails had drawn pressure half moon ridges into her palms that mirrored the purple half moons of exhausted shadows under her eyes. Rhette leaned over and put an arm around Ana's shoulder.

'Yes, enough,' she said, her voice was ragged. 'I'm taking her home. She's done in. To hell with the charges against us. Just find her son. Just find him.'

Half an hour later, after the women had left, Mark led the evening police session.

The search had proven little although the Coober Pedy team had an Aboriginal Officer brought in from Marla to check the area around the house again. He came back to the station to report.

'Anything, Milo?' Dave Ballinger asked, his voice was tired as he rose to shake the proffered hand of the tall Aboriginal man.

Lex's black eyes widened. Crikey, he thought, that was a bit racist. The only thing he knew about Milo was that Grace, his wife, put the dark chocolate powder into milk for the children. They loved it.

Milo caught the Lex's look and smiled as he shook his hand. 'I've always been called Milo,' he said. 'My Pitjantjatjara name is unpronounceable to most white fellas, and you lot too, and I wanted Milo from the first time I tasted it as a kid. Still like it better than the beer all you blokes drink.'

Dave broke in as a chuckle progressed about the room. 'Sorry Milo, you can talk about that later. What did you find?'

'The tracking wasn't easy. Too many boots, feet and dog prints had covered most of any tracks left there, but I don't think the little fella wandered off. I went a long way out from the house, way past where your lot looked. Nothing. No little footprints had walked away. But there was a motor bike track that was newer. Someone had stopped and looked at the place a short time. Someone who'd made up his mind then pushed off with the bike to do something in a rush. Impatient foot pushed off. Left a ridge in the sand.'

'You're saying abducted? Not wandered off. Abducted.' Dave demanded.

'That would be my thinking. No way I could tell that the bike had the extra weight of the child, but another track was where the rider had stopped close behind a vehicle. Put his bike on the stand and got off it. Your boots covered what he did next, but the bike was probably left with the engine running. When it moved again it went slowly, probably quietly, before it accelerated away at the end of the street.' Milo's hands played the scene's as he spoke the words.

'You got all that from?' Mark said, his voice quiet in amazement.. We've been over that ground a hundred times...'

'He's the best there is,' Dave said.

'Been doing it awhile...' Milo said. 'And my conclusion is the boy was abducted by someone on a large motor bike. A Harley by the treads.'

'Nothing left there. No cigarette butts?' Lex asked.

'Nah, nothing else. He was careful.'

It was too late to put up 'Crime Scene' tapes but Milo had confirmed the suspicion of abduction.

Ana's chase after Quinn had been vindicated.

'You look like shit Mark!' Harry Shaw said as he came into the conference room. He'd just arrived on the late plane with the Major Crime team from Adelaide.

Lex grinned as the two men embraced in the back slapping way that male friends do to offer support and concern. They had a history like the one he wanted to form with Mark. Early days yet but he respected the younger detective more each day they worked together.

Harry pulled out a chair and reached for a sandwich from a tray in the middle of the table in one movement. He transferred the sandwich to the left hand to offer his right to Lex as Mark introduced them.

'I heard about you,' Harry said as they shook hands. 'The new big black guy from South Africa. Good to meet you.' He nodded towards Mark. 'Our friend here always seems to get himself into the middle of things. Buggered if I know how he does it. We've had to bail him out all the time. Your turn now it seems.' The expression of the open face of the detective was both friendly and yet serious.

Lex grinned. There was no racism in Harry's comment and he

was immediately comfortable with the tall muscular man who's presence dominated the room. 'Yes,' he said. 'Working with Mark is interesting...'

Harry took the sandwich in one bite, swallowed and grimaced. 'Cripes, they always give us bloody stale cheese sandwiches. Can't anyone get ham and mustard for a change?'

The men relaxed as the day's tensions eased with some food and the common knowledge that they were a team. At the end of a terrible day with a child still missing and a known criminal plaguing them, only their professional attitude would tie them together.

'Tomorrow...' Mark said.

Rhette forced Ana into bed, a sleepless bed, but one she had insisted Ana go to be in any shape for the continuing search in the morning.

# Chapter 32

At seven the next morning Lex opened his email in the Coober Pedy Police Station to find a message from Jessica Taylor.

It was brief. "Lawyer Erica Marryat is listed as Tyler Grayson's representative in the Port Augusta Magistrate's Court hearing today. He's the Whyalla customs man caught smuggling drugs. Isn't Mark's ex, Erica, a top brief? Interesting she's representing Grayson."

Lex looked across the room to where Mark was surrounded by officers and the Rescue Squad. He hit 'reply' and typed.

"Good pick up. Get the Port Augusta dees to follow up. Photos of people attending would be useful. Keep me posted. I'll pass this on to Mark."

'You bastard!' Quinn gasped as the large bikie pushed a foot into his armpit as he lay on the bed in the remote dugout. The man reached with totally tattooed arms and grasped Quinn's left wrist.

'Shit... I know what's coming...' Quinn tried to hold himself rigid but the moment he relaxed to take a breath the bikie jerked his shoulder bone socket back into place. The replacement thunk of tendon and muscle was audible. 'You fucking enjoyed that!' Quinn said through a clenched jaw as he got his voice back after the jolting pain of the manipulation.

'Yeah I did that.' The big man said as he put a collar and cuff sling on Quinn. 'Keep your bloody arm still if you want it to get better.' He looked over at Lucy. 'She's my woman, the woman you're using.'

Lucy moved beside the bed. She tapped a syringe, found a vein and pushed a morphine dose into his right arm.

Quinn slapped her hand away. 'No more after this, whore,

149

I've got to stay conscious. Get the fuck out and look after the boy.'

She shrugged. 'Stop worrying, he's asleep.'

Quinn had been brought in the night before. Banged up and bleeding. Obviously in pain, spewing venom about women and whores from whatever had happened to him. Gone were any soft leftovers from the relationship Lucy had hoped they were forming and obviously the frustration was making him nasty. He'd immediately ordered her mobile phone be taken and stopped others communicating to the outside world. He had an unspoken rank that they obeyed.

'Sure. It's better than being near you,' Lucy said.

'Do it, bitch. The boy's your only ticket.'

An hour later Lucy hugged the little boy close to her body as he cried in fright. There was a violent storm raging outside and the thunderbolts of noise reverberated through the underground rooms. No rain softened the storm overhead but to the locals there was the dim hope that the morning would be cooler with the passing of the low weather front. It didn't, and the morning was as though the storm had never happened.

Erica sat up in the vast bed that occupied the top atrium of Dieter Hood's converted warehouse building by the old Sydney docks. An apartment building that didn't look like an expensive home. The scruffy outside didn't matter, but what did matter was the opulence of rooms, a swimming pool and courtyard, inside. Everything was covered by the roof, one that could be opened, but it also kept out prying eyes, especially those in planes and helicopters. Not many people knew he lived and worked his criminal business from there. Legitimate business was conducted from an office and rooms in the Sydney CBD.

With Dieter still apparently sleeping she slipped out of bed to use the toilet. As she passed the only desk in the apartment she was forbidden to look in, she saw that his leather briefcase was open on top of it. Unusual. Unusual also were the legal court papers she immediately recognized, that were showing. She didn't touch anything until she saw her name. It stood out like a beacon. Her eyes sought the top of the South Australian Court document.

'In the case of Tyler Grayson,' she read. What! She'd never heard the name or him. She glanced back towards the figure on the bed before gently easing the paper further out from the case. In the Port Augusta Court. Her eyebrows raised. She'd never set foot in the place and she didn't intend to start now. Her arena was Adelaide not the lesser Country Courts. What the hell was going on?

'Come back to bed woman.' Dieter was propped up on one elbow looking at her naked and lithe golden body. It was a command always expected in the morning. She shifted her body in an attempt to cover her invasion of his briefcase and papers. Maybe if she went apparently eagerly to satisfy him she could find out what was going on.

She went back to bed and endured the sex while her mind worried over her name listed on the Court documents and if he'd seen her at his desk. There would be consequences if he had seen her.

She jumped as a car horn in the street sounded more loudly than she imagined she'd heard before.

The consequences started immediately.

'And?' was a question lightly put. He'd seen her at his desk. Seen her looking at the Court documents.

'I'm not going to Port Augusta for any case...' She jammed her hands into her armpits.

'But you are. This is important. One of my friends has got himself into a little bit of trouble. He needs a top lawyer to get him out of it.'

Rot, she thought. Dieter would not ever have heard of this Tyler Grayson until something went very wrong. Now he was trying to use her as the best legal representation to deal with whatever it was. 'But not to Port Augusta? The local lawyers can get the case moved to Adelaide, easily,' she said.

He gestured towards the bedside table on his side of the bed. 'OK, I'll grant you that,' he said. He paused as though thinking. 'All right. The local lawyers can do the Magistrates Court. You don't need to worry until the case gets to Adelaide.' The nod again towards the drawer containing the box she craved. 'Take it easy...relax. It'll be alright,' he soothed.

Shit! Erica thought as she got off the bed and scuttled to the 'lollies' as they called them, waiting in the silver box. She fumbled the little syringe and put a tiny dose into the muscle in her arm. She wasn't mainlining yet. It wouldn't be too hard to get off the drug.

She glanced at Dieter. He looked smug and self satisfied. She felt the power of him like an aphrodisiac; dangerous, deadly and exciting. She could convince herself she loved him even now. But there was a small problem that she hoped probably would be overlooked in the Court Notices. Her name on the Tyler Grayson's brief. She'd work on Dieter to employ someone else when the time came for the trial in Adelaide. Reputation was everything in the legal system and so far hers was and looked clean.

Had Dieter put her name on the brief as a control mechanism? Erica wondered. She wouldn't put it past him. The questions brought on a wave of fear, almost a dizziness of worry.

The rush hit and she didn't mind very much any more.

# Chapter 33

Port Augusta is almost always hot.

North, east and west winds blow in from the vast Australian inland carrying heat like thrusting sword shafts against the city. The winds jousted with the sea, hulking in shallow patches and for all intents and purposes the scorching blades of air won. Only a wind charging in from the south, from Antarctica, could prevail and yet even that cool air had to pass through the funnel of the Flinders Ranges mountains beside the Spencer Gulf and the vast expanses of Eyre Peninsula to get to the streets.

By late morning the Port Augusta Magistrate's Court on Flinders Terrace was hot. The air conditioners only worked efficiently within the sanctity of the court rooms. Before they could find solace from the heat, the myriad of lawyers in their suits, clerks, people waiting for judgment of lesser matters and bystanders had to pass through the metal detectors in the outer halls. Even once there, in the court, the coolness was soon a memory as the mass of sweating and nervous humanity sat emitting their own heat, and the stink of a few unwashed and un-deodorised bodies rose in an invisible miasma towards the ceiling.

The Magistrate got it better. His rooms got most of the cooled air.

The court cells got nothing of the cool air.

Tyler Grayson was sweltering. He'd felt the heat during the transportation in the closed van into the court from the Port Augusta Goal and stress of standing in the dock while the people he knew and betrayed thrust dagger eyes at him. Then there would be an interminable wait while the Magistrate made the committal hearing decision.

'Bugger and shit!' he said into the face of the local lawyer who had come to the cells before his appearance. 'Where's Erica Marryat? The bastards promised she'd represent me!' he ranted as the lawyer stood; clutching the papers of the very new brief he'd been given.

'She'll be in Adelaide after I get a trial date and have this matter moved there...' Perspiration beaded a brow so young it hadn't had time in years, or experience, to wrinkle. 'Don't worry.'

But Tyler was worried.

This replacement lawyer had made a bumbling mess of his address to the Magistrate to get the trial shifted to the Adelaide Supreme Court after the prosecution lawyers had produced evidence that they were most likely going to get a guilty verdict and with it a prison sentence. He'd cited diabetic health issues, but the Magistrate had dismissed this as nothing that could not be dealt with in the prison system. Tyler then offered the more substantial call that his client was facing the likelihood of a very long sentence, if convicted, especially given that he was a Customs Officer. Therefore, he tried to emphasize, the weight of a convicted judgment would be heavier on an officer of the law, more so if it were given in the Port Augusta Court.

The Magistrate, irritated that the request was so ponderously put, retired to his cool chambers to consider it instead of automatically allowing the transfer of the prisoner to the Adelaide Remand Centre and the Adelaide Supreme Court for trial. He would give his decision after his lunch of a chilled salmon salad and a glass of white wine. It was also good to get out of his sweltering court robes for a while.

Tyler Grayson was returned to the cells.

He wasn't feeling well. It wasn't just from the heat and stress but he was getting very low on insulin. They had given him an early breakfast before Court and now this wait made the regularity of his medication a thing of the past. Since his incarceration his diabetes levels had jumped all over the scales. The wrapped cheese sandwich from a local café thrust through the bars waited unopened. He needed his shot first before he could eat it. Or anything.

'Where the fuck's my insulin injection?' He slumped in a nauseous heap. 'Why the hell couldn't they give me my kit to do it myself?'

Grayson knew the security answer to that question but it didn't matter in the shock of comprehending the weight of evidence against him and knowing what 'guilty' would mean to his life. He had to complain about everything, being caught, being in prison, the useless lawyer appointed to him when he was promised the Adelaide defender, and naturally the heat. However his insulin was top priority at that moment.

To escape the rants of his prisoner client the young lawyer went looking for medical help. A uniformed prison officer arrived. He was gloved and after obvious fumbling Tyler grabbed the syringe and bottle from him and measured the dose himself. He pulled his prison uniform shirt aside and jabbed the short two centimeter needle into his stomach, pushed the plunger and injected the contents.

Many bikies have unusual hobbies.

A local gang member had tanks of poisonous snakes; King Browns, tiger snakes and especially the more lethal taipan that were found in the deserts around Port Augusta. He was also adept at milking them. He'd mixed the toxins, predominantly that from the taipan, and filled the 'insulin' bottle when told to do so by the late night burner mobile phone call.

Delivery was easy in a prison officer's stolen uniform and he'd walked, with a no nonsense attitude, into the cells area.

The idiot victim had done the injecting job himself.

Easy...

Half an hour later Tyler Grayson was already a dead man when he was returned to the court room to stand again in the dock.

He swayed then projectile vomited the sandwich he'd eaten all over guard standing next to him. The guard reacted, cursing and pushing away from the prisoner in revulsion. A chaos of noise erupted. The judge banged his gravel demanding silence, officers shouted and moved in all directions, some towards him protectively suspecting even a break for freedom, or away from the mess the prisoner was spewing. An acid vomit stench expended outwards on a wave of putridness that sent people on the public benches gagging.

But in a moment of rigid comprehension Grayson stared glassy eyed at the judge. His hands moved from clutching the bars of the dock to grab at his stomach. As his face clenched in a rigor of pain he slid to the wooden floor in a heaving convulsing heap.

There was nothing that anyone could have done for him. A fraction of the dose he'd injected was enough to kill him, and a whole court room full of people for that matter. The collapse was inevitable, irreversible especially as no medico could have guessed what had been injected instead of insulin.

It wasn't a pretty sight.

His case was closed.

# Chapter 34

Ana was so torn. She felt she would scream if anyone said anything at all to her.

Pietie!

Her body ached with the pain of the physical loss of him. The warmth, the wriggling boy giggles that were Pietie.

Where was Pietie? She knew he would be expecting her to find him.

She knew he was with Quinn.

He'd taunted her with it. Told her that he wanted his own son back. His son, the boy she remembered only now as 'Clinton' because Quinn had said his name. She'd repressed that name as she'd thrust that last day on the houseboat into the dimmest place in her brain and being. Thrust Peter's death, with the memories of the refugee camp so long ago, and taken a new blank life page when she'd started the journey north to Darwin.

Oh please, her whole being screamed, where is Pietie? Bring him back to me.

Had everything changed because she had met Mark again?

Was that her punishment for marking that new page with an old memory? Because of him was Pietie gone? Her logical left brain said no, but she shut it out letting the emotional right brain scream yes. There was guilt burning into the back of her throat; guilt, an honest reaction that was pulling her apart. The hatred and fear was so strong that it had let her almost kill Quinn when she'd had the chance. Her action so stupid that at the end of it, he'd escaped.

Was it her fault that Pietie was still missing? Maybe dead? She bit into her bottom lip again drawing blood. The metallic taste thrust the memory of when Quinn had tried to choke and kill her into her mind. That was nothing compared with the pain she felt now. Then she had struggled against the darkness. Now... she struggled against an endless black pit.

But she'd had to flee when the other bike came. She could not admit to herself what she might have done if she'd not been interrupted. And Rhette was her accomplice only because she'd refused to let her go alone on her wretched idea. That was wrong too and she felt guilt at implicating her new friend.

She should have called Mark. Anyone – not tried to act on her own.

And Mark.

She could see the betrayal in his eyes. See him trying to understand her actions. See him torn apart as a man of the law with what she'd done. Seen his exhaustion in the search for Piet. Fear, guilt and remorse made her turn away from him, unable to be touched, unable to hear what he said. The earth had fallen away between them, a chasm dug and widening with the stilted words they now spoke to each other.

Ana looked up and was surprised to see Rhette sitting opposite her at the kitchen table. She tucked her elbows into her sides and awkwardly pushed away the plate of food that was there. She didn't remember it being put in front of her. She stared into the depths of the food feeling it engulf her.

'Any news?' she asked from way, way, far away.


'I don't know you!'

Mark was exhausted. Done in. As he stood opposite Ana in the kitchen of Doug's house his clothing more crumpled than usual. His cheekbones stood out in a face grey with fatigue and worry. He'd had to see her even though it was almost midnight. It had taken that long to clear the next day's preparation log of searching for Piet and trying to organise the capture of Quinn. He still smarted that Ana had found Quinn, captured and tortured him, and then let him go. OK she'd been forced to let him go. The 'what ifs' of her actions were a mountain of almost insurmountable worry in his head and imagination.

He was almost as angry with Rhette as with Ana for being a part of it. He knew that he could be in deep trouble with the police hierarchy if and when they found out what had happened. Their concern would be the mission. Finding Piet, capturing Quinn and finding out more about the drug and opal connection.

But now he had to see Ana.

Had to sort out his feelings for this woman he thought he knew and loved.

Damn the time of night. He knew she'd be awake.

He'd pushed past Doug who answered the door. Strode to the kitchen and flicked a 'get out of here' look at Rhette. She got the message and after a glance at Ana, left the room.

The words just flung themselves out of Mark's mouth. 'I don't know you...' he said again to the woman who sat huddled in the wooden chair that now looked too big for her, who straightened as he charged into the room.

Her hands reached. 'You have news? Pietie...?' she said.

Mark stopped in his tracks. Shit, he thought. That's all she was living for. News of Piet. 'No, I'm sorry. Nothing yet.'

Ana's hands flopped. Her whole being looked like a fish out of water, flung up by the storm of events and left to dry and whither on the empty desolate beach that was her mind and person.

Mark's anger dissipated. He couldn't be the wave that tore at her again, pounded the fragile shell he'd thought she was within.

'They're still searching?' she asked. 'Searching for Quinn? He's got him. I know he's got him. The storm last night would have frightened him. He doesn't understand thunder and lightning. He needs me...'

'They're still searching. I couldn't stop the people if I tried. Some are on foot around the town listening, hunting for sounds, but they can only do so much in the dark. It's dangerous for the searchers too with the mine shafts everywhere. At dawn it will start again with full forces of police, the rescue crew and SES. But Ana...you've got to...'

'You said – you don't know me!' she cut him off as though she could, with the exhaustion and worry, only comprehend one statement at a time. Her voice took on a harsh and determined note. 'No you don't. I'm tough. I survived bullets in a refugee camp. I survived Quinn's hands around my throat. I survived the arrows and knives on the houseboat. I survived when Peter was killed. I survived on my own when Pietie was born...' she said as tears ran down her cheeks. Her voice crumpled as she said her son's name. 'Pietie... Pietie...'

Mark took her in his arms. The body that had been warm and womanly before was hard now, angular now, all ribs, elbows and knees. Her eyes had sunk into bony ridges below hair that straggled, black and white. The wave that he was worried about tearing at her now tore at him as he held her. She was so rigid there was no fit anymore. With a shuddering sigh she gave a fraction and he could meld her into himself. After a few moments he began to speak quietly as her head rested on his chest.

'Stay,' he said. 'We're doing everything we can. And I've got an Australia wide search going on for Faye Bishop. You remember her? She was Quinn's defacto. Clinton's mother. We'll find her and ask her for help. She may let Clinton speak to his father; he'd be about twelve now. Maybe...'

'Yes! Yes! Try her and the boy. Try anything.' She stopped. Tensed. 'Faye couldn't get away fast enough when Quinn was arrested. She was off on the bus to Adelaide then on to who knows where. Gone the same day. That's why he attacked me at the prison,' Ana said. 'He thought I'd helped her get away.'

'Well, we'll find her. Then we can only ask her to help.'

'Find her. You know how to find someone who doesn't want to be found?'

Mark found a smile and ran a finger down the remnants of the tears on Ana's cheeks. 'Yes I think we can find anyone we really want to these days. This will be all out because of Piet and you. I'll call in every contact I have and so will everyone else. Federal and state, the lot.'

'I guess you can do it better than I could as a psychologist.' There was a hint of another relaxation. 'Don't tell me that you would break the law getting information. I thought I was the only one who did that…'

'Maybe I can bend the law a fraction where necessary, but…' Mark said.

She cut him off. 'I mean about Quinn today. I wasn't expecting things to happen like they did, you know. I was so angry I was ready to do anything to get information…to get Pietie back.' Her eyes clouded.

'And you and Rhette could have been killed or worse.' Mark took her face firmly in his hands. There was an edge to his voice. 'Don't you ever do something like that again,' he said.
He held her gaze. 'Ever.'

Ana's toughness pushed resolve into her backbone. She straightened, pushed away from Mark's hands, stood and walked out of the room.

Mark felt the rejection. He swore at his own ineptness, his rigid police ethics and slumped from the house.

There was no place for anything but Pietie in Ana's life.

# Chapter 35

Johnny Fox was requested to see his boss.

A request was an order, a summons no matter that the call from his secretary was her simpering voice on his mobile.

As usual he used the back delivery entrance to Dieter Hood's warehouse premises in the inner Sydney suburb. He was early so he could spend a few moments to settle himself before he found out what new job the summons brought with it. Dieter Hood liked punctuality, for his men to be on time, not early and certainly not late. As Johnny pulled up into the drab parking section he had the time to reconnoitre the area, as usual.

It was some place.

No-one would know of the other hidden garage section. There his boss parked his array of Mercs, a Bentley or two, a couple of Harley motor bikes. His cabin cruiser was big enough to have a large galley and an upmarket four by four to tow it. He's probably got a Ferrari stashed away somewhere here by now, Johnny thought. Once he'd been to the garage when Hood was feeling expansive and been amazed - as he was expected to be. All this, he recognized, was a subtle display of Dieter's wealth that power gave him and maybe a suggestion of a promise.

Johnny drove a 'hand me down' Mercedes from Dieter but it was a car he never expected to own or drive given his poor Balmain childhood. The car suited him and a Merc wasn't such a stand out car in a city like Sydney.

A tradesmen's entrance led to an old open lift that shook its way only down to a basement storage area. Concealed through another steel double locked door was an alternative lift that hummed its way up to the office area on the first floor. A key system, one that Johnny didn't have, opened up to the second and third floors of the warehouse.

He wouldn't mind a setup like this one, he thought. If he played his cards right and eliminated all opposition this could be his one day. Johnny Fox knew how to play his cards, and except for the one occasion when he'd actually gone to trial, he'd stayed apparently clean. His police sheet was supposition only and he'd kept the Boss a phantom figure. Meanwhile Fox slipped here, slipped there, the threat of the organisation as he had been for decades. No charge laid had ever stuck and he meant to keep it that way.

Fox straightened his tie and smoothed down his navy suit as he hit the lift button to the first floor business area of the building. He felt the thin frame of his body. He was still loosing weight and, although Sydney was sweltering in summer heat, he needed a woolen vest under the suit shirt to keep warm. Dieter insisted that he dress as a business colleague and that meant the suit and tie any time he was with him.

Jane, Dieter's secretary smile was as simpering as her phone voice had been as Fox sidled up to her desk and playfully flipped one of her trademark long dangly earrings. She had hundreds of pairs of the jewels, mostly expensive, that marked her as the trusted secretary, and cousin, of Dieter Hood. 'Keeping it in the family,' Dieter had said one time. Keeping the legitimate front in the family, and Jane's bookkeeping abilities were adequate to deal with the import and export business he used cover for his real other business. If Jane suspected anything she wasn't saying – not with the salary and gifts she received as one of Dieter's family.

Johnny knew of only one other family member, another employee, his pilot brother, Sean. The latter had a fixation with gaining wives in succession and was unpopular with Dieter who spent time bailing him out of the latest marital experiment. A good looking bloke, Fox conceded and thankfully he was sterile and there were no offspring to cloud up a business succession line. Fox'd carried a bit of a torch for one of the women. Watched her get messed up by them and drugs. None of his business but he'd masturbated with her in his mind over the years. It wasn't in his job description to get involved with the boss's women.

His only opponent was Quinn, a new comer, and until now the golden boy. In this type of business it was useful being supposedly 'dead' and one day Johnnie Fox wanted to make that 'dead' a physical actuality. It would be a pleasure to do it.

'How's the man?' he asked. He nodded towards the closed office door as he ran a finger down Jane's heavily made up cheek.

Jane squirmed like a virgin schoolgirl at the touch. 'Good. He won't be long. He's on the phone. I think he is...'

Fox noted the call wasn't going through the telephone system that Jane controlled. He leaned towards her and inspected her latest earrings. Opal, he thought, so she's got the opal export part of the business officially underway.

'These are new...nice!' That's all he needed to say to allow her to chatter on and glow under his attention.

'Aren't they? I love them, especially these green ones. Dieter has promised me red stones when he gets some. He's marvelous. He had them set into these earrings for me. As a surprise.' She caressed the loop of gold and opal dangling from one pendulous earlobe.

She was flirting with him. 'That's great,' he said and smiled a brief smile. She didn't seem to notice the insincerity of it and flapped her fingers at him.

Pity she was an old broad, Fox thought, and the jewels were wasted on her. There was a time when he considered making a play for her, just for the sport of it. It might have been more interesting to have played dress ups with all the earrings draped over a naked body if she had a figure worth while even to look at. She was never like the image Fox held in his mind of another woman.

The scenario was impossible he knew; Dieter Hood provided his secretary cousin a tiny flat to live in on the ground floor of the building with 'security' doors he could control remotely.

A small luxurious place and Jane never knew she inhabited a prison.

'Come in, my friend, come in,' Dieter ushered Johnny Fox into his sound proof office with a hand to the shoulder that, to all intents and appearances to trusting Jane, was a friendly hand.

The moment the door shut behind them the hand tightened into a hard grip. It seemed to separate Fox's bones.

'What the fucking hell's going on with Quinn and the South Australian set up?' Dieter demanded. 'The Whyalla drug busts. Shit, at least Quinn fixed the customs fuckup but he had to deal with too many other things there. Can't he control the people he sets up to do the chemistry and grow the crops?'

'I had...'

Dieter's colour was up as his hand waved at Johnny to shut up. His face was reddening by the second. 'Your message said he'd kidnapped a kid. Why in the hell did he do that?'

Again the hand tightened.

Dieter wasn't ready to hear any excuses.

Johnny Fox had to stand and listen to Dieter Hood's usual tirade of the difficulty in running his organisation without good staff. It wasn't the time to discuss Quinn and his fears that Quinn was trying to move up in the boss's estimation over himself. Trying to muscle into the number one position. Better just let Quinn crucify himself with his current diversions and the situations that caused.

With luck he'd be given the task of fixing Quinn soon. He'd thrown one small spanner into Quinn's works with the kidnap report and it was good to hear of the results.

One piece of useful information came out of the steely rant was that Dieter Hood was planning to fly his private plane to Coober Pedy to pick up the parcel of opal. He didn't trust Quinn with that delivery.

'Yeah, boss, a good idea,' Fox added his barb to Quinn's back.

Dieter Hood, with a shrug of his shoulders as if Fox would understand, suddenly said, 'I should've known that it's only fucking family I can trust. It's time I get Sean more into the business. He's cost me a bloody packet over the years with his procession of expensive women and keeping him happy with one aeroplane after another.' He paused, seemingly looking past Fox.

This, if it meant what he thought it did, left Fox stymied. What was Hood planning? Was his own loyalty and contribution worth nothing?

'Yes,' Hood said as he ushered Fox out the door with once again an apparently friendly farewell for Jane's benefit. 'Get ready to fly to Coober Pedy tonight. We'll do the business there. Perhaps we can pick up some nice opal too.'

Yes, thought Fox, millions of dollars worth of opal for the family business and another trinket for Jane.

Family.

And the smile towards Johnnie Fox didn't reach Dieter Hood's eyes.

# Chapter 36

Above Coober Pedy a star studded night sky lingered.

The storm had cleared in the hours before dawn, but in the dugout room where Quinn lay, there were no sign of it. The bikie gang's covert stronghold lay behind a shop front selling car spare parts. That, like all the other rooms hidden there, had no windows to the outside world. The entrance, especially, was well concealed.

Quinn's room, the guest room was large with a bed pushed against the far rock wall. A bedside cupboard held a huge assortment of magazines on motor bikes, porn and naked girls, and not much else. Opposite the bed was a huge flat screen TV set into the wall, its electrical cables draped like sagging spaghetti to a single socket. On the floor dozens of DVDs, again reflecting the tastes of the usual occupants of the room, were stacked. Violent 'R' rated was the norm. There was, however, a small pile of Disney cartoons and the odd wildlife vid. One could never underestimate the tastes of guests. A light bulb burned low.

A totally incongruous object, to any outsider, in the guest's quarters was Quinn's huge black and silver Harley Davis motorbike. Despite the dents and scrapes on the paintwork and chrome from his accident it still loomed enormous and threatening taking up a large area of the room. Oil stains on the stone floor said volumes that this was where other precious vehicles had been parked before. It lent an aroma of oil and leather and the pungency of fuel to the room.

Quinn's damaged leathers were slung over the seat and his locked saddle packs bulged.

'Lucy? Where the hell are you?' Quinn bellowed.

Lucy came into Quinn's room. She was angry. When George

had left the previous night after attending to Quinn's shoulder he'd let slip that the boy she was looking after was the child that all Coober Pedy was searching for. She'd be up for assisting in the kidnapping if they were caught. If she were caught it would mean prison time for her. Lots of it...

'Yes,' she said without her usual smile.

Quinn scowled at her. 'Get dressed the way you were before. How I want you. I hate women in pants. Go on, get changed bloody now. Then come back here.'

She shrugged. She was comfortable in her shorts and halter. It looked good. But these bikie men either wanted their women to dress 'feminine in dresses,' in other skimpy clothes or to look like their men in leathers. OK so that's what he wanted. She changed back into the green dress, going commando as expected, without the ruined shoes, and returned to the room.

She hadn't changed her attitude.

'The boy,' she said frowning, 'they're looking for him. I don't want any part of what you are doing.'

'You'll fucking do as you're told. Care for the kid properly too. Feed him right. Keep him quiet though...I can't stand whining kids.'

'He's asleep...' she was cut off.

'Yeah, OK then. I'm still in pain from this blasted busted shoulder.' As Lucy moved towards the cupboard with the drugs he said, 'And I don't want any more of that stuff.   Distract me woman...' His good hand moved towards his fly on his black jeans. 'Do me.'

She knew what he wanted. Bloody men, she thought as she moved to comply. Any time for sex. Being serviced. She assisted him to drag his jeans down. It took a while to distract him and as he got close to orgasm he said, 'Get on me bitch. You're not going to waste my load.'

When it was done he kept her on him. Still rocking now gently to ease him down she said, 'About the boy...'

Quinn eyes went flinty then granite hard. He brought his knees up into her back. Imprisoning her. 'I'll be the only fucking one to tell you about the kid...' he said through bared teeth.

'But!'

Quinn lashed out at her with his closed right fist. His angry sweeping blow caught her on the temple and smashed her head into the rock wall.

He heard the crack like someone hitting a coconut shell with an axe. She slewed sideways her head distorted; her body limp after the one shudder that pulsed through her.

He knew immediately she was dead.

'Shit!' He struggled to get himself out from under her slumped crumpled body. To free himself from her, the bed and the bed sheets.

Quinn stood. He shrugged up his jeans and one handed forced the zipper up. His steps, still uncertain, either from the pain of his shoulder or shock at what had happened, were stumbling and ragged as he went to his Harley. He pulled a key from a leather strand around his neck and opened the locked storage bags. His gun, time for his gun. He fumbled to open the mechanism to make sure that the gun was loaded. It was. He might need that gun if he encountered the woman's partner. He knew that despite the rigid hierarchy of the organisation the members got attached to their disposable bitches.

Quinn straightened and took a deep breath. He shouted. 'I need help in here...'

A bikie came into the room. Started towards the bed and the still form.

'The whore attacked me,' Quinn said. Cords of annoyance were rigid in his neck.

'You've killed her?' The mans eyes went wide.

'Just get rid of the bitch's body.'

'Lucy...'

'Was that her name?' Quinn said.

# Chapter 37

Mark, alone in the squad room, looked at the crime scene board that detailed everything they knew about the disappearance of Piet Foster, aged three years. Someone had underlined the 'three years old' notation seemingly making the possibilities bleaker than ever.

He found himself repeating in his mind what was written on the board and had never felt so confused over his thinking before. He was looking for answers that he just didn't want to formulate.

One: Pietie had wandered away and had fallen down a Calwell mine hole near where he started from and he was dead at the bottom of it. This had been ruled out by the tracker but they had to leave that as a possibility. Besides that in the heat of the past two days he couldn't have survived. They'd search and researched every known hole in the area going further than three year old legs could be imagined to go.

Two: someone like the two British monster boys had taken him and put him down a hole. Unlikely Mark thought. The kids in Coober Pedy had safety drilled into them all their lives and he doubted that this could or would be a thrill killing. Unless it was kids from outside the town, he'd have to think about that, but again it was unlikely.

Three: Quinn had the boy and had killed him and thrown the little body down a shaft further out of town. A strong possibility that he shuddered to think about.

Four: Quinn had him and was holed up somewhere in the town. If this last one held up then he was determined to find them. If Quinn had killed the boy then he vowed to make him pay for it. With his life if necessary.

And Ana?

How was he going to face Ana again if they couldn't find Pietie...?

Mark gasped and flinched ready to ward Lex off when the big black man's hand grasped his shoulder.

'Didn't you hear me come in?' Lex said. The smile that creased the open face faltered. 'Sorry if I startled you. You were far away, man.'

Mark swatted back at Lex trying to cover his confusion and the welcome break in his thoughts. 'Yes, I was.' He seemed to shake himself. 'It's good that you're early. We've a long way to go today.'

'Harry's coming with coffee. Be in soon. And the local boys'll be in as well for the meeting. They're ready to go. Dave Ballinger knows the area better than anyone. He's been here for years according to the local men.' Lex straightened out a map of the town on the desk.

Mark said. 'I met Dave for the first time this week. Been talking to him on the phone regularly though. He's about to retire soon and I'll miss his expertise and knowledge.' He pushed his tousled hair back as he looked at the map. 'Making anything of the search area?'

'You'll never believe me but there are only wide open spaces and craters out there. Like the bloody moon. Gives me the creeps.'

Mark pulled his thoughts into line. He seemed to be operating on automatic. He quipped. 'What, the African veldts deserted you? I thought you were ...'

'If you're going to say used to chasing lions when I was a kid then you've got it wrong. I've never seen a lion out of the zoo. I'm a city man.'

Lex watched in satisfaction as some of the tension eased from Mark's face at his response. Now was the time to talk to him about Ana, but Mark leaned back into his chair and said. 'I've heard a rumour from the local boys that there's been a huge opal buy here in the last few days. Not the corporations, a private buy. Following up what we discussed about opal being used as drug currency I want to know more about it.'

'Sure thing,' Lex said.

'Follow the money trail. Find out as much as you can. The usual, check with the banks. The dealers and quiz the local boys. It's often the money trail that gets names and results.'

'I'll get onto that straight away.' Lex waited a beat as Mark settled back towards his computer screen. He wasn't a person who pushed into other people's lives but he felt the need now. 'Have you talked to Ana? I mean really talked to her...'

The tension went back into Mark's jaw-line. 'No,' he said. 'Things have changed and I'm not ready to yet.'

'You're completely mad! Nothing's changed. You still love her and she's in trouble, worse than ever before... Her kid's maybe dead.  Nothing else would be on her mind. She'd be like that lion you were going to talk about, ready to kill to protect her cub.' Lex reached a hand towards Mark shoulder again, this time as though he was going to land a punch in emphasis. 'She needs you, Mark, not someone who's judging her.'

'What she did was so ... against what I believe in ... so against the law.'

'This's bloody nothing! Sure – it was stupid. But hell it was gutsy, and it could have killed her and Rhette. I'd want my woman to fight for our kids, or me.'

'Maybe...'

'Forget maybe. She needs you.'

Harry Shaw pushed the door open and dropped a paper bag of bakery pastries he held under his arm onto Mark's desk. More carefully he put three cups of coffee down beside them. He glanced at Mark. 'Hell, you still look like shit! Not sleeping? Ana keeping you busy as a diversion?'

Lex's eyebrows headed towards his bald dome, his eyes followed. He glanced towards Harry. Your friend, you talk to him, the look said.

'You're kidding. You haven't made up with her properly yet. You stupid bastard!' Harry thundered. He landed the hard punch on Mark's shoulder that Lex had resisted.

'I will. I will, after the briefing I'll go out to see her again.' Mark looked towards the door as the congregation of police officers and mining searchers trooped in. It was almost a relief to have them ready to work rather than be chastised by friends.

Dave Ballinger came in and took off his wide brimmed uniform hat. Unusual; the man usually had his hat welded to his head, he had every time Mark had seen him. He noticed the sun cancer lesion spots across his forehead and knew the reason why.

Mark nodded to Dave to go over the crime scene board and bring everyone up to date. There was little change. The faces were tight and serious as Dave pointed to the photo of Piet, so young, so fragile, on the board. There was a whisper, a rustle as paper maps were opened and spread. Fingers traced the marked street already searched, hands expanded out as it was discussed that today they would just widen the search area and continue questioning about the bikie involvement.

Yesterday they'd searched the spare parts shop they suspected was the new bikies headquarters and found nothing obvious. They'd search again. This time they'd try for a warrant from the magistrate at Port Augusta and tear the place to bits if need be. It mightn't be an easy task to get the warrant but they'd build the best case they could on very little real evidence. It could take twenty four hours to get the paperwork.

Mark said, 'Lex you can stay here and do the computer work on the warrant, and cover any other matters.' That'll keep you away from the open spaces with big bad roos and ferocious camels there, he thought. A smile touched at the corners of his mouth as he saw Lex had read his intentions.

Ballinger put up a hand as he read a text that had silently come in on his mobile. 'They've found a body in a shop. It's been identified as Frank Mason, the opal dealer. It's definitely a homicide.'

'Change of plans.' Mark grabbed his coat. 'Harry, you go with Dave and check this out. He's got to be there and you can assist, take over if it's routine so that Dave can keep on with the search for Piet.' His eyes went to both Lex and Harry. 'I'll let Ana know where we're at...'

# Chapter 38

Rhette opened Doug's front door to Mark and the morning heat leaked in as he entered.

His slight shake of the head and his grim expression told her that there was nothing new in the search for Piet.

'At least you're here again. That's something,' Rhette said abruptly. She led the way to the kitchen.

Ana had made an effort after Rhette had almost pulled her out of bed. She had showered and her dark hair, with its distinctive white streaks, hung wet to her shoulders. She was sitting with her hands clasped between her knees as if she didn't know what to do with them after she had twisted the wheels on the little car that Lex had given to Piet almost off. She looked up from the toy, took an unsteady step towards Mark and sagged into his arms.

'Anything?' she said. She held on to him as though she would fall if he let her go.

'No not yet, but everyone's out looking.' He brushed her hair back and buried his face into the wetness and the warmth of her neck. 'I'm sorry,' he said. 'So sorry. I was angry and said those horrible things to you last time.'

'I'm sorry,' she echoed. 'I was stupid...'

Rhette banged cups down on the bench and flicked the kettle switch. She turned on Mark. 'Enough of the 'sorrys'. What's happening? This is only the second time you've been back since we got Quinn. Ana's been devastated. Phone calls weren't enough.' She filled coffee cups and plonked them down in front of them at the kitchen table. 'Sugar there! Milk's there! And Ana eat something. I'm not wasting my time cooking for you if you're not going to eat. Doug's out all the time too and...' Rhette's gaze flitted from one to the other and back to the table and the things on it. 'Shit!' she said. 'I've only known you both for a few days but what you have together was feeling good. Now Pietie's gone and I can't see you two like this. Get over the sorrys and support each other.'

Instinctively Mark and Ana reached and each took each other's hands. Their sorrys were cut short as Mark's phone vibrated in his pocket.

'Sorry,' he said, not sure if he should let his face show the irony of yet another apology. 'I'd better take this.' He went to the next room and they could only hear a few words of his conversation. 'OK,' they heard as his steps started back to the kitchen. 'The place smashed up but you think this is a professional hit. An odd one though.'

`'Nothing to do with Pietie then?' Ana's face closed in again.

'No...' Mark's phone vibrated again. 'Sorry,' he said again needlessly as he turned aside to answer it.

'We've got another case as well. A young woman's body was found this morning. Out near a place called Seven Mile Road. Harry and the local boys are there.' He started to close his phone, hesitated, then left it open for them to look at the photo that had come to him. 'It's not the prettiest...'

Rhette cut him off. 'That's the woman who Quinn was with at the opal shop,' she said.

'Yes,' agreed Ana. 'You're right. It's her! O no! If she was with Quinn, and he's killed her, what has he done to Pietie?' Her hands gripped, scrunched, then pleated the material on her trouser legs. Her eyes were wide with pain again.

'We don't know that! We don't know that Quinn has him. We don't know if he killed this woman.' Mark enfolded Ana in his arms. 'You identifying this woman as being with Quinn may help us.' His lips were in her hair and his eyes met Rhette's over the top of her head. His thoughts were spinning. The total policeman was back again. 'We'll be able to get a warrant we need to search one particular premise now. This could get us closer to Quinn and Piet, but I've got to go now.'

He kissed Ana and as Rhette walked him to the door his steps were more sure and forceful. 'Thank you for looking after her,' he said. 'You're a true friend.'

'Just get Pietie back,' Rhette pushed strands of her mop of red hair back behind one ear. 'I'm not going to apologise for my scolding either. You two needed your heads bashed together.' She said with force.

'Shit! Men!' Mark heard as Rhette slammed the door shut and he was out in the morning light where the heat was building.

Just maybe they had a breakthrough, he thought. The professional hit could be Quinn's work. With that assumption they could move heaven and earth to locate him.

They had Quinn's DNA signature and he was no longer a dead man.

Quinn was real.

No longer chasing a ghost.

He'd been seen and he was in Coober Pedy.


Mark pulled his car into the site by an iron galvanized fence. The place where the woman's body had been found was desolate; red-yellow sand and dirt with not a skerrick of vegetation. There was the smell of turned dry earth and the flies had already discovered her and hummed the tune of new death. It was now a police site, her privacy protected by a large white tent erected by Dave Ballinger and his men. Yellow tape outlined the whole area from the grey fence to the dirt road.

Lex and Harry met him and led the way to view the remains.

She lay there still untouched; her green dress creased but covering her body properly as though someone had at least smoothed it down and given her a little dignity in death. Not just dumped her in the night. She could have been, instead, just tossed her down a mine shaft to be found sometime - if ever. If the person hadn't been disturbed in burying her they may never have found the body in the vastness of the area. Next to her was what appeared to be a partly dug grave in the sand and a pile of folded clean sheets, again indicating that some care was going to be taken with her. Her head, its profusion of golden hair marred by two head wounds, lay at an untidy and an unlikely angle. An air of youth hung over her.

She hadn't died of natural causes.

Mark felt his usual mixture of emotions at a murder scene when seeing the victim for the first time. Sadness. Anger at a life terminated and a gritty determination to give the person justice; even if she was a cohort of Quinn as Rhette and Ana had attested.

After a quiet look at the remains and area where the corpse lay the police trio moved outside the tent to ensure that they didn't contaminate the scene in any way before the forensic team arrived to 'do their stuff,' as Harry put it.

'This burial was disturbed,' Mark said aware that he was stating the obvious. 'Who called it in?'

Harry pointed to an elderly man and his Jack Russell dog who had now been shepherded away from the scene. Someone had provided him with a camp chair and he sat shaded only by a broad rimmed hat while his little dog sat under the chair. Perhaps that same someone had put an enamel cup of water, now empty, for the dog there too. As he slumped on the chair they could see that the old man had either dressed quickly into his shirt and shorts or he wasn't an advocate of wearing underpants.

'He did.' Harry unnecessarily consulted his notes, a grin on his face, as they moved towards the witness, 'John Parkinson. He's a local miner; well really he's a professional opal noodler. He makes just enough, with his pension, to keep him living in the tourist park. He said his dog scratched at his caravan door asking to be let out at about four this morning. The dog did its pee but then took off towards the park fence.' Harry nodded towards an iron fence behind them. 'He said he got his torch and followed. The dog was making a bit of a racket and he wanted to quieten him. He's not officially allowed to have a dog here but the park people, he says know about Percy and leave him be. As long as no-one complains. He said he could hear a noise over the fence and he climbed up to have a look. Shone his torch over a bit, and called out, the usual, Anyone there? Obviously there was no answer. He stayed a while calming his dog before going back to his van.'

'Why didn't he call it in then?' Mark said.

'He doesn't have a mobile. He grumbled that his pension's not that good for the expensive type of phone that'd work out here. Anyway, he said as he got back to his van he heard a motor bike start up. Then about seven he got up again when he now had to pee and had a good look over the fence. He went to the park office, waited until they opened at seven thirty, and used their phone to call us.'

Lex said, 'I know, if he'd had a phone and called us earlier we might have got the bastard who was burying her.'

'A pity,' Mark said. He turned towards the old miner. 'Mr Parkinson, you can go for now. Get out of the sun. Thank you for your co-operation. An officer will take a written statement from you later today, or tomorrow, and we may need to speak to you again so please stay in Coober Pedy.'

'You know where to find me,' was the reply before he shuffled off mumbling about the dog needing another drink.

The detectives stood, backs to the sun and heat, but oblivious to it as they concentrated on their next moves.

'At least, with Ana and Rhette's ID that she was with Quinn, as you said on the phone, and the report of the motor bike, it looks like a bikie crime. We're probably not going to get much from them.' Lex said.

Mark shrugged then his chin jutted. 'It's enough information for that search warrant to get into that spare parts shop. Lex, that's your first priority. I want it today. Get past the legal privacy claptrap that their shonky lawyers will put up. OK, I don't care what you say in the report request. Just make it strong. If we can get into that store front, as Dave insists it is a bikie stronghold, then we've got a chance to get Piet and Quinn.'

Dave Ballinger had come to the group and overheard Mark's last comment. 'The bastards would've moved on by now to another place. They've always got more than one bloody rabbit hole in Coober Pedy,' he said.

'Yeah?'

'More like warrens of them. Much of the area under the town is tunnels. Dug as miners scraped out rooms to live in, then extended as they found opal, or wanted more rooms. Remind me to tell you about when they moved the old Italian Club when this is all over...' Dave laughed a weary non humorous, laugh. 'Then you'll have an inkling of the extent of underground mines and tunnelling here.'

'OK. So, you have a notion of the other places? OK Lex, include other suspicious addresses or premises in your warrant order.'

As Lex went towards his car to go back to the station Mark turned back to Dave.

'Yeah, and from what I've seen and heard, I think it is bikie related too. I've seen the woman about Coober Pedy with one of them. I noticed her because she didn't seem like the usual type of woman who went with them,' Dave said.

Mark raised an eyebrow as a question. 'How so?'

'She was softer. Not the hard, I'll kick the shit out of you if you cross me, type. She could smile, and I didn't tie her in with them until I saw her with George Gordon one day. They seemed to be a couple, and I'll bet that he was the one burying her. I'm not totally sure he'd kill... But you can't always guess about people, can you?

'You may be right. You know your own town. This has the feel of Quinn. He's a psychotic bastard. I know that from his past kills,' Mark said.

'We'll probably never know. George Gordon will be to hell and gone far away across the desert by now. I've put out an alert on him, but he knows the region and he'll be hard to apprehend.' Dave said.

A police van pulled up. Two men from the Forensic Team in white overalls got out and ambled across to the detectives.

'You got here quickly,' Mark said as the men shook hands.

'We were in Glendambo on a road death job that had a few extra questions to be answered. Finished up last night and the call came through just as we were leaving. So here we are,' the lead man said.

'You must have hiked?' Dave said.

'Two fifty's not far when you can use the siren and lights. We technical boys don't get the chance to use them that often.' He grinned. 'Always wanted to be a fireman when I was a kid.' There were smiles of amusement as the forensic men looked pleased with themselves.

'How far away is the pathologist?' Mark asked. He shifted his stance, feet impatient. His sense of humour was less than the men's and he just wanted to get on with things.

'Wally Gideon's coming with him on the plane from Adelaide this morning.'

'The Chief?' Harry questioned.

'Yeah. With the government cutbacks he has to do the rotations too. I think he likes it, but we'll do the preliminaries and get the body back to a cool morgue.' He flapped at a fly. 'Be better for the autopsy without the flies too.'

The specialists moved into business mode. After a nod from Mark they went into the tent for a first look at the body before going back to their car for their equipment.

'Harry, you stay with them. Get a chain of evidence set up and all that but mostly get anything they can tell you about her and the scene. There's got to be something to help us. Dave, will you find out the woman's name. Someone must know who she is. Anything that might give us another address Quinn could be hiding.' He paused. 'This killing may also be Quinn's death certificate if he had anything to do with it. But if they kill him then what about the boy?'

# Chapter 39

Later that morning Rhette and Doug sat together in the kitchen, an echo of elbows on the table.

Ana had gone back to lie down and rest on her bed.

With the suddenness of their re-uniting as father and daughter and the shock of the little boy's disappearance, there was an unspoken agreement that they would leave explanations governing actions in their past lives for now. Until then Doug was the practical man; a man who would do what he could to fix things. Rhette didn't mention, not yet anyway, that this was one of the problems the family had to contend with in the past. Emotions he'd run from, maybe, as she realised now as a response to Vietnam and his only way of dealing with things was action. This time he was not running away.

She leaned forward in her chair. 'So you reckon that Quinn's injuries will only hold him in Coober Pedy for a few days before he's ready to make a run for it?' she said.

'You described choking him, and he had a crook arm.'

'Shoulder. He busted his shoulder when he came off the bike.'

'OK. Shoulder then. It makes little difference. I reckon you only got him because he was thrown in the accident.' Doug's forefingers made air indentations at the word "accident." 'Had the wind knocked out of him? From what Ana has said about him he sounds tough. An ex con on the run, a bikie and maybe a hired killer. I think he'll be heading out as quickly as he's able. It's too hot for him here now.'

'What. The police will get him if he stays?' Rhette asked.

'Pietie's disappearance is now an abduction and Quinn's the leading suspect. That's what Mark said. I'd guess also that the dead woman they've just found is linked to him too. They'll move on every known and unknown haunt of the bikies. The local cops know who's likely to crack and grass him amongst the bikies. He's an outsider and no matter how high up in the hierarchy he is he's possibly vulnerable.'

'You know a lot about these people...'

'Yes, I know the people and the area. I've been here a long time, remember...'

There was a pause. Neither wanted to be reminded of the long period that Doug had been in Coober Pedy; for their own reasons.

A truce was a truce.

There was a newspaper on the table and Doug pulled it towards to them. He fished out a blue pen from his pocket and started to draw over the printed page.

'The police and mine rescue boys have been looking close to Coober Pedy.' His pen traced a cross with the initials CP in the middle with a circle around it. He drew a double thick line representing the highway through the cross as he said, 'He can't have gone on the main bitumen or they'd have got him by now. There's only one main road through the place.' He drew a spider web of lines radiating out from the central cross. 'I think either he's got the child holed up in the town...and that situation can't continue.' The pen tapped at the cross. 'Or he's going to take one of the tracks towards the outer smaller mining camps.'

'Like yours,' Rhette said.

'Yes, there are dozens still in use. Even in the hot weather like now.' More drawing. This time he broadened some of the webs, 'These,' he said, 'are the tracks that are used all the time by the big mining consortiums. He'd stay away from them. The traffic of the big vehicles would mark those tracks. He'd be able to see them.'

'So you're suggesting that Quinn, if he went out of the town, he might hide somewhere, such as in a camp where they miners have left because of the hot weather. Sounds plausible. But how would you know?' Rhette smiled the question at her father.

'It would be trial and error. If I were the cops I'd start looking at tracks. Looking for ones that I thought wouldn't, or shouldn't, be in use now. Even a motor bike track would show up by disturbing the dry dust surface. Different tyre tracks too from the usual utes and trucks.'

'You're going to do it?' Rhette asked. 'Have a chat to Mark and the cops. Put your theory to them?'

He paused and ran a hand down his stubbly cheek as he considered. 'I thought I'd give it twenty four hours. Time for Quinn to recover a bit and make a move. Now that time's up and I reckon things are heating up for him. He's going to have to get out... if he hasn't gone already.'

'Pietie...?' Rhette left the question unsaid.

Doug shrugged, the question unanswered. He tapped the pen against the paper. 'I'd also go north because that's where you idiot women followed Quinn before. He seems to be attracted to the north.'

She echoed his tap-tapping but with her finger on the paper. 'Your camp's that way too, north isn't it?'

'Yes.' Doug drew a cross on the map he'd drawn, and then sketched in other major mining areas and the rough roads that led to them. He wrote in a GPS identification code. 'This's my position. My claim's away from the others. I've hardly even got a track that anyone else would know about. The copper Dave Ballinger's been out there to see me. He'd remember where it is.'

Rhette's eyebrows rose. 'Had a brush with the law too?' she smiled.

'Nah, nothing really. I forgot to reregister my truck a few years back and Dave came out to remind me. We found we had a lot to talk about. He's a Vietnam vet too. I was there early in the war; he was at the end of it. We catch up in the pub sometimes too. He overlooks the fact that I live out there on my claim...not supposed to do that according to the rules.'

'You blokes stick together...?'

'Vietnam made us different. We needed to stick up for each other.'

There was a pause as Doug's thoughts seemed to drift away

from their conversation. Rhette smoothed the newspaper and pointed to the GPS mark. She drew him back with the smiling question. 'You're not worried that the search will find your mine with the opal seam you've left there waiting to be dug again, are you?'

Doug said. 'Sure that's only a small consideration. I've got many other areas pegged and they're all on the survey maps. I just want to try something to help now.'

'You're an old man now, Doug. Just pass on the idea to the police...'

'Yes, Yes... Maybe I'm too old to go chasing after villains.' It was a long time since anyone had told him he was too old for something. Had even thought enough about him to do the telling. To care. 'OK, I'll just pass it all onto Dave. Relax,' he said.

Doug stood, paused a moment again before he bent to plant a brief kiss on his daughter's forehead. Rhette smiled. That felt good. 'You're off to see Dave and Mark then?' she said.

'Later, I need to think it out a bit...' Leaving Rhette sitting at the table Doug retreated to his room. He shut the door and lay on the bed.

His thoughts churned back. As always. Ever back...

Months after the fire, the air in the local Hawker Community Hall shimmered.

The buzz of blowflies traced their endless rectangles near the roof and the long demented wail of a crow moaned high above. Outside the hall, a dog lay in the shade of a rusted tank stand and waited. Inside the small crowd shuffled on metal chairs under a row of slow moving ceiling fans that just pushed hot air against their faces and moved the dust motes into languid echoes of the flies. They'd all gone to the local hall to see about government money. To restock, rebuild, if possible after the fire.

A line of officials in hot city suits sat up on the small raised stage ready to consider the views and propositions for recovery that were put forward. Bankers, government agencies, federal and state alike with the farmers and graziers.

In the hall kitchen Gina had found a large washing up dish, a good splash of water and a plastic jug. To keep Rhette cool and amused. The child squatted playing and singing quietly as the speeches and proceedings droned on and on. Many of the hot officials on the stage found their attention wandering as they watched the little girl take off her gingham sundress and her sandals as she paddled in the dish. Her golden two-year-old body glowed as she poured water over herself. They smiled when her giggles and a squeal of delight echoed around the vast hall as she sat down in the dish. The water welled out and across the floor. She traced finger patterns and stomped her feet in the water before making small footprints on the dusty floor boards.

Perhaps it was Rhette and her water dish combined with the smell of baking scones that made the officials relax that hot day. They took off their suit coats and ties and the meeting went ahead. The community was drawn together.

That was before the accident; three years later.

Gina had never wanted the horse but Doug convinced her, as he always did, that the children, their two daughters, and the baby they were expecting should have a pony. He remembered Gina carefully trotting around the home paddock on the brown mare; hair flying and sometimes with one of the girls perched in front. Then the terrible day when of the mare's fore hooves lashed out at a snake and they'd found Gina's small figure lying still in the dirt. Hip and pelvis shattered. There was blood between her legs and the longed for new baby, perhaps a son, was obviously lost.

Gina screamed once into his face and was silent. She had been silent through the long trip on the back of the truck to Blinman and the Flying Doctor flight. And silent through the long hospitalization in cold white rooms and in the months before she left the city; thin, white faced and quiet still, to come home to their rebuilt house.

It was never the same.

There was a ghost between them and the intimacy of their love was barely remembered. Gina, with relentless pain, faded before his eyes and he couldn't bear to look at her. Finally they walked off the land, gave it all up and had gone back to the city.

To the city and his guilt, his failure and eventually his new dream.

Doug's escape to opal.

'No!' Rhette hissed, keeping her voice low. 'So you're clearing out. Again!'

Doug faced up to his daughter. There was an air of resolution about him. One that hadn't been there before.

'I decided I was going to start looking for Piet myself. Doing it like I showed you on the newspaper map I drew. The coppers have their own theories. Probably wouldn't listen to an old codger like me...not even Dave. Too busy.' Doug shrugged away from Rhette's restraining hand. 'I've been cooped up here with you two women ever since this began. I need to get out there. I can help with the search.'

It was later; Doug had left his bedroom and paced the front room, the only room where the daylight bore in already, a hot searchlight.

'No, you're doing it again. Just like you did all those years ago when the going got hard after Mother's accident...' Rhette said.

The truce was broken. It showed the levels of anxiety they were all under with the child missing.

'That's a load of shit...' he said. 'We'd lost the farm and...'

'And you took off. Chasing opal. Chasing your dreams!' There was a sneer in Rhette's tired voice as she interrupted.

'Well I got opal, didn't I? Opal and money? Enough...'

'Yeah but too late for Mother... and Kate.' Rhette stopped with a sharp intake of breath. That wasn't fair. Not really. It was going too far. She turned away from her father's startled stare.

Doug's face sagged into deeper lines. 'Well, this time I can do something positive. Go after the little boy. Follow my hunch,' he said.

'You're going to do it anyway so you might as well go now. Leave us to fend for ourselves. What if the bikies come here again?'

'This time you call Mark and the police.' Doug put his hand on Rhette's shoulder and spun her to face him. 'You'll do that won't you? Not anything stupid like going out with Ana again?'

Ana's voice was low as she stood in the doorway. 'It was my fault before,' she said. 'I put us in danger.' She came further into the room and stood before Doug. Her voice implored. 'If you have any ideas please...'

'I'm going to do the search Rhette and I talked about this morning.' Doug went to Ana and his large rough hand engulfed her small pale ones. 'I can't just wait here with you. I know the area so I'll go and do my bit.'

'Do it. We'll be alright.' Ana turned her head looking for Rhette to support her. She reached out and gripped her arm. 'Please let him go...'

'Well, if this is settled between you two, I'd better pack some sandwiches and stuff for you to take.' Rhette conceded after a hard look at her father. 'We'll let Mark know where you've gone too. That way if you get into trouble then they can find you. I guess that I'm so worried because we've just got back together again. There's twenty years for us to work through and you're not a young man any more.'

'Is that all?' Doug embraced both women. 'Rhette I've been up here long enough to be able to look after myself. I'm not that old!' His smile turned into a serious expression. "I'll be armed and I can use a gun.'

'So Vietnam was of some use... you could've fooled me,' his daughter said. A smile had returned to her face and voice. It wasn't easy to show concern to this man again. Now that she'd found him her feelings were jumbled. It was going to take time.

The tension eased.

Doug went outside and checked the locked rifle box in his Land Rover. A .22 rifle and a heavier gun. 'I hit what I aim at,' he said as he brought a smaller box into the house. 'Have either of you ever fired a pistol?' he asked. He opened it to show an Army service revolver and ammunition.

Ana's eyes widened in horror then a look of resolution firmed her features. 'Show me,' she said and reached to grasp the weapon.

'You just hang on...' he stopped her.

'It's alright. I'll look after this,' Rhette said. 'I know how to fire a pistol.' Ana's hand pushed towards the revolver again. 'I'll show you too. I've even got a license to use a fire arm. Later...when we have a few moments after Doug's gone.' It wasn't the time to worry her father that she had a pistol, all still neatly parceled as Harry had given her at the Adelaide Hospital before her flight to Whyalla.

'Well, I expect that you won't need it,' he said. He checked the mechanism of the weapon. 'It's clean and unloaded.' He turned the pistol to show the safety lock, 'and this's on. You should tell Mark that it's in the house too.'

'Show me how to load it,' Ana said as Doug opened the box of ammunition and shook out the bullets. The harsh clatter they made on the table was reflected as steel in her voice. Her dark eyes were flint hard.

Both Rhette and Doug looked at her sharply.

This was an Ana they had not expected again. An Ana like the person who'd taken off after Quinn.

'Wait. I'll show you later,' Rhette repeated. She replaced the ammunition in the box, pushed the guns to the centre of the table, and moved towards the kitchen. Ana and Doug followed her into the darkening room. Rhette slung her arm about Doug's shoulder. 'I think you should wait until the morning before you go,' she said looking at her father. His face was tired and the lines were etched deep below his sparse grey hair.

Ana interrupted, her voice was as weary as she looked. 'Yes, you have been so kind... Get a good night's sleep before you go...if my Pietie's still alive...then...Quinn...' She slumped into a chair.

'He's still alive and that bastard's got him.' Rhette finished for Ana. She started banging pots and a frying pan around. 'Don't just stand there.' She said to Doug. 'Get us something to drink. A beer at least. A wine. We all need to eat something.'

Doug looked relieved as he went to the fridge and pulled out a bottle of white wine. 'You have a glass of this now. I'll keep a bottle of beer for Mark. He'll be along later I'm sure and I'll get going tomorrow. I'll do as I said. Go north towards my camp. Criss-cross the tracks until I find something.'

# Chapter 40

Erica pouted and then set her carmine lips into a determined line.

'No!' she said with emphasis.

She was dressed in a navy business suit ready to fly back to Adelaide, her office and the briefs that were waiting to be prepared for her next court appearance. She tidied a flick of silver blonde hair into the chignon she wore at the nape of her neck and settled the gold chain in the breast cleavage of her cream silk blouse.

Hood glanced in her direction. 'Don't argue with me...'

'No!' she repeated 'I'm going home to Adelaide. My flight's booked and I have important appointments tomorrow morning. If I don't make the flight today I'll be too late for them.' She walked to pick up her brief case from the desk in his warehouse suite of rooms and placed it beside her packed suitcase.

'And I tell you, you're coming to Coober Pedy with me tonight.' Hood's voice was quiet, firm. He pointed a stabbing finger at her in emphasis. Then turning his back to her he gave brisk instructions into his mobile phone. He clicked it off. 'I have business there and I want you with me.'

'No...I don't want to go to that god-forsaken place.' She put the pout back onto her face. A beautiful face that hid the extremely successful and formidable lawyer brain behind it. 'And in addition I have court cases I have to get on with. My Associates can only do so much in preparation.' Erica leaned forward and slid an enticing hand under the lapel of his suit.

Hood slapped at her hand. 'Dammit Erica! No! Tonight you're flying to Coober Pedy with me.'

Erica tried again. Changed tack. 'No... But I'll be back soon.' There was a hint of seduction in her voice.

Hood barked. 'You're coming! That's fucking final!' The implied 'or else' gritted through the air like flying hot shrapnel.

She stepped back from the sharp rebuke. He pulled further away from her and stood up from his office chair. Took a moment to smooth down his hand stitched suit coat as though eradicating her touch.

The words hung in the air and she shuddered. He dominated her and she loved it and hated him and herself for it. Passion, limitless wealth and power emanated from him, from every word and every movement. Every time that he allowed her the use of the 'lollies' in the silver box.

Johnnie Fox had a doctor's appointment that day

He'd been loath to make it and less inclined to keep it.

He'd known about his cancer, the total breakdown of his body, and the knowledge that he had six months, maybe a year at the outside, to live. If he was lucky.

Shit happens, he thought.

Life and death was common place to him and he'd terminated a few lives for Hood over the years. For him his health was the lesser of the predictions and promises in his life. After his conversation with Hood, he was pissed off that now Quinn had pushed ahead of him and that the pilot brother was further up the hierarchical ladder than he'd ever been. He just flew them around, and chased skirt, for shit's sake! He'd fix the bastard Quinn, even if he had to do it with his own hands, but otherwise there was nothing ahead for him. Fixing Quinn would be his epitaph.

Fox sat in the sterile surgery. He'd given up listening, and with the cold of the air conditioned room seeping through the fabric of his suit into his bones, he heard only that he had less time than had been predicted earlier.

He'd seen another doctor anyway who'd sorted a pain relief implant for him. Fox almost smiled as the man across the desk tried to tell him about using pain medication. Shit, he thought, he could get more hard drugs and stuff than the idiot could imagine.

He didn't need these platitudes being handed out to him by this young man in a white coat whose stethoscope hung decoratively out of a pocket. The doctor was trying to be kind, empathic, but he knew nothing. Shit all.

Fox got to his feet. 'That'll be all then,' he said. In a stride he was at the door. Hand on door knob.

The doctor gaped at him. 'But there's palliative care, things I can set up for you...'

'Nah,' Fox said. 'It's no other bastard's business but my own. Waste of my time. You can all go to hell.'

He strode out past the receptionist, who was standing waiting for him to sign a Medicare docket, and outside into the air that felt cleaner. He grinned at a thought. They could go to hell too about the medical bills. No longer his concern.

Erica pouted again as they arrived at Sydney Kingsford Smith Airport to fly to Coober Pedy.

This time the pout wasn't just about going to the far away inland town. Her next pout of the day was aimed at Johnnie Fox, who she disliked immensely. She made it her business to ignore him as much as she could. He was going to Coober Pedy with them.

But she'd been 'rewarded' when she had managed to change all her legal appointments for a week, and agreed to go to Coober Pedy with Dieter. What turned her pretty nose up at the airport was what was waiting for them, north of Terminal 1. It wasn't a sleek executive jet that she thought Hood should fly in but a stubby single engined turbo-prop aeroplane.

This time Hood watched her pouting with amusement.

His Cessna Caravan 208 had cost as much as a Lear Jet, but it was his aeroplane of choice. It was his work horse, and piloted by his younger brother Sean, it achieved all aspects of his business perfectly. It carried his legitimate cargo – or the illegitimate cargos of drugs, firearms or whatever he was trading. The versatility and the ability to take off and land on almost any airstrip were paramount to his needs. What was special about the Cessna was that unlike most aeroplanes, and all jets, it had a left hand roll sideways rear cargo door instead of the usual shell shaped hatch that opened up. The 208 provided easy loading facilities. It was also an escape to ditch cargo, even in flight when necessary, that made it perfect. He'd recently had the engine modified to provide more power, something his brother Sean approved of immensely.

Sean, the enigma of Hood's realm to his other staff and gang, was apparently content to be invisible. He just obeyed his brother's orders without question. He had his uses. Pilot and bodyguard when necessary. All Dieter had to do was to keep him clear of marriageable women. Three wives and three divorces was more than enough. Money-wise anyway.

'Fuck them, shack up with them, use them but don't marry any more of them…they're too expensive,' Hood had said.

After the last costly divorce Sean had apparently complied with his brother's orders. Dieter didn't know that Sean had lately developed a passion for playing the poker tables. It was costing him a packet too. So far he was breaking even. It couldn't last. Money and Sean weren't ever going to be on the same page.

Erica waited while Sean and Fox carried all the luggage into the plane then boarded and settled into one of the luxury leather seats behind the pilot's console. She pulled open a locker and verified that there was suitable food and champagne to sustain them for the long flight ahead. Fox and Sean loaded cargo into the rear bay then came aboard. As the pilot settled himself into his seat Dieter nuzzled a kiss into her neck before he sat and adjusted his own seat belt. He reached over and placed the silver box into her hands. It was a wonder, he thought, that a person with the intellect that Erica had, could still respond by calling the drugs he was slowly increasing the purity of, as her 'lollies.' Increasing her dependence. It confirmed that he could control his women. No matter what they were or who they were. He was always the master in the relationship.

With the control tower's permission they taxied to the 'East – West' runway and nestled behind the bulk of a Qantas 737 waiting in line to take off. As the runway cleared Sean lifted the

Cessna away from the turbulence from the 737's takeoff and out over Botany Bay then headed west into the setting sun for Coober Pedy.

Johnnie Fox, settled into his own seat, ate his own plastic wrapped ham sandwiches and slept.

In Coober Pedy the hunt for Piet and Quinn stagnated for the night as tired police officers and other professionals came in from the town and opal fields to file their reports and to plan for the coming morning searches. Most of them headed home for a few hours sleep.

Quinn found that his welcome with the local bikie chapter was getting more and more tenuous.

The Chapter was in turmoil. With the prospect of repatching with an incoming American chapter, and the possible changes that the mining companies would bring if they started to drill for a vast underground reservoir of shale oil beneath Coober Pedy, their continuing existence might become problematical. At least their focus would have to change from 'business' with opals to oil. The latter was bigger than they were accustomed to. The bikie gang was further torn with inner conflicts and opinions about the future and dealing with a Sydney boss made the complications worse.

The leaders called a meeting and decisions were made.

'Get to fucking hell out of here,' the Master at Arms member said to Quinn. He shrugged huge shoulders in a black greasy t-shirt. 'You've got twenty-four hours and that's only because of the kid.'

'I didn't mean to kill the woman. It was an accident.'

'Yeah, well we had to stop you from getting a blade across your throat so count yourself fucking lucky.'

'Where...?' Quinn stopped. The senior member was flanked by a phalanx of twin burley shadows.

'You are a risk, a bloody risk and we don't want you here. Twenty four hours...' the voice ended in a snarl. 'Find yourself some where else to stay or get the hell away. We don't give a shit where you go and you can tell your boss that we won't deal with him again either.'

Quinn was quiet as a tough heavily tattooed female member attended to the dressings on his cuts and abrasions from his encounter with Ana and Rhette. His shoulder was still painful but he knew he had to manage to ride his Harley.

He had no option but to go... by nightfall.

# Chapter 41

The aeroplane landed at the dirt strip that was the Coober Pedy airport runway, close to midnight. Red dust rose in an unseen cloud behind the wheels as they thumped down, and then became a diminishing veil aft as the navigation lights flickered into it. With the terminal closed no one was watching, or interested other than the driver of their hire car. He'd lounged against the car so that he could smoke the only cigarette that their early arrival had allowed. He shredded the butt under a boot and waited.

The plane taxied to the small airport building.

The door was opened and Erica shuddered as the air from the outside darkness gushed into the plane. It was warm, hot even and stank of diesel and avgas. She could sense the vast surrounding dry desert out there. Without the comfort of city smells of fast foods, of restaurants, of concrete and the wafting aromas of the harbour's salty waters and gardens, she felt lost. She didn't belong. Her territory, her unit, was on the esplanade of the seaside suburb of Glenelg in Adelaide or lately with Hood in Sydney.

As she went down the steps from the plane her stiletto, sling back heels sank into the sandy and stony ground and highlighted just how far away from her comfort zone she was. She hopped on one slim ankle to free a pebble from her shoe and grabbed for Dieter's arm to steady herself. At his tired and irritable grunt she withdrew her hand and said nothing. She waggled her foot until she had freed the stone and hobbled after him. Within seconds her fine blonde hair stuck to her forehead in the heat and her sense of belonging to this alien place ebbed further away.

'This'll cost you in opals,' she thought. Coober Pedy meant

opal and she was going to have some as payment for being dragged here.

A booked car took them to the Desert Cave Motel, to a special suite of rooms, underground, that the owners kept exclusively for the big buyers of opal, the business tycoons and the people who could afford to be in the opal town without anyone else knowing they were there. It was just opulent enough to satisfy Erica and she was further placated by the imported champagne and strawberries that awaited them.

Dieter and Fox conferred into the small hours of the morning in the sitting room. Erica retired to the huge bed with the blue satin sheets. She could hear the voices rising and falling in the next room, Dieter's angry, as usual, and Fox a murmur below her hearing. She slipped her hand into the luggage and found her special little box, and tasted. She was determined that she would feign sleep when he finally came to bed; not interested in his company or the sex he would demand if he thought she was awake.

As it was, the drug taste helped and she slept very soundly...

At four thirty in the morning Hood chucked the burner phone into the hotel's waste disposal chute.

He clenched and unclenched his hands. He'd made contact with Quinn, after they had discovered that opals weren't at the drop Fox had set up. Now he'd bypassed Johnny Fox to go to the bikies hangout although Fox had stood beside him as he made the phone call.

'Let me go, Boss,' Fox said. 'I can get the opals from Quinn.'

'You'll kill the bastard if I send you,' Hood said. 'He's going down with all the problems he's caused. But later, when I say so. And you can do him but only after that. I want to collect the product from him. In person.'

Fox shrugged. There were times that Hood needed to take matters into his own hands. 'OK, Boss,' he said.

'I'm taking Sean with me.' It was a flat statement.

There it was again; the brother Sean being promoted to

responsibilities he didn't want, over Fox.

'Are you sure, Boss? He can't protect you from the bikies like I can.'

'I'll be armed and someone has to stay to make sure that Erica is protected.'

Fox hesitated. Sean had the worst of reputations around beautiful women. Maybe the boss wasn't confident that his brother could be trusted to keep his libido and flirtations under control and his dick in his pants. He wanted to laugh out loud. The fuck-faced brother could be trusted with Hood's life but not around Erica. Some confidence Hook had. Was it all just a knife edge balance of drugs and power? This packet of opals had to be paid for even though they had not retrieved the drug package from the Whyalla wharfs. Little or no product had come from the drug labs in Whyalla or Port Augusta. Quinn had pissed in his own nest in more ways than one. Now the Boss was perhaps in the shit too from the overseas consortiums.

Fox drew breath and said nothing.

Not his problem.


Just after dawn Hood and Sean returned to the motel but almost empty handed. Hood looked grim and charged, wordlessly, through the front rooms to his bedroom to where Erica lay sleeping. There were sounds of his cursing and objects being smashed through the thin walls of the suite.

Johnny Fox kept his head low in his own bedroom, listening. He smiled. Serves them right, he thought. From what he could hear it seemed that Quinn had divided the opal package in two and had hidden one, keeping it as insurance.


About seven o'clock that morning Erica stretched, arching her back, before leaning over to the bedside consol and switching on the overhead fan. It wasn't needed but she luxuriated in the coolness as the moving air licked around her body. Dieter Hood still slept beside her, and she ran her tongue around her mouth.

Yuk, morning breath. Morning teeth.

She slipped out of bed and went towards the bathroom to brush her teeth.

Dieter's clothes and toiletries were strewn around the room, her own case was tipped up and her expensive hair dryer was smashed on the tiled floor.

So that's how it is, she thought. Things have gone wrong again. She'd learned that it was better to say nothing and just ignore his moods. It would cost him, dragging her to Coober Pedy and now her dryer. She brushed her teeth and put the hair dryer into the bathroom bin.

Dieter usually wanted a taste of what sex they'd had the night before in the morning and her cleaning ritual would cover the fact that he didn't ever bother to brush his teeth until after he'd had it. She inched back onto the bed and again pretended to be asleep as he stirred.

The sex; it couldn't be called lovemaking although it pretended to be, was masculine and powerful telling Erica that he was the boss. Dieter made the rules. She was sexually experienced and attempted to use her own strength to fight back. But, at the sweating end of the session, he had forced her to the orgasm that she had wanted to deny him. He'd won. Afterwards they lay back, panting with exertion, not touching. He didn't need intimacy after sex and she was hyper sensitive to being touched again when the sex was over.

She escaped to shower while he looked at the morning news broadcast on TV.

'You're not to leave the motel,' Dieter ordered as his room service order of eggs Benedict, toast and coffee arrived. He tossed the motel brochure towards her plate of muesli and fruit. 'There's plenty to do here. Look shops, opal exhibits and you can buy what you want. Anything. I'm going to be doing business and I need to know where you are. Especially if I decide to move out in a hurry. Understand?'

She didn't, but at times, it was better to just to do as she was told. It kept the peace and he'd told her last night that their stay wouldn't be long, if his business went well.

Erica scooped up the opal brochure. 'Anything I want?' she said.

'Yes, and you'd better get small opal earrings for Jane. For services rendered, for both of you, but remember I'm here on business and I may want to leave quickly.' Hood said.

OK, she thought. So things haven't gone well, but there's always a 'get something for dear secretary Jane.' I'll shop early. Erica pushed her blonde hair into a sleek style off her neck and flipped tendrils to frame her face. Dressed in slim jeans and a deep sapphire coloured silk blouse, she picked up his credit card. This'll cost you in opal; she thought as she let the suite door close behind her. Her high heeled sandals clicked on the parquetry floor of the passage as she made her way to the foyer. I've always wanted an opal ring and matching solid opal earrings. The smashed hairdryer was worth an extra opal pendant as well as being replaced.

She learned quickly about the opal values to buy the best pieces on offer. In the shop she found that opal doublets were quite nice; fancy enough for Jane's earrings and much less expensive than the pieces she chose for herself. Hers were solids with reds that flashed within the green depths as she turned the stones under the lights. She waited; reading a chic magazine, while the jeweler set the stones in a gold pendant.

# Chapter 42

It was after eight and the seven thirty morning report and police daily work schedule was drawing to a most unsatisfactory close.

There was nothing new on the whereabouts of Pietie Foster. Either the child was dead and his body fallen or thrown down a shaft or he had been taken by persons unknown. Mark doubted the latter but one never knew, given the cases that existed overseas. Children were reported stolen to sell on order. A horrific thought. One that he hadn't discussed or suggested to Ana.

It had to be Quinn who had the boy.

The press hadn't yet caught on yet to Quinn being alive or the story that went with it. Their Google investigations however, when reporting that Mark was involved in the investigation of the lost child, dragged up the history of Rick Charlton and the court case that followed Mark's arrest of his late boss, the cop serial killer. That reference was going to be forever linked to Mark's name in the papers and on TV. So far they had made the connection of the missing child with Ana Foster, a witness at the previous case, but they had not found her whereabouts in Coober Pedy. They hadn't been able to put her through the trauma of being interviewed on TV or parading her as the tearful distraught parent.

Quinn was still missing and the police didn't know whether he was in Coober Pedy or to hell and gone.

The drug connection with opal as payment had yet to be proven although Lex was working on that aspect.

All in all it weighed heavily on Mark's shoulders as he went back to his desk and clicked through his computer screens.

Suddenly Mark sat still and scratched his chin as a thought struck him. He reached for the land line phone, a more secure communication than using his mobile. Listeners these days had ways to overhear mobile conversations. He dialed.

'Della,' he said as the Whyalla Customs CO answered. 'Mark Llewellen here. Did I read in the Tyler Grayson arrest report that the drug package that you caught Tyler Grayson with had spilled white powder? Was there loose powder anywhere?'

An intake of breath, then silence. 'Yes,' she said. Through the phone her voice was not much more than a whisper.

'Shit, I'm sorry Della. I was so caught up in my thoughts and enquiry that I forgot the outcomes. Tyler's death must have shaken you. I apologize... I'm a bull at a gate sometimes.'

'It's OK, Mark.' He could hear the strength that came back into Della's voice. 'You Dee's are always like that. What were you asking again? Spilled powder before we tested it?'

'Yes, it occurred to me that Grayson may have taken a sample to test before you nabbed him and slit open the package.'

'There was. A small sprinkle of powder loose in his rucksack. And on the chart table.'

'It may link into a huge opal sale here in Coober Pedy.' Mark said as thought he was thinking aloud.

'But the package we got Grayson on was only worth about two grand...'

'Yes, but what if the powder was just a test sample? What if there was a bigger payload?' Mark's questions hung in the air before Della responded.

'You think that there could have been more dumped where the ship was berthed?  A big package the old Dee didn't see dropped?'

Mark's voice took on a more excited tone. 'Yes, Della. That's exactly what struck me. We have a consignment of opal exchanged here that was worth millions. Five to eight million. Maybe ten.'

'That's a lot of money. Are you thinking that these opals were to pay for more drugs?'

'Yes. Any unusual divers or action along the wharf?'

'I haven't noticed anything and no fishermen have reported

that they've snagged anything unusual either.' She gave a low excited chuckle. 'I've not heard that the old resident wharf walrus's been acting funny either. He's not obviously been into any funny stuff…'

'OK then. It's a hunch. I'll get Jessica involved and order a diver to have a quiet look along the wharf area. Keep this totally out of the public eye, would you.'

'Will do. If people ask, even nosy fishermen, I'll just tell them that one of my boys dropped his watch overboard when he was checking a ship. Happens.'

'Thank's Della. I owe you.'

'It's all good,' she said. 'It would be the answer why and how Tyler was tempted by such a piffling amount of drugs. He never confessed to anything. This makes a lot more sense. Especially why they murdered him.' She paused. 'You did get the pathologist report? About the injection of multiple snake venoms instead of his insulin?'

'Yes, I did. It was an exceptional piece of toxicology. Must have been quick too for Tyler…'

'No! It wasn't. It was a horrible death…I was in court. Messy…vomiting…convulsions. I was there to see it.'

'I'm sorry Della. I seem to always be around when things go bad for you.'

'Yes, Mark. But at least I can talk to you about it. You don't give me platitudes.' Her voice was quiet then she paused a beat before she continued. 'I'll get right on with putting a dive team together with Jessica.'

Mark hung up, and then sat holding the phone for a beat. Criminal work had its victims and they weren't all so evident to outsiders.

'Lex!' Mark yelled from his office. The tall black man moved with surprising speed on silent feet to lean into the doorway. His face expectant. Mark's call had been with a level of urgency.

'Had a thought' Mark said and outlined his phone conversation. '…and Della's following it up in Whyalla. Just maybe there was a bigger shipment of drugs dropped from that ship last month. What they got before was just a sample.'

'Sounds like a possibility. A good one. It'd explain a bit,' Lex said.

'And I didn't need a game of computer patience to come up with it either...some of us can think outside the box on occasion with out chasing cards games,' Mark tried for a joke. Any joke to relieve some of the tension that the whole station was under.

'Didn't know we were looking into boxes...' Lex said.

By ten thirty Doug was ready to leave to follow his theory about where Quinn was, and therefore where Pietie was. With Rhette upset about him 'going off again when things got tough' as she put it and Ana almost catatonic with worry, he had begun to doubt his decision to go. Mark had cautioned him against doing anything on his own but the police had no legal jurisdiction to stop him.

What if Quinn or a bikie came to the house looking for Ana? The fact that the two women now had a gun also worried him. This could be more dangerous to themselves than to any one else. But them not being armed in the current situation?

What if...?

More what ifs...?

The possibilities made his head hurt. He needed to do this and he was prepared, armed and he had every sort of supplies he felt he could need for any contingency. His background as a bushman, a miner and an army Vietnam Veteran gave him that confidence. A confidence shared by Ana; and Rhette even acknowledged she knew what he was proposing. But agreement? He didn't have his daughter's agreement. As an extra precaution he'd arranged with the women that if anything of interest was happening around him he'd open his satellite phone to them. Keep it open and then they would contact Mark too.

Was he ready? Doug couldn't answer that. The reconciliation with Rhette was the best thing that had happened to him and he wanted her approval and to be there for her in the future. Late fatherhood hung on his shoulders like a tender silken wrap but because he was so unused to the responsibility of it he was drowning under its weight.

It was already hot this morning.

37 degrees centigrade in the shade; where there was shade. And it would get hotter.

Black kites were circling over the town in their usual spiral formations catching the heat updrafts from the hot land to the waiting clear sky above. Away to the west horizon a sheen of cloud made rain promises it would not keep, and he heard a thread of mining machinery whine on the dry breeze. The door banged behind him as he went out to his Land Rover to leave.

'Wait, Doug!' Rhette called and rushed out to give her father a hug. 'Take care,' she said.

'I'll be careful,' he said and his face creased into a smile as he folded his arms about her. 'I will, I promise.'

# Chapter 43

'Anyone home?'

The call emanated from a short, stocky and swarthy man balancing a slim computer, a bulky overnight bag and two cartons of fresh orange juice in his arms as he leaned against Mark's doorway jamb in the police station. 'This place is a fortress,' he said. 'I had a very difficult job getting past the officer at the desk downstairs until I could find my card.' His speech was pure, with few verbal abbreviations.

'Immy! What in the heck are you doing here? Mark said. He leapt up and retrieved the overnight bag and one of the cartons that was in danger of falling from clutching arms. Putting the bag against the wall, he shook hands before he pulled out a chair and motioned his visitor to it. 'How have you managed to escape the depths of the Major Crime section? I thought you were super glued to your desk.'

Imran Kadir, sorted his juice cartons to one side and positioned his slim computer carefully on Mark's desk and opened it. 'Yes, that is usual,' he said. 'But maybe they thought that I was loosing my tan and needed some time out here in the sun.' A smile inched across his face as Mark chuckled. Imran was known for his precise wit, usually against himself and his heritage.

'They thought you were looking pale, did they?'

'Yes but I've only been changing one office for another, although I should increase my tan now I'm out in the field.'

'OK, why are you here? Not that you're not welcome and I haven't seen you in a while...' Mark brought the reasons back to business.

'I'm looking into the origins of opal correlating with ice, heroin and cocaine that have appeared here and elsewhere in

Australia lately.' Imran's words were concise. As Mark sat down again at his desk, his colleague continued. 'Opal. China and Japan are fanatic about opal and buy it from Coober Pedy and other sources, such as Lightening Ridge. Recently most has come from here and the differences in the opal are easy to test. We questioned why. Is it just because Coober Pedy is a bigger supplier of better opal or is there another reason.'

Mark was used to Imran's question and answer reports. They got to perfectly analyzed and reasoned conclusions. He waited then took a pen, grunted when it didn't work and rattled in the desk drawer looking for a replacement. Set then, he started to jot down notes on a note pad.

The Data Analyst looked up from his screen and shook a hand above Mark's pen. 'No need for that I have a report prepared. I just thought you would want the verbals.'

'Yes, please, your verbals are easier to understand than your reports.' His mouth twisted into a smile as he looked sideways at Imran. 'Too many big words.'

'Just so. I understand. Simply put, bigger opal parcels are being offered from Coober Pedy. There was also an interesting bank transfer done in the last seventy two hours. The receiving end was here but the sending end bounced around the world via different servers, different banks and countries. I'm always fascinated by these transactions.' A look of smugness crossed Imran's face. There was no way in the world that Mark could have got the complex bank transaction information as quickly.

The latter nodded. 'Interesting. It could well tie in with the murder of an opal dealer here yesterday.'

This seemed to satisfy the analyst.

'Then the drugs,' he said. 'Most heroin comes from the Golden Triangle, but you would know that. It's sold chiefly to China and America. Cocaine is from South America. The cartels are running just a little scared with local government and USA crackdowns...' he smiled at his small joke. Mark acknowledged the cocaine crackdown verbal link. 'Here different drugs are the main game and the gangs have become involved.'

'Different drugs?'

'Ice mainly here. Made here from imported components and rural Australia is flooded with it, as well as the cities. It's the cause of a greater percentage of our crime statistics.'

'Are you linking these with bikie gangs?' Mark said.

'Yes, especially now that there has been re-patching of some Australian gangs with the American ones. And these are especially violent gangs.' He leaned forward to mark his point. 'Don't let their soft propaganda they are spreading via the media tell you anything different. They are as bad as they get.'

'Immy, I'm going to introduce you to Lex Osei, one of my detectives from Whyalla. He's made that possible link by deduction and you may have the evidence to confirm it.' Finally maybe some potatoes to go with the shred of meat, he thought.

'There was a report from him on the line and I look forward to working with him.'

'Great. But you're not to bag him for head office. Or the Feds. He's too useful to me...' Mark said as he tapped Imran on the arm. 'Keep your hands off him...'

The short detective stood from his chair. 'Introduce us please.' Taking his laptop, Imran followed Mark to Lex's desk.

Ten minutes later Mark went back to his office and retrieved the cartons of juice and the overnight bag to deliver them to Imran. The two men were already engrossed in computer screens with Lex and Imran nodding together over charts and data. He placed Imran's belongings beside the desk and left them.

Mark quipped. 'You won't have time for solitaire cards with Immy here,' to Lex. The big South African flushed and shuffled in his chair. Mark was fascinated to see his black skin darken. The computer games could take some explaining to Imran, he thought.

A new report would be on his desk in hours and he reckoned that the detectives would also be out in the field getting new samples of opal, earth and whatever else they sought, for confirmation with the drug samples they could obtain from the locked police safes. He stood back and reckoned that he would definitely lose Lex to Major Crime Headquarters. Great advancement for Lex but just when he was getting used to the detective.

'Lex,' he said. 'Please spare time to work on the Frank Mason case and the woman's murder. The local guys and Harry are up to their ears in it, with Piet's disappearance.' He waited a flicker to see the detective duo look at each other. Their theories were compelling but now there was more immediate work waiting. The myth of the first twenty-four hour investigation being important to police was real. That's when the clues were hot. 'Take Immy out with you. He'll get the sun he's asking for then...'

Imran grinned as puzzlement crossed Lex's black face. 'Certainly Mark, I'm here to assist in any way I can.' he said. This would be a joke to share with his colleague.

Lex cut in. 'Imran's bought some telephone spy ware that might help us. I'm guessing that the bikies, and especially Quinn, use burner pieces here but the Coober Pedy phone cover isn't like the cities. Maybe they're using other phones. We may get a lead to their headquarters whereabouts. And there's Google maps and satellite tracking. Just maybe we can get something from it. He's got contacts there too.'

'So there's a possibility that everything we're dealing with may be interconnected. Had that thought myself,' Mark said. 'Quinn, opals and drugs, the murders and Piet being kidnapped. It all revolves around Quinn. Leaves out the top crims though. The bastard Quinn surely doesn't have that amount of power...'

'And that's why I'm here. Not just to save your butt again.' Harry stood in the doorway. He grinned at Imran, and extended his hand. They shook. 'Immy, good to see you.'

Mark said. 'I thought that headquarters was just insecure about my handling of these cases, not that I'd once again be the glue to it all.'

There was a chuckle in return from Harry. 'Get a load of him. Sun shines out of his butt.' He became serious after trading another glance with Imran. 'I've been shuffled from Sydney about a gentleman, and I used that term loosely, named Dieter Hood.

That's an Australianized name he's chosen. He's Middle Eastern and a master crook. Been just out of reach for years.'

'That's where Rhette Ryan comes into it?' Mark asked.

'Yes. She was an insider until we acted too fast. Almost got her killed and we didn't get Hood in the process. The bastard you know as 'Quinn' didn't come onto our radar until things started here. We naturally assumed he was dead that time on the Murray River. There's been a ghost in Hood's organisation and now we know who that mongrel killer is, thanks to you and that small slip he made in Whyalla.'

'A horrible run of coincidences if you ask me,' Mark said. 'I don't like it at all. But maybe we'll have the chance to get Quinn for you. That's a good call in saving my butt, I reckon.'

'And Hood is here in Coober Pedy somewhere. I feel it in my bones,' Harry said.

'I met him in Adelaide a year or so ago. Interesting, I met up with my ex then too. Erica Marryat,' Mark said.

'She's the one we've been following in our efforts to get Hood. She's ready for a fall...' Harry said with a sideways glance at Mark.

Imran cut in. 'We have someone who tells us a bit now and then about Mr Hood. I'm hoping for another information drop soon.'

Mark raised eyebrows but Imran Kadir wasn't saying any more.

# Chapter 44

Target, the leader of the Coober Pedy Chapter of the bikies, knew a dead man walking when he saw one.

The bastard standing before him, Quinn was that dead man. He still breathed and he still cursed. For now. He still thrust orders into the midst of the phalanx of men who again stood behind him as they waited for Quinn to go. They were all armed and Quinn's gun, he'd made sure of that, was still locked in his saddlebag.

Quinn's dye was cast and they would not hear an appeal.

To Quinn everything that was happening seemed to be deliberate. Unreal. As though everything was in slow motion as perhaps it had been for his past victims.

'Fill my bike with petrol,' Quinn said.

Approved.

The leader nodded. The Harley, still on its stand in the room, was topped up from a can; the extra fuel tank too. The stink of petrol pervaded the area.

'Get into your leathers.' Quinn's leathers, still red dirt stained and scratched from his altercation with Ana, were thrown over the bike seat. He struggled into them, his shoulder still worrying him although he tried not to show any pain. The dented helmet waited for his head.

'I need food.' Two packets of sandwiches were given to him. Quinn unlocked the saddlebag close to where he stood and squashed the food in with another large package that remained there. His water bag was full.

'I want another gun.'

Refused.

Target raised the hand with the bull's eye tattooed across the knuckles covering a prison inking of 'hate'. The message was clear;

try me if you think you can take me. You're nothing now. You're lucky to be leaving here alive.

'The boy?' Can I leave him?

Refused.

Target's woman came forward to intervene. Before she could open her mouth a fist was thrust against her ample leathered bust. She stumbled a step back, recovered her balance and stepped up again behind her man. Her eyes were red from apparent tears at the repeated refusals.

'How in hell am I supposed to take him with me?' Quinn's eyes sought out Target's woman. She looked hard at him and shrugged. You kidnapped him. Your problem.

'What the hell am I supposed to do with him?

'Kill him then. Toss him down a shaft. It's been done before.'

The bikies gave him time to digest this fact. They had time; he didn't.

His problem.

Quinn turned back to his saddlebag, pulled out and opened the opal package. Thank the stars that he'd managed to halve the package he'd got from Mason. The extra minutes he'd taken to split the opal, to find an equivalent amount of lesser stone, and to rebind the remainder before he'd left the opal dealer's shop after killing him, was worth his life now. His life; not Mason's, he'd thought as he'd stepped over the sprawled body, counted. The Boss may have thought he'd collected all the opal from the agreed drop, but Quinn had got himself some insurance. Insurance against the time he expected to be facing Fox's gun. It always paid to have something tucked away.

'I've got money. Opal to pay for everything.' Quinn said. His was a thick voice of desperation. There was a sharp intake of collective breaths when he showed them what the package contained. They knew opal, and the probable dollar value of the huge and spectacular stash there.

Target hesitated then reached into the pile of colour. He took a handful and dropped it on a work bench beside him.

'We'll take what you owe us. Enough to move to other

headquarters since you've fucked this one up. Enough for a share for each of us. New bikes.' There was a murmur of greed from the men. 'Enough for Lucy's grave if we ever get her back to bury. Enough for her man to get over you killing her, you bastard. Enough to buy our silence.' The package had diminished by less than a quarter and commandeered opal was spread across the bench like a flattened and spread rainbow arc of colour.

Quinn waited expecting Target to take the lot. He didn't. His woman moved forward again and Target pushed her back. He stopped and then with a grin at her, he deliberately took another smaller handful of opal and added it to the rainbow.

'OK,' he said, 'but there's some for the women who've looked after the boy.' His eyes bored into Quinn's. 'We're not thieves.'

Quinn had suspected they were going to kill him for the opal. This was just a ruse, not taking it all, to get him out of the bikies dugout without a fight. Still, he conceded, the country boys could be a bit different to the city chapters. His gaze defiantly went from one face to the next of the leather clad figures. 'I'll pay the rest of this stone to any bastard, who can get me and the kid out of here safely,' he tried to stall. To bribe.

The bull's eye tattoo was thrust up into his face. The fist huge before his eyes. 'There's only one fucking bastard here and that's you. Get out! I've been patient but that's bloody well run out...You've caused us nothing but fucking trouble. Our new Chapter won't be dealing with the likes of you ... or your bosses.'

So that's why everything had collapsed, Quinn realised. Why Hood was refused entry last night after he'd been to the drop. It was usual that Hood and Fox visited their cronies. They'd even shut Hood out. Quinn was going to be lucky to leave the place alive. And it was probably because of the kid that he was going to be let go free. They didn't want the further risk of the boy being found with them, not from the local police and kidnapping wouldn't go well with the new American Chapter. Not with the yarns they were spinning to the cops and public that they were a non criminal soft gang. The public might have lapped it up the positive publicity but they knew better. The Coober Pedy gang and Target was eagerly anticipating the profitable drug years ahead. Target despised being subservient to Hood and they just had to get Quinn out without fuss to start the new regime.

'The fucking cops are everywhere. Probably watching here. For the kid's sake can I stay at least until its dark?' Quinn was finally pleading for his life.

Refused.

The squad of bikies closed in around him.

Quinn backed away and saw that Piet had been brought into the underground room. He looked sleepy but was still clutching Bear and the hand of Target's woman. He hadn't seen her leave the room. The boy was dressed in his little blue play suit, the one that Quinn had grabbed him in. One shoe was missing.

The woman held a green tartan rug. She thrust it forward. 'You can wrap him in that. Put him up front as you ride.' She still didn't look happy about Quinn taking the child but it was out of her hands.

Target spoke to one of the men standing behind him. 'I'm going to get you out through our other tunnel entrance. Not the shop front. You should get away OK from there.'

It was a concession. Probably, Quinn thought, because the police were watching the shop as he'd suspected. The gang didn't want the fact of him being there confirmed. It was a wonder the police hadn't got a warrant already to tear the place apart.

A procession followed as Quinn was urged ahead of Target, the woman now carrying Piet, and a bikie pushed the huge black Harley through a tight passage of low ceiling rooms carved out of the ground. Through doorways that were concealed and padlocked behind furniture.

There was no going back.

They halted at a final doorway and Quinn straddled his bike. As men supported the machine a cushion was placed on the petrol tank and Piet, wrapped in the blanket, was put on top of that. There was no way that Quinn could protect and hold the crying child inside his tight leather jacket and he would have to manage, or dispose of the child, to get away.

The child slumped against his chest and Quinn knew that they had drugged him. Drugged, the woman's way to protect the child against what they expected him to do. Toss him down a shaft or abandon him to the heat of the day or, to the other extreme, the cold of the desert night. Advice pushed into his thoughts as he attempted to manage his bike and his shiralee. His unwanted burden...brought on by his own act of revenge.

Quinn's helmet was unceremoniously thrust onto his head by one of the men holding the bike upright.

'Start the bastard up,' Target said.

One arm holding Pietie, Quinn kicked over the Harley and the engine didn't respond. He kicked again as the effort jarred to his shoulder. The engine roared.  A second and then a third motor bike engine were kicked into life beside him and the Harley bellow drowned out any final words Target or Quinn might have said.

The escort was ready.

Not a triumphant Bikie procession but a couple of the tough underlings to make sure he went the right way.

The door opened into a blazing late afternoon sun and he was pushed out.

Quinn wanted to do a wheelie, to blast them with the sounds of defiance, but as he took off gently, he struggled. His damaged left arm worked the clutch and his right the throttle. Thankfully, he knew, the engine would adjust to the clutch as his speed picked up but he wobbled trying to adjust the balance to hold the terrified and now struggling boy in front of him.

The two outriders shepherded them until Quinn and Pietie were two kilometres out onto a minor track going north. At that point they peeled off and left Quinn to his own devices.

# Chapter 45

'He's not dead...! I'm his mother. I'd know if he was dead. I'd feel it. Quinn has him. I know he has!'

Mark held Ana while she anguished aloud. There was nothing he could say except to agree with her. If Pietie were alive he had to be with Quinn and or with the bikie gang. There was no other way it was just too long since he's been taken. All other options were gone. She swayed back and forth, her fingers clutching at his hands as though they were the only straws she had to cling to.

'I must go, darling Ana...' he started.

'Yes, go, find him. Then bring him home to me...' she said.

Wally Gideon, the Forensic Chief, came into the office within minutes of Mark's return to the police station.

'I've done the initial post mortems. May I?' he said as he sat beside Mark's desk and put his password into Mark's computer. Wally looked tired. 'Here are the interim reports on Frank Mason and the young woman. Both are definitely murders. You can read them or ... which verbal do you want first?'

'Mason.'

'This one's interesting.' Wally's mouth skewed sideway in a puzzled look. 'He was king hit from behind, but that didn't kill him. Blood pumped into his brain meninges for a few minutes and the swelling would've killed him, given time.' He corrected his statement as Mark's eyebrows rose. 'Blood bled into the brain between the covering layers after he was hit and before he died. That easier to follow? OK... But he actually died of asphyxiation. Something, maybe even a pillow, was pressed into his face cutting off the oxygen to his lungs. There weren't pressure marks of hands over his nose and mouth so it was unlikely to have been manual strangulation. No signs that he fought back.' He stopped as though he was thinking aloud. 'Some interesting marks on his neck though. A bit of a mystery at this point although my assistant suggests that something may have been put over his head to cut off the air. Plastic maybe... '

'So he was out to it when he was finally killed? If he'd come to he could have named his killer?'

'I doubt if he'd ever have regained consciousness, but his killer mightn't have known that. He was being very careful.'

'Covering his tracks,' Mark suggested.

'That was Dr Myers opinion,' Wally said.

'Dr Myers? Jimmy Myers? I worked with him before. He was more than helpful in the Port Lincoln case when we were chasing Quinn last time. But I think that bastard's definitely the killer here. We suspect he was the person who was the go between with the big opal deal,' Mark said. He made no mention that Quinn didn't turn out to be the Port Lincoln serial killer. Wally Gideon and Myers were well aware of that fact. But now it was their department that had identified Quinn's DNA; brought him back to life, so to speak.

'Yes, Jimmy's still one of my best young pathologists,' Wally said with a smile. He remembered. The previous case inference wasn't lost on him.

'He still in town? I'd like to catch up with him...'

'You'll have to wait a bit; I had to send him back to Adelaide. Other ordinary cases await his scalpel. You can't hog all our resources with your murders.' Wally said as a slightly teasing smile creased his face. Pathologists often have unique and dark senses of humour.

'These are more than enough...' Mark started but was cut short when Wally's smile faded as he clicked the mouse and a second screen replaced the first.

'Now the young woman. Her ID at this stage is just "Lucy" as was suggested. Anyway, she was hit, again very hard and probably with a fist. Then her head hit a wall, or something very solid. There was only one blow and the angle was from the front and side, hitting the head on the left side, against a wall on her right.' Wally's fist imitated the blow making a smacking contact with a filing cabinet next to the desk. 'Completely smashed the thinner bone over the temple.'

'Nasty. The fist used again. Anything else that could link the two? Mark asked.

'Not at this stage. Not from the pathology. The woman was partly dressed only, no panties, and she had very recently had sex. Unprotected sex. We'll get a DNA sample without problems from that and give you at least one name if it's on file. So maybe it's a crime of passion as they say, killed by a current lover or killed by a past lover. I'll get the results done asap.' There was a pause as Wally drew breath.

Mark cut in. 'Thanks Wally for coming in to talk about these cases. Now I'm up to date. The boys will have gathered more crime scene information today. But just listening, I get that both died due to being hit. Hit hard. OK one with added assistance,' he conceded. 'We can tie the woman to Quinn as she was witnessed with him earlier this week. She was a bikies woman named Lucy. We haven't got any more as the chapter has clammed up.'

Wally's eyebrows rose. 'Well, I wouldn't have guessed that involvement from her appearance. No tatts and in death, disregarding the misshapen head, she had the appearance of a lovely person. One can never tell...' he mused.

'Can you also look for DNA other than the sperm? There may be a link with Ana's missing boy, Pietie. You've been brought up to date with all that I expect.'

'Yes, I have. It's the one main topic of conversation and gossip I've heard about since I've been in Coober Pedy. You, Ana Forster and the little boy. I'm so sorry and I'll get scrapings done and tested from Lucy as a matter of urgency. If she handled the child since she last showered then we could be successful. I was going to say lucky,' Wally admitted, 'but that isn't appropriate now.'

'From what people have said, Lucy might've been a good carer for Piet if Quinn has him. How and why she was murdered just adds to the pain of it all.'

Wally got up to go. He stretched. 'I'm flying the bodies back to Adelaide for more tests as I said. No one has so far claimed either of them. Another interesting factor. The boys have done observations, fingerprints etc and these should be with you this morning.'

'Thanks again. You're a great person to talk to and you've given me facts not blather. It could all be Quinn and what I need most is to get him and most of all Pietie, alive.'

'It's not looking good is it...?

'No. Wally, it's not.

Half an hour later, just after noon, Mark sat with Lex, Dave Ballinger the Coober Pedy senior man, and detectives Harry and Imran at the long conference table in the media and public announcements area.

'Well, I'll be damned,' Harry exclaimed poking fingers towards a tray of sandwiches. 'It's not just stale cheese here! There's ham and mustard, egg too. The gods must have heard me. All we need is some good coffee to go with them.'

'Do get your grubby fingers away from there,' Wally Gideon said as he came into the room. 'Sorry I'm late but at least I'm here in time to set a bit of decorum not to mention some sanitation with these Major Crime boys.'

There was a much needed chuckle around the table. Already all of them had expressed in some way, their concern to Mark regarding Ana and Pietie. A nod across the table, a slap or touch of the shoulder from each man. Word got out and the police fraternity supported each other.

'Yes, help yourselves, there's coffee, tea and water. Cake too,' Mark said. He nodded towards Lex, 'it's not as good as his missus Grace's cake, but it will have to do. Can we eat and talk do you reckon? I want us back outside asap.'

Harry led the sandwich grab.

Mark gave Dave, as the local man, the go ahead.

'I'll start with the search for the boy,' Dave said, food in one hand, coffee in the other. 'It's very apparent that he's either gone, given the timeframes, or he's been taken. The tracker says the latter. The bikies have totally silenced up, both about the boy and the murdered woman, Lucy. I do know that George Gordon, her man, has gone from the area. He may be a chief suspect and I've put out the word and description to all states on him. My instincts are that he didn't kill her except maybe as an accident. In the bikie world they were a quiet couple and he hasn't much of a rap sheet. Nothing violent; a bit of weed and traffic offences with the Harley. He's a crazy man on the bike.'

'Thanks Dave. Your take?'

'George's gone, sure, but if Quinn is with the bikies then it may be because Gordon could've retaliated when Lucy was killed. My money says that he went because he couldn't stay. It's a bikie hierarchy thing and Gordon's only middle rank. I think Quinn is involved in both, the boy's disappearance and Lucy's murder.'

Mark looked along the table. 'OK, Lex, you're next.'

'Imran and I had set up as a team to look for the money trail. Then all the murders turned up. I had to go into the wide open spaces and be an outside detective again. So far I have escaped the wild dingos and rampant camels everyone's warned me about.' He waited for a small chuckle and shuffle to subside. 'I think that the murder of Frank Mason was a hurried killing and there was an attempt to make it look like a robbery. Only one display case of opal was broken into and not much taken going on what was left. The cameras were smashed on the way out but the security chips etc were not touched by that. We've been able to get an image of a man in black with a full face mask, a bikies helmet from the look of it. It's mostly there. Mason was hit from behind, he fell and the body was hidden as the killer reached down to it after the punch. The killer smashed the display case then picked up a plastic bag. He went back to the body and bent down again. The killer waited then straightened up and he put something from the display case into the bag before leaving. Mason must have had new technology security cameras because it is all there.'

Dave Ballinger broke in. 'We've had security system salesmen up here this year. Opals worth big money and most of the traders upgraded.'

'Well, the murder could've been done as in an old movie. Shaky but it's all there; and I think it's Quinn or at least one of the bikies. Not quite clear enough for a positive ID because of the helmet but the images are amazing. We'll all be out of jobs if these cameras get into common usage,' Lex said.

Harry hefted another sandwich. One bite demolished it. Two blissful chews and a gulp of coffee and he stretched and straightened back into his chair. 'I went mainly to the Lucy burial site. Obviously the first thing we all noticed was that it was started with care and the process was disturbed. For some reason I found it sad...' He looked around as his cohort of detectives murmured.

'Yes,' Mark said, 'its cases like this one that make me want to give the victim an accounting,' he trailed off aware that he was sounding soft. 'No dammit,' he finished. 'That's what we're all here for.' He laughed as he heard Harry's 'Yada Yada Yada' of agreement. Tough old Harry also had a soft spot. Detectives; a conservative bunch really always trying to put the world to right.

Turning, Mark nodded to Imran.

'Lex and I have chased the money angle through the computer banking trail.' Eyebrows raised in question as Imran continued. 'You all were aware that between Lex and Mark some interesting ideas have surfaced. In short, drugs are coming into Australia from the East and the Middle East, mostly via the previously innocent shipping of grain and ore from Whyalla and Port Lincoln. From there it is easy to road them to Sydney and Melbourne. In addition ice and crack are being produced through the prison and parolee networks and join the drug procession to the Eastern States. The new aspect was the payment being done with opals. Clever, as these are especially sought after, popular and profitable, in these regions. The perfect trade commodity. Legal and advantageous to the miners. We have been able to track an opal bank deal through interesting countries and banks to an organisation we know well by one of the aliases. Vincent Hood and Associates.'

Harry interjected. 'I like the meat, Mark, I've been after them for years, but have you got the bloody potatoes yet? I need the full meal to get an arrest order. Supposition isn't proof of the linkages.'

'Yes, but I believe we're getting close. Jessica from Whyalla texted me to say that the Customs and our boys have just hauled a big package of drugs out of the sea under the iron ore wharf. It's huge, half a ton of the stuff. It links to the crook Customs Officer, and from there to a lawyer, Erica Marryat, who I've witnessed works for Vincent Hood. She didn't show up in the Magistrate's Court but she was on Tyler Grayson's first court ticket. He was the Customs man murdered at that session,' Mark expanded for Imran's benefit.

Again there was a murmur from around the table. The proof of poisoning by snake venom was a Cleopatra idiosyncrasy and fascinating. It had gone out on all police emails and discussions. Mark continued, 'Another link we're almost sure of is Quinn to the murder victim Frank Mason. Probably to the woman, Lucy too, if we are lucky with the DNA, and it might just link in with the known case of murder and arson where we know Quinn was present. He probably ordered it.'

'A lot of that's circumstantial, Mark. Will it hold up before a jury?' Lex asked.

'I think it will…eventually.' Mark said as he and Harry exchanged glances.

# Chapter 46

'I'm going to the police station,' Ana said. She picked up a brush and quickly pulled her straight hair into place. As always, the large white streak in front of her hair glowed at the touch of the brush. But it did little to hide the extra years that exhaustion and worry had etched into her eyes or to cover that stress had stretched the skin tight and gaunt over her cheekbones. Her chin jutted. 'I can't stay here another minute.'

Rhette took the car keys out of Ana's hands. 'Well, I'm driving...' she said with a twitch of her lips that alluded to the last time Ana had driven the car and chased down Quinn.

Ten minutes later they were at the Police front counter where a young constable announced them by phone to the detective's squad room.

The two women looked around the reception area to where a group of obvious reporters, camera and notepads laden, waited with them.

A reporter stepped forward and spoke to Ana.

'Coober Pedy Imparja Channel. You're Mrs Foster? Mother of the missing little boy aren't you?...' he said gently. 'We're crossing to go on air right now. Would you say a few words please? It might help...'

Ana hesitated.

The young Aboriginal man was respectful and seemed genuine in his concern.

She glanced at Rhette who shrugged one shoulder in a 'can't do any harm' look. As other channel cameras were hefted Ana took a deep breath and grasping Rhette's hand she looked straight into the camera. 'Please find my Pietie. I know that many people are looking for him, and I'm so grateful to them, but someone must know where he is...' Her voice trailed off. 'Please...if you have him or know something, please...'

The Imparja reporter was jostled aside as the more experienced city crews sought their own news clips and TV bites.

An interstate reporter, a man intent only on his own career and his dream of a more highly rated radio talkback show and golden microphone, pushed to the front of the pack. 'Mrs Foster!' he shouted in her face. 'Do you think he's dead, Mrs Foster? Did you kill your son yourself and throw his body down a mine shaft?'

A shocked silence from the other reporters lasted a fraction of a second before, from behind him, individual calls came from all angles. 'Mrs Foster, here...!' 'Here!'

Ana's hand went to her throat in horror. She looked down as if she was swamped by the noise and kinetic energy of the reporters. Rhette pulled Ana's slight body into the protection of her shoulder as the lights of the TV cameras flooded the area and still cameras flashed. 'Stop it! Back off - all of you!' she said loudly.

Mark and Harry came charging through the door into the area. The cameras swung in their direction. 'That's all,' Mark said as he saw Ana's shocked face. His teeth clenched as he took her arm. 'Thank you,' he managed to keep his voice polite to the array who now jostled more vigorously. The country reporters could be kinder to a woman in this situation, but the two police officers were fair game to get the news story they wanted. Especially from the city men.

Questions were hurled at him.

'What's the latest?'

'It's been three days. The boy can't be...'

'Has the kid been chucked down a mine shaft like the other one?'

'Is it true that he's been kidnapped?' a loud voice demanded above the others' calls and shouts. 'You know the person who's got the kid?'

After a nod from Mark, Harry firmly elbowed a way through the throng to the restricted area door, used his pass card to open it, and pushed Ana and Rhette through and into the passage.

Mark turned back to the reporters. 'That's just your speculation,' he snapped. 'We've told you all we know at this time. The search is going on with police, a police helicopter, the dogs and the volunteers and we are covering all avenues. Mrs Foster is under enormous strain and you need to give her some space… There'll be an announcement when we have something to tell you. Now please leave the station.'

The questions continued, still noisy.

Mark's hands curled into fists and he found he was having difficulty keeping his hands by his sides. He frowned especially at the loud shout from the interstate station representative he recognized as usually abusive.  Mark nodded to the desk officer who had come forward to try to restore order and to get the reporters out.

'Sorry Sir, they…'

'Just get them out of here!' Mark shouted as he swiped his card at the door lock and left the area. In moments he had caught up with the women and ushered them into the conference room. Rhette dragged a chair forward for Ana who was shaking uncontrollably as she fought back tears. Harry poured water from a jug into glasses and put them before the women.

'You OK now?' Harry asked Ana. He stood with a gentle hand on Rhette's shoulder.

'Guys, give Ana and Rhette a few moments to compose themselves,' Mark said. With one arm around Ana he abruptly picked up the jug and slopped water into another glass. He drank it to give himself time to recover his feelings and temper. 'The bastards were waiting out there… Dave, can you make sure that this doesn't happen again?'

Dave Ballinger grunted. 'The local bunch are OK, but the case's attracted the city boys…' He turned to the women. 'I'll do my best to protect you from them, but it's not always possible. There's a back way out.'

Mark introduced Ana, then Rhette, to the men in the conference room.

Rhette gave a startled gasp. She stood back in alarm as Imran rose in respect at meeting the two women. 'You were at the hotel when I went after Hood!' she blurted out. 'I saw you up on the top level with Hood and his mob.' Her blue eyes darkened with anger. 'I saw you drinking with them...' She looked about the room as though she was suspicious that this man was a danger to her. Worse, an informer to Hood.

Harry butted in before Kadir Imran could respond. 'Immy's OK. Relax woman. He's with Major Crime.'

'Well, that night he seemed to be with Hood.' Her tone implied disbelief.

'I was not with the gentleman you speak of. Just observing him and his companions.' As usual Imran's voice was quiet.

Rhette's eyes fired, she flicked back strands of red curly hair. Harry touched her arm. She turned her back on Harry not taking her eyes from Imran. 'What's he doing here then?'

'That's police business, Rhette.' Harry said.

A thought barreled into her mind. A spike of frown lines deepened between her eyes. She blurted, 'Hood's not here too is he? What'd he be doing in Coober Pedy? He's not after me...?' She slumped against Harry and grabbed for his hand.

The big man covered her hand with his. 'If he's in Coober Pedy he's here on other business,' he said.

'Those reporters,' Rhette pulled her hands free. 'Those cameras. They'll show me too. If Hood sees me - I'm done. He's got a kill contract out on me.'

Hood stood rigid in the middle of the executive motel lounge room. A "Breaking Local News Flash" had just appeared on the TV. Rhette's fall of flaming red hair was immediately visible in the crush of jostling reporters at the police station.

'Fox!' Hood shouted and strode across to thump the door leading to the adjoining rooms. 'You were supposed to have terminated that bloody woman at the hotel.'

Johnny Fox sauntered into the main suite.

The TV was blaring but the voices were drowned out by Hood as he continued to shout for Fox.

'Boss...?' He glanced towards the wide flat screen in time to catch sight of Rhette and another woman being ushered towards a door by two plain clothed policemen. He recognized Rhette immediately, and one of the coppers. Obviously Hood had done so judging by his outburst.

Hood said. 'That fucking bitch! She's the one who testified against us in Sydney. She disappeared. Probably into some bloody protection scheme.'

Seemingly impervious to Hood's harangue, Fox watched as the camera swung away from the women to the younger policeman. 'Yes.' he said.

'I've been waiting for her to bloody well surface since then. I gave you a direct order to 'do her' in Adelaide last month. Why in the hell's she still breathing?'

Finally he could get a word in as Hood drew breath. 'She was gone by the time I got where I thought she'd be...'

'You incompetent bastard, you never told me you didn't get her.' Hood's face was clenched in fury and thrust close to Fox's. 'I thought she was fixed as I'd ordered.'

'When I got back to our hotel you were occupied, fucking one of your little bints. You never asked about it when you were finished with her. Or afterwards.' Fox's voice was flat. He raised a shoulder in a shrug.

'You should've done it. The bitch doesn't deserve to live.'

'Well, as it turned out it seemed better to just let her be. She'd gone from the hotel. Leaving significant corpses behind you when you've been schmoozing for customers in a new city wasn't a good idea, I'd have thought.'

Hood's mouth relaxed from the hard line. 'You don't get paid to think,' he said. He struck Fox's thin shoulder, his hand heavy but his voice lighter. 'Maybe you're right. You've always counted the bodies haven't you?'

'Yes, Boss, my job's the body count...'

Erica Marryat appeared in the doorway of the master suite in a deep blue satin and lace dressing gown, her hair wrapped in a towel. 'And he's supposed to note who you fuck when I'm not with you, is he? You said you'd leave those young pussies alone since we've been together?' She pulled the sash firmly about her waist and tied it off. Her chin was high, her glare a rapier, and it was obvious she was dressed under the gown. 'You said…' A mobile phone summoned from behind her. 'I'll get that.' she said.

Hood moved quickly and spun her around before she could move. 'No. I'll get it,' he said. 'I told you no phone calls while we're here. No one's to know we're in Coober Pedy.'

'But…' Erica shrugged away and Hood's hand gripped her towel bound hair. It fell free and her dry hair with it.

The mobile phone's ring tone ceased.

'Who knows you're here?' He demanded.

'No one.'

'And I thought you were resting. From the heat. That's what you said you were going to do.' Hood's brows lowered in suspicion. 'And you weren't dressed when I saw you last. Where've you been woman? Or with who?'

'No where. No one. Down to the hotel shop. For more opal.' She turned the accusations on him. 'You said I could buy whatever I wanted.' She tried a pout in her lips and voice.

He wasn't buying it. 'Have you been with Sean?'

A derisive laugh escaped her lips. 'As if…' she said. 'Give me a break.'

'Well,' he paused. 'No phones and tell me where you're going.'

Erica started to protest. 'I'm not a child. Not your prisoner. I have clients I have to speak to. Court cases waiting.'

'Listen we're going to have to leave tonight or tomorrow morning. Probably in a hurry, so stay here. In this suite. Understand!'

Doug Napier cast back and forth across many of the tracks that lead away to the north of Coober Pedy.

The terrain was undulating beds of alternate sands and siltstone, heavily corrugated and endlessly blinding with white and red colours relentless reflecting in the harsh sunlight. It was harder going than he had suggested to the women and to Mark, as there had been no rain in months and the mishmash of dusty ruts and tracks told him little. Less than he was expecting. Where the ground wasn't broken up by vehicles and heavy machinery it was baked as hard as concrete. Traceable tracks didn't exist there. He'd left the safety of the established tracks leading up towards the dog fence looking for that single motor bike wheel track in the ruts.

Nothing.

He was beginning to doubt that he could find Quinn as he'd hoped and promised. As the day wore on he continued to fight the wheel over the pitted country, and sweated. The sun rose higher and hotter. With no air conditioning in his old Rover he was sweating profusely and the steering wheel slipped and jarred in his hands. His shoulders ached and he could feel the reddening of his bare thighs where the sun bore into them through the windscreen.

He pulled up. Still nothing. He drank again from his waterbag. Even in the esky the ice had melted and water was barely cool. He decided to retreat back to his own mine dugout until there was some heat respite with the coming of the night.

Doug suddenly felt old. Older than he'd admit to himself. Where was his bush craft, he thought, as he drove again across the familiar yet daunting moonscape of mine holes, Calweld shafts and mounds of waste refuse? He was used to the familiar track he drove on to and from Coober Pedy not lurching across the pitted land of holes and mullock heaps. He'd done that when he was younger but now, having reconnected with Rhette, his current resolve was less than he'd allowed himself to admit.

Was he again just escaping the raw emotions of the child's loss as he'd done before? The idea wormed into his brain, a probe that left Doug doubting his own reasons. Shrugging that aside he recognized that the most sensible thing he'd done was to take his satellite mobile with him. Fully charged and set to dial Rhette and Ana at the touch of the screen. That was the concession he'd made with Rhette, that and to show her his own mine GPS reference plus his intended search pattern on a map.

Doug reached his mine and parked the Land Rover by the door to the tunnel that was his home, before now. After heaving the esky out of the car he unlocked and entered the cooler area. He sat down heavily on his bed and swung his legs up. Lay back. Cripes, I feel knackered. Too old for this roaring off in rescue, he thought.

# Chapter 47

Quinn bit back the bile that rose into his throat and filled his mouth with the taste of acid.

Damn that Foster bitch, he thought.

Her blasted brat had finally stopped whimpering. That was something. The women had drugged the boy and at last it had worked to keep the little body still and quiet. That was something too. Were they expecting him to dump him down the nearest shaft? Drugged up so he'd never experience and be conscious of his own murder. With the damaged left shoulder Quinn could only use that arm to hold the boy against his chest, leaving him to steer and ride the Harley with his right hand. He wasn't ready to answer the question. Dump the kid to his death or... Not yet.

The fast escorted ride out of town had been a struggle and he'd wondered if they'd been seen.

By the cops. By anyone.

Whether the bikies had made an anonymous phone call to the cops telling them that he was gone, to take the heat off themselves. Wouldn't put it past them, Quinn thought. They didn't want to be linked to the boy. Not any more in any case.

Now he had slowed down considerably to get his bearings. The sun was getting lower in the western sky and, as he was heading north and west, he was feeling the punch of heat into his eyes. One of the bastard bikies had pinched his designer sunglasses and, without them he squinted, as he pushed the bike as fast as he could in the ruts on the tracks left by the big mining companies. He continued on, still using the mining tracks outside Coober Pedy. He was very aware that the police would be looking for him on the main highway leading north to Darwin and south to Adelaide but he needed to join up with the Anne Beadell Highway that led to Laverton in Western Australia. He remembered that the old highway was almost due west from Coober Pedy but his idea always was to punch north then double back to find that road. If he could get past the opal mining area fenced in by the Dingo Fence and the railway line, keep west onto the track, then he felt he could escape the dragnet. The Anne Beadell Highway meant possible margins of safety as he knew that the vast area was criss-crossed with tracks leading further north.

In prison he had learned the lesson that a person had to research the area he was in if he wanted to have an escape route and before Hood had sent him to Coober Pedy he'd done just that. A rough mental map of inland Australia lay in his head.

During prison terms, before his escape via the Murray to Sydney, Quinn had heard rumours of drug running gangs operating from northern Australia. Crims boasting, he'd thought, but these gangs were his only hope now. Would the remainder of the opal cache he'd kept back from Hood buy him passage? Buy him position in the drug cartels there? He had his own sale contacts in Sydney and Melbourne and the ice market was booming. Spread out into the rural towns as well. Plenty of room for him if only he could get away and set it up.

But first he had to get himself a better set of wheels. A four wheel drive of some sort, something that could do the rough tracks and the highway he had researched. Be ready to jump other travelers to change vehicles and to get supplies. It had worked on the Murray River where he had broken into houseboats for food and grog. He muttered aloud and hitched the child on the petrol tank higher as the small body started to slip in slumping sleep. He'd need to make a decision about the boy and soon too.

Suddenly the track turned briefly due west into the setting sun and he was blinded. Cursing he skidded sideways and got a foot to the ground. He kept the bike upright and released the throttle. As the Harley's engine quietened Quinn heard the sound of an aeroplane.

Shit, he thought. The bloody cops!

He looked around for somewhere to hide on the track.

Nowhere. Nearby just level ground all around.

Nothing.

But way off the track he could see what looked like an open cut mine. Maybe he could hide there, in the cut. He slewed his bike through the gibbers and dust off the track and made for the mine. Where the height of the cut cast deep late afternoon shadows, he pulled his bike into the shade and shut off the engine. With Piet still in his arms he let the bike rest against the cut. He swore again in pain as he struggled off the machine. His legs relaxed and his back slipped down the straight angle of the cut until he was seated, legs splayed. A rattle of stones and dirt followed the leather of his jacket and a dust cloud rose. One handed he pulled his helmet off, put the bike on the stand, and leaned back.

Quinn could no longer hear the plane.

Pietie murmured in disturbed sleep, or the sudden silence, and snuggled into his chest.

On impulse Quinn pushed the boy aside and laid him, still wrapped in the tartan blanket that the bikie women had given him, on the ground. Piet stayed asleep and Quinn avoided looking closely at the baby features and the eyelashes that curled below the soft wide forehead and head of dark curls. He cursed aloud again. The bloody kid was getting to him.

But the boy wasn't Clinton.

Not his own son.

His boy was as fair haired as he was. Clinton looked nothing like the bitch who'd whelped him and who'd taken him when she got the chance to get away. Just his echo. Another Quinn. Could he make this boy into Clinton if he took him? For a moment, in his exhaustion, he let the past escape from the corners of his mind. A corner he'd closed off except for the search for Clinton.

Now the images surfaced. Port Lincoln. He thought of the shack outside the town where he'd lived with Clinton and his mother whore after getting out on parole after a long prison stint of ten years. His kid. Just looking at his son cemented his path to immortality.

The bastard cops appeared out of nowhere and arrested him for murders he didn't commit. His bitch Faye disappeared with the boy as soon as they had taken him away.

Then Ana Foster.

He'd got his hands around that bitch's throat at the prison when she wouldn't tell him where his defacto was going with his son. The escape from the prison van taking him to Adelaide for trial. Many killings that followed; he didn't remember all the faces in the blur as he had fled east along the Murray Valley towards Sydney. His one predominant focus was to survive then to find out where Clinton was. Ana had been there on the Murray River, on fucking holiday, when he was trying to get away. If they caught him he knew he'd be up for the murders but first he had to find Clinton. No one and nothing else mattered except finding his son. Hardly even himself.

But the moment after he'd killed Ana's stupid husband, being shot and almost captured when his body hit the river, the bullet in his guts, he was determined to fight for his life.

He'd hidden over the weekend in the river construction works of Lock 6 while the cops looked downstream for his body, and somehow he'd managed to get out of the water. He was lucky, though. The bullet had missed his vital organs. He'd stayed amongst the reeds until he'd dried off and then hitched a lift from a woman who'd detoured off the road looking for somewhere to buy oranges. The stupid bitch had been mesmerized by his looks and taken him all the way to Sydney. There he'd killed her in payment for the ride. Another stupid woman ruled by her cunt.

Then he'd met up with Hood and his gang, not hard nuts to crack when he'd done them a past favour, a contract killing, in the years before he was put away for rape and a killing. While he worked for Hood he continued his endless search for Clinton. He'd got word out to all the bikie gangs Australia wide but the bitch Faye had taken him and gone underground. He'd never got a hint of where she was living.

Not until he saw Ana outside Whyalla.

Maybe Ana had helped Faye. He was sure enough then to try to strangle it out of her.

And now he had her little bastard.

He was shocked by her attack on him but the bitch knew he had the kid and he was a winner there. Let her suffer.

Quinn suddenly realised that in his inaction he was drifting, off to sleep even, wasting time. Letting his thoughts of the past dominate his resolve. He had to move or be cornered by the police. Decision about the kid later too, he thought.

First get a new vehicle. Then get going north, eventually when he could get past the Dog Fence and onto the highway with that stupid woman's name. He forced his brain to visualize the map of the area again.

Quinn opened his locked saddlebag looking for a drink of water. Way down was his Glock 8mm gun, solid and reliable. He pulled it free of its soft leather wrapping and checked the magazine. Empty. The bikie gang had managed to get into his bags while he was asleep or drugged out and find his gun. Bastards, he mouthed. He flexed his left shoulder trying to ease the pain, stiffness and discomfort of the injury, and the thought came that they'd been scared enough of him to empty his gun while he was out. Gutless pricks, he thought as he found a clip of eight bullets, and the many spares that were secreted in another wrap. He slid them into the chamber. Now he was ready for the first time since he'd been forced out of Coober Pedy. Lifting the tough material of his jeans he shoved the gun down into the top his right boot.

It was a snug fit but now he was ready. The pain dissipated as power surged through him. Armed, he felt good.

He levered himself to his feet, grabbed the drugged sleeping boy, and swung him across the petrol tank. His boot kicked away the bike rest as he started the huge motor. The boy's body jerked in protest at the roar but Quinn ignored it. He pulled out from the shadows and headed north-west again on the track he'd previously left.

That's when Quinn was seen.

Above him the police plane, heading back to the Coober Pedy air strip for fuel, spotted a man on a motor bike. The pilot radioed ahead to the police with the observation. The call was put through immediately to Mark.

'Thanks Ray. Is it too late for you to go out again? You've done a lot of flying hours already today, haven't you?' Mark asked.

'It probably is for me. Getting dark soon. I can't land. There's not a clear patch anywhere with all the mines and diggings. Not even on the so called roads out there... I can only report what I see. Hang on; got another call on the other channel coming in.' the pilot said and cut the transmission. 'It's our police chopper...the airport's in sight now and I can see them. It's just landed.'

'Great. I'll see what their ready position is. Thanks Ray...' Mark said.

'I caught that,' another voice cut in. 'Ray put you on speaker.' He gave the helicopter call sign then said. 'Nick Johnson here. We'll need to refuel. We'll get the co-ordinates from Ray and be ready to fly again in, maybe half an hour. My co-pilot Kerran's been sleeping like a log all the way from Adelaide so he'll be your pilot when we're ready to roll again. See you then...' There was a murmur of comment from another voice as the connection was cut.

# Chapter 48

'Harry? Got a minute?' Imran said as he came to the door where Harry and Mark were strapping on body armor vests.

Harry shrugged his shoulders into a more comfortable position and broke the chamber of his pistol to check again that the bullets were in place.  Fully loaded. He looked up briefly to Imran. 'It's on,' he said. 'We've got a sighting of Quinn.'

'Any sign of the boy?'

'No, the plane was too far away from the motor bike to see anything clearly. Just a big man on a big Harley heading north. I'm hoping its Quinn. Then we might know what happened to Piet.' Harry hefted his gun to its holster. He glanced towards Mark who was ready but still taking a moment to begin thumbing numbers into his mobile phone.

'Well, good luck.' Imran paused. 'We've got the positive link between Quinn and Hood so it would be expedient if you could take him alive. Might then find a clue as to why Hood's warehouse stronghold in Sydney is in flames. The men watching the place have just reported that there was a mighty explosion and it's burning. Puts a whole new complication on things...'

Harry stopped. 'Hood's place has gone up?' he queried.

Mark brushed past the two detectives. 'Leaving here in ten. I'll meet you at the car with Dave.' He said to Harry.

'Be right with you...' Harry said. He turned an instant back to the Iranian detective. 'Immy, gotta go. Find out more about the fire. Keep on it. Who did it and why... interesting.'

'I will do that,' Imran said, his language precise as ever even as he called to Harry's retreating figure. 'As you say, interesting.'

'There's been a sighting of a man on a motor bike. North of

Coober Pedy.' Mark said quickly and quietly when Ana answered her mobile. 'We're going now. By helicopter. Stay where you are and I'll let you know immediately we have news.'

'Anything at all? Anytime?'

'Anything...'

'Take care...'

'Love you...'

'For Christ's sake Mark, keep that stuff until we get home with the boy.' Harry said from the door as he headed downstairs. 'We'll get him.'


Quinn's bike bucked and spun over the rough jumble of tracks, shafts and looming mullock heaps left by the outpourings of the Yorke Hoysts. The odors he could smell through his helmet were of red dust and stone but suddenly permeating through it he caught another whiff. Shit, the bastard kid's pissed himself, he thought and instinctively he shifted the burden of the child's body away from his chest. Even this desperate by habit he didn't want the stink of urine getting into his leathers.

Another reason to get another vehicle.

And to get rid of the kid.

The coming night was inching in from the west; and the wheel rut shadows darkened before him making the way even more dangerous. He pulled up again and stamped a foot down. Dust rose but he ignored it and scanned the deepening dusk looking for a light, any light. One that could mean a vehicle he could steal.

There it was, still to the north where he wanted to go. Finally a break, and about time. He idled the engine to quieten the bike and, with extreme caution, crossed the few hundred metres to the light source.


Doug got to his feet, aware that he had drifted to sleep when the beat of the Harley engine had pushed thought and evaporated his dreaming. He shook himself further awake and grabbed for his .22 automatic rifle. Not a deadly weapon but in his experienced hands it would hopefully be sufficient. He'd chased away too many enthusiastic noodlers before with it before. It would have to be enough.

As promised he clicked on his mobile phone to Rhette and Ana. As he put it into his shirt pocket he hoped that the women would just listen and not speak if who he thought was coming appeared.

# Chapter 49

The shadows cast by the mine walls had taken on the shades of night. Dark becoming black as the light was gone and the scant twilight fled after the sun had set leaving a dirty red smudge in the west. The blowtorch heat of the desert air palled but the hotness was still thrust up from the dirt and stone that had soaked in it all day. The cold could be near freezing overnight when the desert clear sky sucked the heat away.

Doug's Land Rover held its shape against the dark, solid, as Quinn eased his bike with its cargo to the rear of the vehicle. He set the heavy Harley against the mine cut wall. Nothing moved although Quinn could see the glow of a LED light from inside an entrance. He slung Piet, still swapped in the gang blanket, over his left shoulder keeping his options open to reach for his gun with his right hand.

'Anyone home?' Quinn called softly as he moved to just outside the influence of the light from the mine entrance. He stopped and waited.

'Yeah,' Doug answered. 'Who's there?' He stood silhouetted against the light, at once feeling exposed and vulnerable. Shit, he thought as he stepped back into the shadows. I'm supposed to be army trained. Did my army stint. I'm not some stupid civilian. He waited for a response.

'My name's Ben Jackson. I was heading back to the town when I found the kid everyone's looking for. Beside the track, almost ran over him.' Quinn said. His voice sounded genuine.

For a beat, a millisecond, Doug wanted to believe him. He could see the shape of something over his shoulder. 'Is he OK?' he said and he went towards Quinn, as the stranger brought the bundle to the ground.

'He's alive but I haven't had a squeak from the little bugger.'

'Bring him inside where we can see him. There's a bed here.' Quinn followed Doug through the mine entrance to the hollowed out room. The bed, covered with a grey blanket, was against one wall. Quinn lay the boy down and smoothed the curly hair back from his brow, then stood back as Doug came forward to look. 'That's him alright,' Doug said. 'We'd better get word back to his mother and the rescue teams. Everyone's been frantic. Been out looking for the little fellow myself.'

'I was lucky to find him. Don't know how he got so far out of...' Quinn stopped as Doug started to cough to cover the sound as Ana's urgent voice then a gasp issued from his mobile phone in his pocket.

Rhette kept her hand over Ana's mouth. 'Shut up!' she said. 'Just listen.'

Ana struggled. Pulled free. 'Pietie's alive!' she whispered. She swept her hand up pushing her hair back off her face. A face that glowed in relief.

'You have to be quiet.' Rhette's face was a mixture of delight and apprehension as she now held her fingers over the phone speaker. 'Quiet to help him stay that way. And Doug too...'

Ana nodded. She'd be quiet. She whispered. 'It's Quinn. Definitely Quinn.'

They sat, huddled over the mobile phone, fingers against their mouths as instinctive reminders not to speak.

Doug grabbed for his phone but the sounds were gone. Cut off. 'I'll contact them now.'

'No!' Quinn's voice was steel. 'You'll contact no one!'

All pretences were off.

Quinn backed out the mine entrance into the darkness.

Surges of adrenalin seared through Doug's body as the fight or flee impulse flooded in. He pushed Piet's sleeping body against the wall and reached for the .22 rifle he'd hidden on the floor at the end of the bed. Everything was sharp and clear. Pietie was OK but this man had caused all the heartache to Ana, and Rhette too, and it was going to stop. He was going to stop it. Every past action where he'd taken the easy way to avoid family responsibility, to look only to his own dreams, was swept away. With a glance towards the still boy, his new family since Rhette was back in his life; he cocked the gun and strode out into the darkness.

'You're not going to do anything stupid, old man?' Quinn's cold voice oozed out of the night to Doug's left. 'I just want your car.'

'No,' Doug said. He lifted the rifle to his shoulder. He could see just enough of Quinn to aim. 'Why do you want my vehicle? You have the bike.'

'You've got the boy...' the voice was hedging. Evasive. Very quiet.

There was a scrape of leather, a click as the shape changed. Quinn had his weapon and was now crouched.

Doug adjusted his aim lower.

A different shape hardened out of the night.

The dingo.

Somehow it was there, again. Out of the past. A feral smell spread as a miasma. A growl.

Doug hesitated.

Quinn didn't. 'What the fuck!' He shouted and fired. The dog yelped, leapt high, folded and dropped.

The sound of the shot was sucked away out into the silence.

The next bullet will be for me, the thought rattled into Doug's stunned consciousness. This is more than real. He took a fraction of time, as Quinn backed away from the dog's carcass, to melt into the shadows outside the mine entrance. Out of the light. Past training had kicked in.

Quinn's attention was back on Doug. 'Your car. I want it,' Quinn repeated.

Doug could feel the presence of the gun aimed again at him. 'Take it. Just go.'

There was another beat, and in that instance Doug knew that he was in trouble. Deadly trouble. He was out gunned and his new resolve couldn't match that of the killer waiting in the darkness. A goosebump of cold crackled and swept across the skin of his hairline and neck. He had to act. His finger tightened on the .22 trigger and he fired.

Doug never heard the instantaneous second shot as Quinn fired.

Both men staggered.

Doug Napier went down. Quinn's heavier bullet punched through his sternum and into his heart.

Quinn automatically shoved his gun back into his boot then brought his hand up to the sharp sting he had felt in his neck.

Fucking hell, the bastard got me, he thought as he stepped into the light and looked down at his hand.

Blood. Dark red, almost black in the LED light. His fingers returned to his neck and traced the wound. Blood welled out and he knew that the rifle bullet had probably hit something important. Maybe the jugular vein, he thought calmly. Maybe it's just a nick. Maybe it'll stop. One thing at a time, he resolved. The Rover keys. He needed the keys. He pulled his leather jacket up tight around his neck and went back into the mine.

Quinn stopped short.

The boy, Piet, stirred on the bed. Looked up at him with glazed uncomprehending eyes. Dark brown eyes like the bitch's eyes. Quinn snapped his gaze away and searched for the car keys. There they were, on the cupboard by the bed. He turned his back on the boy as he pocketed them. He found a towel and sopped up the blood on his jacket. More blood than he expected. He grunted and wound the towel about his neck. The welling stopped, momentarily.

The darkness swallowed up the third report when the Glock was fired again from inside the mine.

Quinn made a split second decision and fired at the boy who wasn't Clinton.

Night hid the shadow of the man who stopped long enough to reload his gun, who hefted the saddle bags from the motor bike and drove away in the Rover.

Light spewed out of the mine entrance where two bodies lay in the dirt.

The world was slowing for Demetrius Quinn as he turned more west than north. The map in his head was becoming muddled as the blood seeped away from his brain through the wound in his neck. The Anne Beadell Highway he wanted was south from him now. His current heading was towards the railway line and beyond that the Dog Fence.

Rhette's knuckles were wedged into her mouth. Her other hand still clamped over Ana's.

Two shots. Perhaps an echo or a third one.

Maybe the sound of a vehicle.

Then nothing. Silence.

The two women looked at each other in horror. What had just happened out there?

The women had heard that definite third gun discharge.

# Chapter 50

Kerran glanced over his shoulder at the trio beside and behind him. 'All buckled in? OK. Right taking off now.' The young police pilot eased back on the helicopter cyclic yoke and it rose, dipped to the north and headed away from the lights of Coober Pedy and out into the night. Over the thud and clatter of the rotors he radioed both the police station and the aviation tower in Adelaide.

Below there was almost nothing. No lights as around towns and cities as, at night, the mines went quiet and most miners went back to their dinners, the pubs and beds. Opal would still be there in the morning. Harry and Mark, in particular, felt the vastness of the desert below and only Dave, seated up front, with his hat on his lap, was used to this phenomenon.

There was a chuckle from Kerran as a vehicle light flickered on the track below. 'Best part of this job,' he said, 'giving people a bit of a fright.' The helicopter's flood lights hit a truck below in a blast of white light. It swerved to a stop and a man got out holding his arm up against the glare.

'I know him. He's OK but he's one we watch. Bit of a scoundrel. Noodles too close to some of the mines after dark. He'd be returning home after one of his forays.' Dave said.

The light clicked off and the aircraft continued on. They intercepted two other trucks and a Land Rover by the same method before they were thirty kilometres out of the town. Dave recognised them all as legitimate miners and they left them to their journeys. No other lights appeared on the route they were taking. This was no consolation but, given the rough land below, a bike would have had to have lights on if the rider didn't want to end up in an accident or down a mine.

Kerran, in youthful optimism, stated the obvious. 'It's hard to sneak up on someone in a chopper. They hear us coming but maybe we could surprise him if he can't hear us over the sound of his bike. Bit harder in this flat country though, no where to hide.'

Mark caught Harry's eye. Yeah, stalemate, Mark thought. Quinn had evaded the police for years. He wasn't a fool and he'd be cagey. He'd stop and listen, find a rabbit hole somewhere. A mine hole more likely.

When they arrived at the position the police plane pilot had reported seeing the man on the motor bike, no-one was there, as expected. It was a starting point and the helicopter hovered, lights blazing, before swinging again north along the trajectory that Quinn was reported as taking. Nothing. They returned to the last position and started a grid search. It would be slower than they wished but it was the only way in the dark.

They were searching the area away from Doug's mine.

'I can't wait any longer. We have to go.' Ana paced the kitchen agitated and upset. 'Why haven't we heard anything more?' She stopped to lean against the table.

'There's nothing we can do, Ana.' Rhette's mind was blank. She sat looking at Doug's phone. Willing it to ring, to hear her father's voice. Anything. 'Leave it to Mark and the police.'

'We heard them say that my Pietie's alive. I didn't hear him. Is he still alive? O Rhette... and those shots. What's happened to him? To Doug?' Ana was rambling and she knew it. The words and questions tumbled out. She moved closer to Rhette and the heads of red curls and Ana's straight fall of black and white hair touched.

Rhette almost pushed Ana aside as she stood. Her body stiff and her head went high. She gripped Ana's forearm. 'Bloody hell! You're right. We can't just sit here. I've got Doug's GPS co-ordinates and our car tracker can get us there. I need to know too.'

The women moved quickly.

Comments flew between them. Get your jacket. Blankets. The first aid kit we bought before... Water. Phones.

Rhette came out of her bedroom with the gun that had been returned to her in Adelaide by Harry. She loaded it and wrapped it in a towel she pulled off the rack in the bathroom. Ana eyed this movement and said nothing. While Rhette put their destination into the GPS in Ana's car, Ana went to the kitchen and rummaged through the drawer for the biggest and sharpest knife she could fine. The last time she'd used it was to carve the pork roast she'd cooked in celebration after Rhette and her father had met again. It seemed an interminable time ago. Before... She took Pietie's pillow and blanket from his bed and his toy truck. For an instant she despaired that he and his bear were lost to her. Then action took over as Rhette called from the front door. The climbed into the vehicle and drove off.

'I hope this GPS thing works. It's taking us down Hutching Street and then onto the Stuart Highway to Alice Springs. That's not the way Doug pointed out the way to his diggings.' Rhette's voice was shrill with excitement but there was doubt there too.

'All we can do is follow it.' She was gripping the steering wheel hard and wriggled in her seat as she drove. 'Turn that voice off, I can't bear it. You navigate from the thing.' She floored the accelerator as they reached the highway and turned right.

'Steady!' Rhette said. 'We'll have the cops after us for speeding.'

Now that they were actually doing something and on the move there was a buoyancy about the two women. A mixture of excitement, anxiety and elation coupled with fear.

Ana slowed but it was hard to keep herself from speeding. The four by four vehicle ate up fifteen kilometres when the arrows pointed to a left turn. As they got to the turn off there didn't seem to be a road.

'What the hell...' Rhette said in frustration.

'No look. There's the Dog Fence. We've been put onto the track beside it. Doug said that the fence wasn't far from his mine.' She turned off the bitumen highway and the twin headlights arrowed into the night and the two wheel track beside the fence.

Their speed slowed as the car bounced and bumped along the

track that was the Dog Fence maintenance line. The two metre high barrier of wire caught the head lights as they continued on across a plain that could have resembled the moon it its barrenness.

'Wait! The GPS has come to a halt. No more arrows. Just pointing to a railway line kilometres away up ahead.'

'Turn the voice back on,' Ana said. She slowed the car to a stop.

'You have reached your destination' the voice intoned then repeated the information. It continued. 'Ahead is the Great Southern Rail line from Adelaide to Darwin. The Ghan Train runs...'

Rhette fumbled briefly with the GPS and snapped off the voice. They didn't want a tourist bite. 'We haven't got to Doug's mine. We're in the middle of nowhere.'

# Chapter 51

Mark's phone buzzed. 'Shit!' he said. He'd left his phone on quiet mode and hadn't heard it over the sound of the chopper.

He spoke into it and his face got serious. He leaned forward and tapped Dave's arm. 'That was Ana. Something's happened at Doug Napier's mine. Couldn't hear it all but Quinn's there. Or been there. You've got Doug's co-ordinates?' At the older policeman's nod, he said. 'Get us there, and quickly. This doesn't sound good.'

Ana and Rhette's luck, good and bad, acted with them that night.

Ana turned off the headlights and the vehicle engine pinged and cooled with the night air. They just stood and looked.

There was a brief flicker of light to the west. In moments it was gone.

Ana exhaled and took another deep breath as she could hear Rhette sigh in exasperation. 'Wait. There's the faintest glow coming from there,' Ana said. Impulsively she pointed in the direction she meant.

Rhette came around to her side of the car. 'You're not looking at a low star, are you?' Overhead the array of stars was impressive. Almost enough light from them now that they had turned off the headlights and their eyes had adjusted to the dark. Almost enough ambient light to see by.

'No. I think it's something else. I'm going in that direction.' She opened her door and the interior light leaked out into the night.

'Wait,' Rhette reached back into the rear section and got out the towel wrapped gun. Before she climbed back into her seat she placed it by her feet.

Ana nodded in agreement. 'Keep a fix on that light, will you. I'm just going to head in that direction and hope that we can get there. There whatever it is. We're not going back. Not until we know.'

It took barely fifteen minutes for the women to reach Doug's mine entrance guided by the light coming from inside. Doug's car was gone and a motor bike was on a stand beside the rocky wall.

'Wait,' Rhette said again as Ana turned off the engine. 'Wait and be careful. This isn't right.'

It was totally quiet.

Rhette was the first to move. She cautiously got out of the car, gun ready, and went towards the lump in the dirt that was the dingo. From the dog smell she couldn't tell whether it was recently dead or a rotting carcass. As she leaned near the remains a trail of cold crept across her neck and scalp. Never before had she felt her hackles rise. They had now. Her eyes were drawn to another shadow just outside that range of the light.

The shadow lying there was her father. Rhette knew it even before she stumbled from her crouching position to drop beside him.

'No!' The brief call was one of desperation. Please be alive. Please! Her fingers found his still warm neck. No pulse. She knew where to look for a pulse. Nothing. With a desperate finality she rolled Doug from his semi prone position on to his back. The stark black hole in his chest told her that her plea went nowhere. Her father was dead.

Rhette became aware that Ana was leaning over her as she crouched beside Doug. The smaller woman turned towards the mine entrance armed with her knife.

'Pietie?' Ana said.

Rhette grabbed at Ana. 'Wait! It could be a trap.' Rhette's mind had cleared. She had no idea what they would find inside the dug out. With her father dead at her feet she didn't dare to hope. 'This time we'll confront Quinn my way.'

Although Ana wanted to rush into the mine she hesitated,

respecting the woman with the gun. If Quinn was there she would kill him somehow or they would die too. Both had scores to settle with that man.

Shaking and with her gun drawn Rhette approached the entrance. At the smallest of sounds Ana pushed past her, dropped the knife and threw herself at the bundle of blanket on the bed.

'Mummy?' Pietie said and both were home.

Through the turmoil that was her emotions Rhette saw there was a bullet hole in the bed near where Piet's head had lain.

How had Quinn's bullet missed the boy when he'd shot dead the man and the dog?

Overhead the chopper honed in on the lights and hovered over Ana's car. Dust swirled grey below thrown up in an instant.

'Bloody hell they're here!' Mark shouted.

They peered down into the cone of the helicopter's lights. 'Looks like there's a body, no, two. A smaller one!' Harry said.

Mark unhooked his seatbelt. 'Get us down there, now!' he said to Kerran.

There was a long moment of silence after the rotor blades stopped spinning and, with guns drawn, Mark and Harry burst into the underground room.

Ten minutes later Mark, with Dave and Kerran left to follow Quinn. Harry remained with the women and the body of Doug to set up the crime scene. He pulled the unresponsive Rhette into his arms and they made a huddle with Ana and Piet.

Police work would come later but now the big detective needed to comfort them all.

# Chapter 52

Quinn's mental map was fuzzy, going awry.

The complication of opal mining tracks and roads, railway lines and the Dog Fence that seemed to not converge anywhere but at Coober Pedy, confused him. City or even other country roads made sense but in the moon scape of the opal fields with tracks going every which way he could no longer get a sense of where he was, or where he should go. His original plan to go north but away from the recognized Stuart Highway just hadn't worked. Now he knew he would have to cross the Tallaringa Conservation Park without a permit, not that had ever worried him, to get back on the Anne Beadell Highway. Somewhere he knew, or thought he knew, there was a railway line he had to cross.

There was little pain from the wound in his neck and Quinn tried to ignore it. Ignore it until the towel he'd wedged into the top of his leather jacket flopped wetly out onto his lap as he fought the steering wheel across the ruts. The towel was heavy and saturated with blood. His blood. He could see it in the light from his own headlights but it didn't matter, he thought, he'd survived worse. The bullet in his guts had hurt; this didn't, so he was alright.

Sure he was alright.

He hiccoughed then yawned as his body demanded more air.

A snatch of a lurid song lyric, the beat almost in time with the beat of the engine and the motion of the car, reminded him of Lucy. Poor Lucy, he thought. Ahead the headlight beams seemed to dance over the ground and made him think of Lucy's green dress. Pretty as it slipped off her body and swished to the floor in a silken and crumpled heap beside the bed. There it was ahead, the bed. A straight line like the mattress. Lucy mistress on a mattress... he sang. He shook his thoughts back and saw that ahead was the railway line. The dress was the ballast materials under the line; the stones were all rocky and wavy.

'Shit!' Quinn said aloud drawn back to the here and now. He had been looking to cross the railway line. To find the opening in the Dog fence. There was the line. Where was the gap; the hole? He gunned the motor and the 'Rover bored up the slight incline, bumped over the twin metal strips to slide down the other side. Good, fucking good, he thought. That's how it's done. Now for the fence he had to find and get through.

He couldn't see it.

Must be here, he thought, somewhere...

With the blood sluggishly reaching his brain Quinn could not think that the railway line had to pass through an opening in the fence. He drove on, weaving his way westward where the fence was many kilometres away. Suddenly in a moment of lucidity he thought to go north again. His mental map said north. He swung the wheel to the right, a good approximation to north and was rewarded when after minutes of singing; now about Lucy in the stars with diamonds that his mother used to sing to him, he saw the strands and mesh of the Dog Fence ahead.

'Yes! Bloody yes!' he shouted to the night.

Quinn pulled the 'Rover up and sat looking ahead as it idled.

Where was the gate? He couldn't see a gate.

The bastards have moved the gate, he thought.

His thoughts drifted and flittered back to the bikie gang. Their word was 'refused.' They refused everything he'd asked for. Stupid pricks.

He decided to show them how to make a gate. He stomped on the accelerator and the Rover lurched forward. The fence was strong and the car just pushed in to it. The bumper bar caught in the wires.

As Quinn revved and revved the engine and pushed against the fence, a bright white light from above blasted the darkness away. The air was filled with rotor beats.

Quinn stumbled out of the door and, gun in hand, ran

towards the fence. His faltering brain said he could push his way through the web of wires.

Through to freedom. Through to find Clinton. He'd let the bitch's kid live. Aimed away from his head, so this should be his payback. He'd live.

Mark and Dave jumped and the helicopter rose to hover. Its down aimed search lights completely staged the scene in light as bright; brighter than day.

Quinn threw his body against the wires trying to push through only to get his leather jacket caught there as his strength and body sagged. He fought his right arm free, turned back and pointed his gun at the approaching policemen.

Dust rose as their boots skidded to a halt.

'Stop!' Mark roared, his gun in hand. 'Police! Quinn, you can't get away.'

'Fuck off copper.' Quinn's voice was a gasping rasp.

Dave Ballinger's hand went to the taser on his belt. He eyed the distance to Quinn. Too far for his taser to hit him. Dave pulled his gun.

Quinn fired.

The bullet missed Mark by a fraction to whistle its death message away into the night.

The policemen dived behind the protection of Doug's Rover.

Quinn struggled again against the wires. Pushing, straining to get through.

A second bullet pinged into the metal, again not far from Mark. He heard Dave grunt.

'You OK?'

'Yeah. The bastard got my hat.' Dave said.

Quinn fired again. The bullet thudded into the steel side of the Rover close to Mark's position.

A shot rang out. A ping. The helicopter lifted higher.

Mark stood and calmly set himself. He yelled 'Stop! Police!' again and shot Quinn through the side of the chest as he turned to aim at the police duo again.

Quinn's body convulsed. His arm dropped and the pistol

thudded to the ground.

Still cautious, the two policemen approached.

Demetrius Quinn's once handsome face was contorted into an ugly mask. His dead corpse hung from the Dog Fence wires.

# Chapter 53

By dawn the two crime scenes were swarming with almost every policeman in the region. The Adelaide Crime Scene troop would arrive by plane and car. There was no rush as the offender was dead and it was just a wrap up of all the physical 'hows and whys.' The examination of all the gathered evidence and how the police acted would wait for in depth analysis, later.

A text of congratulations was received by Mark and Dave, as OICs, from Inspector Giles in Adelaide.

Wally Gideon from Forensics sent another to Mark stating his arrival time, plus the comment that when Mark was around the bodies piled up. Would he please explain?

The police helicopter was grounded. When it was found that Quinn's bullet hadn't hit anything of importance it went back to ferrying the police squads between the crime scene locations and Coober Pedy. Questions would be asked as to why this valuable equipment was allowed to be put within the range of a gun. But that would be later when the bean counters started their post operation analysis.

Also by dawn the early rising Coober Pedy community knew that Piet was safe. It didn't matter initially how, just that he was OK. With that news, and the rumours of the crimes, many of the now elated SES Mine Rescue men and women reported again to the police. The personnel were either sent home to rest after the long search for Piet, or if young and not too exhausted, sent to assist police with transport and security at the sites.

The Coober Pedy people had rallied as usual.

The Salvation Army set up their trailers and tents between the crime sites providing the ever ready sandwiches, tea, coffee, water, shade and fellowship.

With the buzz, reporters from regional stations waited outside the hospital and police station for news clips. One TV helicopter had already risen from the airport, hovering like a blowfly as it took off. It flew over and circled the white tents covering Doug, the dingo and Quinn's bodies. The first one got the pictures and sent them off by satellite. More aircraft would arrive later, more media and more officials to swamp the small airport.

The local Imparja Station got the only brief early interview and CIO Dave stated he'd make an announcement to all stations later. He intended to do it before the odious interstate reporter had time to arrive, if he did. The man had returned to his city to cover some state government potential scandal and missed all the local excitement. The reporter could now decide that it was all below his interests as there was no one to bully and send an underling to complete the story. Dave smiled at his small win, there weren't many against some reporters.

Mark pulled the unmarked police car up at the rear of the Coober Pedy Hospital to check again on Piet and the two women. They had been ferried by Kerran to the hospital after he'd flown Lex to the Quinn site at the Dog Fence and left Harry to take charge of the mine scene.

Mark was totally whacked after being on his feet for almost forty eight hours and until the Adelaide detectives arrived he, and Dave Ballinger, would remain on duty. The exhaustion was physical, mental, emotional and the outcome of adrenaline surges. Again he was discomforted when he had found Ana at Doug's crime scene but elation won over at Piet's recovery.

He sat in the car and remembered the feeling as he'd rushed into the mine and found Ana with her son clinging to her. The look on her face would stay with him always. He'd hardly had time to holster his gun before they were in his arms and later Peitie had held his arms up for Mark to take him from Ana. With the feel of that little warm body against him Mark knew he'd bonded with the little boy, a feeling he'd not expected. It was good.

Then he had turned away to console Rhette, until Harry

arrived back and naturally took his place, his arms around her. Again there was no hesitation.

Time to move, or sleep here in the car, he thought. An enterprising reporter started towards him. Definitely time to get going.

With a wave to the reporter he went inside the hospital and the ward where Ana, Piet and Rhette shared a double bedroom. The boy had been examined and given an 'all clear' physically, despite a few scratches and minor abrasions. He was to be kept in because of the drugs he'd been given. Now he was hungry, thirsty and his initial upset was that he'd peed his pants. The drugs hadn't worn off completely and after being showered, dressed in a hospital gown, fed and hydrated with a large banana milkshake, he settled into the hospital bed for a nap. Despite her protests Rhette had taken the sedative offered to her. The shock of finding her father's dead body had made her shake in reaction and she had finally gone to sleep in the other bed. All this Mark took in at a glance; especially that Ana was curled up around her son on the bed and was watching him sleep. Her face alight.

'Mark...' Ana said. 'Thank you...'

This was a different thank you to the one she had said once before and it was OK. More than OK. With that, how could he tell her off about going out to Doug's mine when he'd said to stay away? Stay home and safe. 'That's OK,' he said.

With typical womanly concern she added, 'You look awful. Terribly tired. Can't you take time to get some sleep?'

Rhette opened one eye to look squarely at Mark. 'You back?' she said, 'and you do look bloody awful.'

Mark reached across from where he was standing to touch Rhette as a comfort, rather than saying something supposedly conventional and proper about her loss of Doug. His sleepy hand brushed her thigh and leg under the sheet. He drew it back. 'Sorry...'

'Thanks. But this isn't the time to flirt with me with your woman in the room...' Rhette was pulling out all the stops to regain her focus. Her accompanying laugh was little more than a chuckle at Mark's discomfort. The smile faded. 'I'll be OK. I have to be and I've learned more about Doug lately than I ever knew. Wouldn't ever have had the chance if things hadn't gone the way they have. And there's Harry again...'

A nurse knocked at the door and came into the room. Detective Llewellen? There's another detective outside asking for you. Says he has information that concerns one of the ladies. May I bring him in here or would you prefer that I find a private room for you to talk?'

Mark looked towards Ana and Rhette. Piet was sound asleep, well off with his bear cradled against his chest. Somehow he'd managed to keep Bear safe. Both women nodded and discretely made sure they were covered completely by the bed sheets.

Imran Kadir came quietly into the room with an apology and a careful murmur of condolences to Rhette. He smiled as his gaze lingered on the sleeping boy. 'Mark,' he said, 'I've just received word on DNA tests you asked to be carried out. The results are that the person was killed by Quinn.'

Rhette's response was immediate. Tense. 'You're not referring to my sister Kate's death are you? Was she killed by Quinn?'

Mark said. 'Why is this so important that you have to tell me now? Can't it wait?' He saw the slight shake of Imran's head as he turned to Rhette. 'Yes. I asked for the police autopsy samples to be tested again against Quinn's DNA. They proved what we had a hunch they might. I wanted to be able to hold Quinn if we caught him alive. These would have done it if...'

'Hood is behind her death. I testified against them but we got nowhere. Quinn was his man.'

'Do you have enough to arrest Hood?'

Imran shook his head. 'We will ... in time.'

Mark interjected before Rhette could say more. 'Is Hood still in Coober Pedy?'

There was a sharp intake of breath from Rhette.

'Yes and they are unlikely to leave before late this afternoon.' Imran said.

'Why?' asked Mark. 'I'd have thought he and his party would be gone by now with Quinn dead? They'd have heard.'

'Their aeroplane has a flat tyre. The mechanics are replacing it with the spare that they carry. But it can be a slow job getting a hoist under a plane of that size and weight.'

Mark raised an eyebrow. 'That's an inconvenience?'

Imran didn't try to hide his smile. He slipped a small paring knife he used for cutting fruit onto the bedside table. 'I had a walk around their plane this morning and the tyre problem was noticed after that.'

# Chapter 54

Just after lunch Ana, Rhette and Piet were discharged from hospital.

'You'll be better resting at home,' the doctor said.

As the senior doctor, he meant it but the hospital would always need the beds they were occupying. Their presence was causing media problems they could do without in the car park. The TV crews and their vans were a particular nuisance. The words came with a smile but his unvoiced frustrations had caused mental expletives.

When he woke up Pietie was the little boy Ana knew. Asking for icecream and another banana milkshake.

The doctor reassured Ana that the drugs Piet had been given had seemingly been slept off.

'Have you worked out what drugs he was given?' Ana asked.

'No, not really. We could have done blood tests but we decided that as he'd been awake and had eaten, it was better just to wait and see. Didn't want to start with the frightening needles after his adventure.' He offered a handful of special 'kiddie' plasters for Pietie's scratches he'd received during his abduction. The boy solemnly chose the smiley face designs he liked and showed Ana. All seemed well.

As Ana was a practicing psychologist the doctor was ready to let her handle any problems that Pietie might have. She seemed to shake herself from the total motherly role to the position of mother-observer. There was help available if needed and Piet should just be left to play in her security.

Mark arrived and took them through the back hospital entrance to his car. There was a brief debate as to where they should go, to a motel or as they finally decided, to Doug's house.

All their clothes and Pietie's toys were there and, although it felt they had been absent for ages, fresh food would still be there in the fridge and freezer.

There were no reporters waiting and they hurried into the cool house and settled at the kitchen table. There was an air of vulnerability between them at leaving the safety of the hospital. Ana was still on edge and Piet wasn't allowed to go far away from her side or to let be alone. When the women went to their rooms for clean clothes Mark played with Piet.

Rhette did not plan to go near Doug's room. That would come later and she had yet to come to terms with the death of the father she previously remembered for all the wrong reasons, she felt. 'At least I got to know him better,' she said when she put the kettle on for coffee in the kitchen. Doug's ghost, if he had one, was hardly to be there as his time in the house had been limited.

'Tonight we dine in style,' Mark said. 'I'll get the pizzas. Dave will know the best place. Six o'clock be OK?'

Rhette later went to Doug's room to check that there were no more guns. A closed door was not always enough deterrent for Piet's inquisitive steps as he was wandering about the house, with Bear, after lunch. He had energy that the adults lacked. She found no more guns but there was an envelope there with her name on it. She sat on the bed and read...

Mid afternoon and Rhette came and tapped on Ana's door. 'Can I borrow the car? I need to go out for a few minutes. Have a look around. Clear my head.'

'I'd come with you but Pietie's just dropped off again,' Ana said as she opened the door to show the boy sleeping all cuddled up with his bear.

'He looks so peaceful.' Rhette said. 'I might call into the police station. Some time soon I'll have to know what to do next about Doug. Harry will know.'

'Are you sure you can't wait until Piet wakes up. Surely you shouldn't have to deal with Doug on your own...'

'I'm OK. Harry'll be there. I do need to go out. Catch you later.' Rhette gave a wave, pocketed the car keys and went out the front door. She shrank back briefly. Here it was autumn but the outside temperature was horrific after the cool of the house interior.

Dieter Hood paced the motel suite.

Just after dawn he'd ordered everyone to be ready to leave immediately. Sean had gone to the airport to do the flight check procedures and refuel. He had phoned back to announce the flat tyre problem. Since then Erica and Fox had stayed clear as Hood paced the motel room.

The TV was on with the ongoing crime reports of the deaths on the opal fields. No names were given yet but Hood knew it was Quinn. He recognized the motor bike, he'd paid for it, and he'd contacted the bikie gang and confirmed his suspicions.

Hood had thrown off his suit jacket and started on the fridge alcohol samples early. It was everyone's fault, Quinn's fault, Fox's fault and Erica got a serve too. The rampage went on and on; the costs of the opal Erica had bought, the loss of the opal Quinn had stolen, on and on. His language was purple and one empty bottle of whiskey from the fridge was thrown across the bathroom.

At least it wasn't something of mine like before, Erica thought.

When Sean rang to say that they could leave in an hour Hood quietened. 'About fucking time,' he said. 'Get yourself sorted for the other destination we discussed,' he said to his brother.

'Aren't we going back to Sydney?' Erica asked.

'No. Sydney's finished. I'm making other plans.' He turned as Fox came into the room. 'You and Erica get organized. Go out to the plane. I've got calls to make.'

Hood made no mention of the explosive fire in his Sydney headquarters that he'd arranged. Carried out with a radio telephone link detonation. Jane, his cousin, had to be dead. She was just collateral damage. He was more worried about the overseas gang reception that would be waiting for him without the delivery of the opals as payment for the drug shipment he'd lost in Whyalla. The whole deal was buggered but someone would have to pay. He knew who the gangs would be looking for. 'Where are we going?' Erica said.

'Fuck it woman, just go. You'll find out when I tell you.'

Twenty minutes later Erica and Fox arrived at the airport.

Rhette sat in the car at the Coober Pedy airport, parked and partially hidden beside a steel hanger.

She knew Hood's plane and she was prepared to wait. Sean arrived and was now in the cockpit. She recognized him and she crouched low in the vehicle keeping well out of his sightlines. She saw another man and woman arrive. They got out of the taxi and quickly mounted the steps into the plane.

Rhette waited for Hood.

No blood red lipstick this time.

No damn it, she thought. Hood should know immediately who she was. Know who was going to kill him. And why. She shook her mane of red curls free and reached into her handbag. Her gun was there. Ready. Fully loaded.

The red lipstick.

She slashed the blood red colour across her lips.

# Chapter 55

'I've just got word that they're on the move.' Imran said to Harry and Mark at the police station.

Harry raised an eyebrow. 'You get word quickly about Hood and his people.'

'C'mon, you know I've got someone in there. Quite recently, and we've got a link. New technology. We don't need wires with satellites these days.' Imran used his vocabulary more easily when excited. 'I know also that Rhette Ryan is watching them getting ready to leave at the airport.'

'What!' Harry yelled. His tired slouch in a chair became a galvanized leap to his feet. He grabbed Mark's car keys and started for the door.

'She's only watching...' Imran began.

'You don't know Rhette. She's got a gun and I bet she'll try to use it.' He paused in his rush. 'Get me some backup would you,' he said to Mark.

'Wait, I'll come...'

Harry's feet pounded his urgency down the passage and people stepped aside to let him pass.

'Hell! The idiot!' Mark said, 'he's left his gun behind.'

Hood arrived in the hire car that had originally taken them from the plane to the motel when they arrived. The driver accepted the generous tip used to ensure his silence and took Hood's bag and placed it at the foot of the aeroplane's stairs. Hood waited perhaps a moment too long to board, waiting for his brother or Fox to come out to the carry his bag aboard. He didn't do that sort of thing when he had the rank and file to do it for him.

Time long enough for Rhette to get within ten feet from him.

'You killed my father. You killed my sister,' she said over the barrel of her leveled gun. Her voice was flat. Cold as an executioner's reading of death charges.

Hood turned slowly towards her. 'Do I know you? I think you have mistaken me for someone else.' He was cool. His gaze apparently on her face and not the gun. He was a man who had survived confrontations before.

'Don't be stupid with me,' Rhette snapped. 'You know who I am.'

'I remember. You were one of Sean's dolly's...' There was a laugh in Hood's voice as his eyes flickered towards the plane entrance where Fox was now standing.

Hood looked up at Fox. 'Kill her and get it right this time,' he said.

Rhette stepped sideways and her gun faltered between the two men. Faltered long enough for Hood to slip a gun out of his jacket and aim it at Rhette. His finger moved on the trigger but his gaze flickered instead to his hit man at the top of the plane's stairs. Better he did the shooting; better his gun pumped the bullet into this confounded woman.

A car roared towards them, horn screaming. Head lights flashing high and low beam.

'Shoot her,' Hood screamed at Fox.

Fox looked towards the car. 'Wait Boss!' He shouted. 'Stop! It's not worth it.'

Harry Shaw hit the brakes and the car skewed to a halt beside Rhette. He almost fell out as he swung the door open, grabbed her and pulled her behind him in one motion. Her back was hard against the car.

Fox had shouted again. The words lost in the hubbub but it was enough for Hood to pause from making the shot himself.

Harry reached under his coat for the gun that wasn't there...

'I have to kill him!' Rhette's scream brought all eyes back to her. 'He killed them.'

Harry prized the gun from her fingers and held it at the slack, aimed towards Hood's feet. Stalemate. 'Police,' he said loudly.

'Put your gun down.'

Rhette slumped, her knees folding.

'Do it, Boss. It's not going to help us get away now.' Fox said. His gun was drawn but also held pointing low.

Rhette's voice broke. 'He killed them. He killed them.' She brought up her hand as if she still held her gun. Gave a sob. 'I've got to kill him.'

There was a rasp of distain, 'I didn't kill anyone. Quinn did and he's dead.' Hood's gun hadn't moved from Rhette and Harry.

Rhette straightened. She pushed against Harry's arm. It was immovable barrier. 'Bloody Quinn was your man. Your killing machine. You killed them,' she shouted at Hood.

'Boss...' Fox called again. 'Let's get out of here...'

As if on cue Sean started and revved the plane's engines and the blast of noise drowned out Fox's voice. Hood frowned up at Fox and with his gun still on those below, he backed up the stairs past him. The plane began to move and Fox pulled the front stair inside the plane and the door latch moved to the shut position.

After a very short run up on the strip Sean hauled the plane into the air.

The police back up arrived, Mark leading the three cars.

Hood's plane was set on a course south.


Rhette sat in the police car next to Harry. Her hands rigid in her lap. Harry reached over to do up her seat belt, his face close to hers. 'It's alright,' he said. 'We'll get them... but not today.'

'Damn you! You should've let me kill them. I'll never forgive you.' She hissed venom.

'Yeah, Yeah. Don't bother to thank me.' Harry said and shook his shoulders as the adrenalin rush subsided.

# Chapter 56

Hood hadn't bothered to buckle himself into his seat. He stood hanging on to the backrest in front of Fox.

'I ordered you to kill Rhette. Or you should have let me kill the bitch. That's the second time she's been after me. She's dangerous.' His rage made his mouth white and his nose purple with engorged angry blood. Hood's eyes were almost manic with the glare as he gripped a handful of Fox's shirt front.

Fox pushed back into his seat away the verbal onslaught. 'Boss, bloody think. If you'd pulled that trigger we'd be still there on the ground, fucking cops everywhere. Not the time or the place. Even if we'd got into the air they'd have arrested us when we landed anywhere. C'mon man, at least we're away.'

His shirt was released and Fox smoothed it down.

Erica fought the impulse to speak. She had watched the scenario but not seen her ex-fiancé, Mark, arrive as they took off. Now she was frightened as she saw Hood's anger. She reached into her little carry bag and found her special box, and tasted some of the contents. That was better. Or it would be in a few moments.

Hood's face was still infused with anger when he turned away to go to the cockpit. Minutes later he came back to tell Fox that he wanted the plane rear door open once they were over the sea. In about half an hour.

Erica slept from her now stronger 'taste' unaware that she had become more and more under the control of her lover as he increased the purity of the drug he supplied. Hood sorted through the remaining opal he had. Opal potch was valueless and Quinn had salted the opal bag he had with the useless stuff. Hood knew why; to cover the fact that he'd taken half the good stones.

'Get me a couple of sick bags,' he shouted at Fox as the twin piles of stone grew. He loaded the bags and put one near the back door ready to dump out. The good opals went into his own bag. He scowled at Erica who was asleep in her seat. Some bloody comfort she was.

'Where're we going,' Fox asked.

'Sydney's finished. I've closed up everything there. New bank accounts, everything. Got a new plan. You'll find out in good time.'

The flight continued until they were low over a sea that glistened with blue innocence below. The plane was south of Port Augusta and over the deep waters of Spencer Gulf, off the York Peninsula coast.

Hood nodded to Fox. Open the door. Fox pushed out then slid the door sideways along the outer fuselage. A surge of air rushed in. Hood passed the bag of potch to Fox and he threw it out.

'Now her,' Hood pointed the sleeping Erica. 'Do it. Put her out.'

Fox stepped back. 'What? No Boss. I won't do that. She's your problem.' Fox had heard a rumour that Hood had disposed of a body before from the plane but not a living person.

Hood's face went red again. 'Fuck you, I'll do it myself then. You get her suitcase ready. It's going too.'

'Goodbye bitch,' Hood said and lifted the sleeping woman from her seat. His action was rough. Hurried.

Erica's eyes opened in surprise; then went wide as fear came into her sluggish drugged brain. She struggled as he dragged her to the door opening. She grabbed at his suit coat and began to shriek in terror.  He steadied. One arm gripped the screaming woman and the other held tight to the door rail. He shook her free of his coat and pushed her out of the plane. The sound of her scream was cut off as the plane surged on.

Her shoe, a silver high heeled sandal lay in the door opening. Hood kicked it out. It spun away and flickered as, for an instant, it caught the sun light.

Fox watched in disbelief. Horror. This was torture. Vulgar and even he, a killer, didn't want to think about what she felt as she fell to her death. Not a clean kill. Not as he killed. No one should die like this.

'Is her suitcase ready? That's next. Wait! She bought opal. I'll have that.' Hood breathed heavily from exertion. He rummaged through the case and extracted the opal gem presentation box, then the gift bag of opal earrings that Erica had bought for Jane. 'The whore had taste I'll give her that,' he said. He pushed the suitcase towards Fox. 'Heave that out now.'

Fox picked up the case and strode to the door.

Suddenly instinct told him something wasn't right. He was in danger. Usually he'd pick up on the feeling quicker but the barbaric act of throwing a woman out of a plane had shocked and muddled his thinking. Fox turned. His back to the sky.

Hood stood with his gun drawn and pointed at him.

'You're kidding,' Fox said. 'If you miss I'll get you...' He began the reach for his own weapon.

'I won't miss. This's pay off for not getting that fucking woman. Or Quinn!' Hood's voice had risen to a manic shriek.

'But...' Fox's gun cleared his holster. Too late...

Hood fired.

The bullet slammed into Fox's pelvis.

His leg crumpled under him. His body was flung backward towards the open sky and his desperate arms grappled in vain for the aircraft door frames. Fox's eyes locked to Hood's for a brief instant before he disappeared on the long drop to the sea. Johnny Fox felt the pain wrack his body but did not scream.

'You're dismissed,' Hood shouted after the falling body. The excitement of killing flushed his empty hard face.

He heaved and closed the door, latched it. It was very useful, he thought, that their plane had this door and not the opening shell shape of most others. The recollection of Erica's disdain at the lowly turbo-prop plane instead of an executive jet she expected came into his mind. He smiled. Maybe now she knew why.

Got rid of trash.

Got rid of evidence.

Got rid of the baggage.

The plane flew on, making a course alteration from due south to east towards the vastness of the New South Wales inland plains. The radar transponder was turned off before that course change and to all intents and purposes Hood's plane had disappeared southwards.

# Chapter 57

Imran pressed the earphones tighter against his head as though this would forge the connection again.

He muttered very quietly and precisely a Muslim prayer for the dead.

'It's finished, he said quietly. His eyes bulged; his skin became the colour of dirty putty as he sat back forward in his chair. 'Our contact has gone.' Imran clicked off the recording device.

Mark, Harry and Lex again occupied chairs in the squad room. They waited, none of them with energy and all existing on second winds, for Imran to speak to them.

He took a moment to compose himself.

Mark suddenly sat up. 'Was your contact Erica?'

'No, but sadly she was a very mistaken woman. Another led by her passions rather than her excellent intellect. A pity. I was listening ... wait I will play you this terrible transmission.'

'Immy, you're not implying?' Harry said as Imran tapped the screen on the iPad he had connected.

At first they could hear only a heartbeat, the thub-a-lub that is the centre of every living person and animal. Imran raised his hand in a 'wait' gesture and adjusted the volume and brought up the voice sounds.

'No one can wear a wire without it being discovered eventually,' Mark interrupted.

'Yes they can, if it is put into the body like a heart pacemaker and interacts with an overhead satellite. I told you there were better technical applications these days.' Immy frowned slightly as the airport confrontation between Rhette and Hood came to their hearing. Then a voice boomed. 'That's Fox,' Imran said.

'Fox, Johnny Fox, was your contact? You've got to be kidding.

He's Hood's killer. His right hand man.' Harry said.

Imran said nothing just indicated that they listen. There were changing responses to the quietened thub-a-lub of Fox's heartbeat as events played out. The sounds rolled on to the conclusion when Erica was killed and her scream faded. Then they heard, as the recording went on to the moment when Fox's voice said, 'This's it...' his heart pulse soared to impossible speeds of tachycardia ... then stopped.

There was an abrupt end of the transmission. A technical silence, tinged with white noise, droned on.

The silence was repeated by the detectives listening.

A stunned silence.

'There was only one shot,' Mark finally said. 'Did the bastard knife Erica?'

'We'll have a trace on the plane. Get them when they land...wherever that is.' Lex said. The whites of his dark eyes flashed as the enormity of a question brought his hand to his mouth as though to close off his words. 'You're not saying...'

'I am. Hood threw them alive out of the plane. He's got the plane to do it. One of the design features is the ability to open the rear door in flight. Usually it's very useful for rescue and delivery purposes and all that and perfect for people like Hood to jettison drugs and the like. I never believed that he would or could throw out living persons.'

There was another silence as the detectives grappled with the understanding of Hood's act. The barbaric nature of it.

'And I wondered why Hood didn't have a jet when I went to the airport. Almost thought I was at the wrong plane...' Harry mused. He straightened. 'OK Immy, you've held your cards too close to your chest. Fox? I'd never have guessed. Tell us the rest.'

'I've run Fox since the trial when they got off the drug charges thanks to a very clever but shonky lawyer. Number of reasons, I suspect, why he responded. He was dying of cancer. Too many smokes and all the rest. He tried to tell Hood at one stage and Hood did not want to know. That did not help Hood in the long run.' Imran's reporting was in his usual precise fashion.

'So it was a dying man's conscience? Didn't think he had one,' Harry said.

'Maybe, but more than that he fell in love. He knew he could not ever do anything about it but he wanted some way to try to protect her.'

'With Erica?' Mark asked.

Imran smiled for the first time since he had listened to the murder of Erica and Fox. 'No, hardly. She obviously had only disdain for him from what I heard. He loved Rhette Ryan. But only from a distance when she met Sean and he saw what the Hood brothers did to her and her sister. He was at the trial, as I said, and sat there listening to Rhette being slandered by the lawyers. Then twice he managed to disobey or not carry out Hood's orders. At his own peril. Once in Adelaide, you were there that night Harry. And today when Hood told him to shoot her. He was also somewhat lax in officially finding Rhette for Hood to carry out the contract he'd put on her. Fox found out where she was in the Police Protection Scheme but he kept it to himself.'

Harry sat with his elbows on his knees, shaking his head in disbelief.

'But he was still a killer,' Mark insisted.

'Yes, he was. He had no option but to pass on Hood's orders to Quinn, and mostly those were orders concerning people who were criminals themselves.' Again Imran raised a hand when Mark began to interject. 'That family in Whyalla. That was Quinn's idea. I heard Fox chastise Quinn for doing it. A shouting match over the phone. He made an enemy of Quinn that was going to be finalised one day, one way or another. If they ever met again, only one of them would be alive at the end of it.'

Mark was silent as the enormity of the day sank in. 'I still can't say that I could like the man...' he said. 'Did Fox know who Quinn really was? That he was wanted by us?'

'No. Quinn started with Hood about three years ago. No one knew him as Demetrius Quinn. He was almost nameless as Hood's hit man. He edged Fox out of that role. Not that Fox minded except for the inferior position it gave him with Hood. He gave the order and Fox relayed them on to Quinn. It did give him the opportunity to hedge and protect Rhette somewhat.'

'It might have changed him latterly, but he's still a killer.' Harry said.

'Of course he was. He was never forgiven for his past actions but we used him to get information to one day get Hood. I will add that he's never personally killed since he's been run by us. Run like a spy too. It was quite thrilling.' The hint of a smug smile flitted across Imran's face.

'But it's finished now. From what I've heard Hood's closed his Sydney base. I'll bet you a dollar to the Harbour Bridge he's going to start up somewhere else,' Harry said.

'Yes, and he's got plenty to do it. Thanks to the internet banking he's transferred millions elsewhere. Probably got a new identity. He's not only closed Sydney he's wiped it out and his warehouse home. Destroyed any evidence we might have found there too. Hood has a sister somewhere, there is only a hint of her but she could be his connection back to Syria. But the Sydney operation is over...' Imran paused. He looked at the incredulous faces of the detectives before adding, 'incidentally there was a body found there, his cousin Jane. Hood is the total psychopath. Not even poor Jane escaped.'

Harry frowned and balled his fist, 'What a bastard!'

Again the pause as the detectives nodded in agreement.

'But we will try to trace the plane, his brother Sean and anything else.' Imran said.

'And I suppose with the government changes in air requirements they didn't have to put in a flight plan? Suppose it's possible that air traffic won't even be tracking him. Sean wouldn't have announced his take off...' Mark said.

'You're right. It's all more lax these days with so many small private planes about. We wouldn't have known Hood was even in Coober Pedy except for Fox as my contact. After that the plane was spotted at the airport.' Imran said. 'They will have turned off the plane's identifying transponder by now.'

Lex indicated the array of devises on Immy's desk. 'So none of this is admissible at a trial here is it. We can't get him on it.'

'We will try when we get him but its all hearsay, no witnesses, no one to collaborate that it is Fox's voice. None of it, but we know and we are patient. We'll get him one day. Like you got Quinn.'

Mark snorted. He pushed his hands through his too long brown curls as he stretched his tired legs. 'We did but it took us more than four years. Too much trauma and too many dead bodies.'

Imran permitted himself a small stretch. He was tired too but there was nothing like the challenge of finding and exposing Hood and his brother. He had patience, and he looked across at Lex. A useful man; just maybe he could coerce his transfer to the Adelaide or to the Canberra federals to work with him, and Harry who would be recalled there soon. There was always a tomorrow in the fight against crime.

Mark got to his feet. 'I'm done. I'm taking pizzas to Ana and Rhette. Coming Harry? You too you guys?' The men trooped out of the squad room. Imran and Lex decided to go back to their motel rooms as both were tired from working the crime scenes and the emotional end of Erica and Johnny Fox. Reports, endless reports to be written after they'd shared a cafe meal together.

Both men knew that Mark and Harry had unfinished business with the women.

# Chapter 58

'Did you bring me any chippies?' Pietie ran across the front room as Ana opened the door to the two men. He hurled himself at Mark.

'I sure did,' Mark's laugh came as a huge relief at the reception from the woman and child. He was still shaken from killing a man, even if it were Quinn, for the first time in his career. 'We've got enough for Bear too.'

Ana stood aside and watched as Harry deftly took the pizza packs out of Mark's hands for safety to let him scoop up the boy. One hand was needed to manage to open the chip bag as Pietie sat on Mark's other arm.

'Good. Bear's hungry too.' Chip in mouth the boy said with a solemn expression. 'Bear has got to have a bath. Mummy says he stinks. I peed on him and there's a horrid petrol smell,' the last words were whispered furtively into Mark's ear. The warm chippy breath wafted to Mark's nostrils and he realised just how hungry he was.

Mark planted a quick kiss as Ana came to him and Piet struggled, as small children do, to get down. The boy ran to the kitchen clutching the chip bag. Mark completed the hug and the kiss was returned, repeated and lengthened.

'We'd better get to the kitchen or Harry'll have scoffed all the pizzas,' Mark said.

'Later then...' from Ana.

'Yes, later...' Not quite the time to admit how hungry he was, for pizza, and their kiss had endorsed his feelings for Ana.

She laughed and led the way to the kitchen. There Piet was already on a chair eating his chips. Behind him Harry and Rhette had little reserve as they kissed.

'At last,' Ana said to Rhette. 'He's been making puppy dog eyes at you ever since the first time I saw you two together.'

'I've known this woman for years. Always out of my league and reach.' Harry said as Rhette smiled up into his face.

'You ugly old sod,' Mark laughed at Harry. 'How'd you score such a beautiful woman as Rhette? You've always been such an old sad eyes.'

'Never mind about the sad eyes, I've been waiting for someone...' he almost said since his first marriage was finished years ago due to work pressures but thought the better of it. Instead he said, 'and forget about the old, I'm not much older than you.'

The couple moved apart and Harry's eyes lingered on Rhette's face before dropping to the pizza boxes. 'Men! Bellies before us,' Rhette chortled, her face flushed. She ran a hand over her mouth and chin, 'I'm not sure I like the five o'clock shadow though,' she said.

'Listen woman, we haven't eaten today. Not a skerrick. Starving in the name of crime prevention.' Harry said. It was almost a lie; the station had provided sandwiches at lunch time, cheese again much to Harry's disgust. Indifferent cheese hardly qualified as food. 'Ditto the whiskers. We've been busy and I thought the designer beard was what you women wanted these days.'

They sat and ate dinner. Pietie's voice chirped when it wasn't full of chips and pizza. Tomorrow I'll get decent food into him, Ana thought as she watched him eat. She could hardly take her eyes off him except to look at Mark across the table through her eyelashes.

She's bloody flirting with me, Mark thought. He saw the colour, a flush basked in her cheeks like a flush of sunset. She was beautiful with the trademark swatches of white hair framing her face. Even the dark moons under her eyes were fading.

Rhette and Harry sat very close together, not disguising their feelings, although there were moments when Rhette's face saddened. The day's encounter with Hood and the shock of her father's death were still there. Her forgiveness for Harry wasn't an issue.

After dinner, with Piet safely in bed, discussions between the four got under way.

The men told the end story briefly.

Detail would come later although the women knew most of it. The men had decided not to mention that Erica and Fox were alive when Hood had thrown them from the aeroplane. Some points of detail were too distressing to be discussed with the public, no matter how close they were. If a case ever got to court it may come out but now wasn't the time.

Rhette had found Doug's will in his bedroom. She had no idea what he was planning to do when he went to 'check his mail' as he'd said, at the Post Office. Or that he had even written a will.

She laid the document out on the table and read the legalese words to them. There was silence at the contents. He'd left everything to Rhette, except a million dollars to the Mine Rescue Team, a million to Ana and Piet. He'd mentioned the special piece of opal that Piet had been drawn to; it was to be his when he was older, if he were found alive. Otherwise it was Rhette's.

Surely he was delusional when he wrote it; they said as one after the other the comments started around and across the table. Rhette turned over the paper where Doug had written a financial explanation. Millions of dollars were in the bank for her, the gifts to the rescue team and Ana were listed. The note included an additional cache of special opals in the safe deposit box that were to go to the South Australian Museum. This was a skull of an opalised plesiosaur, a small juvenile but it was almost complete, was written in brackets with the bank numbers. There were more opal pieces that Doug had cut himself also in the safe bank box. It was an amazing amount listed in dollars and stones for Rhette to deal with, and the shock of it had barely begun to register.

'I can't live with a millionairess. I'm a simple copper.' Harry said and broke the silence into pieces. He almost looked aghast at

Rhette.

'Oh we're living together are we? Well, can you live with a woman with a crime sheet? I've got a past they mightn't like,' Rhette retorted. The 'they' being police hierarchy.

'I can get around that and they'll have to too. Not sure about all those dollars.' Harry made zero signs in the air.  His ugly yet handsome face creased with apparent shock.

'Well it looks as thought it all comes with me, my baggage. Take me or leave me.' There was a pause. 'I've had only a few minutes to think. Doug left us, our mother Katie and me, maybe his abandonment was as a result of his experiences in the Vietnam War.'

Ana quietly interjected. 'Many of the soldiers still have problems with post traumatic stress syndrome. It's ruined many lives, of the families as well as the men's.'

'It probably was something like that. I don't know. Anyway he left us to chase a dream and maybe this is his way to pay us back. I only wish that he'd come home to us before, been with us instead… ' Harry took Rhette's hand. 'There's only me left now. But there are friends and people who helped me when I was on the Police Protection Scheme. The flying doctor service that got me safely out of Adelaide. Doug's bag's there, it was with his will, and maybe he's listed his old comrades who still need a hand. I'll follow it through. There'll be enough left to drive Harry mad though, she said.

Harry's groan was interrupted as his phone buzzed. 'Sorry I though I'd turned that off,' he excused himself, and left the room.

Harry returned.

'That was Immy,' he said. 'They've lost track of the plane. It disappeared off the screens. Been reports of a fire ball explosion south of Kangaroo Island that could have been a plane, or a meteorite hitting the atmosphere for that matter.  There's been a hanger fire and cars stolen out a property near Hay in New South Wales, and police reports of a plane answering to Hood's was sighted over the Grampians in Victoria.'

'They'll keep looking?' Mark asked.

'Sure. But most likely the first we'll know of Dieter Hood, and brother Sean, will be an increase in crime somewhere.' Harry said.

'It'll keep you busy then? You, Imran and the feds.'

Harry slapped Mark's shoulder. 'While you and Ana are all cosy somewhere, most likely in Adelaide rather than Whyalla, we'll be chasing the big stuff from the eastern states.' He slung his arm about Rhette and his look was hopeful. 'Maybe I won't be going back alone either.'

'You're amazing Harry! I haven't even had the chance to tell Ana that I've been recalled to the majors and you blab it out.' Mark said. He reached over and slung an arm about her slim waist. It felt very good even in his exhausted state. She smiled into his eyes.

'Major Crime can't do without you.' There was a laugh in Harry's voice, 'You do act as a crime magnet so they want to keep you under some sort of control...' he said.

Ana and Rhette exchanged glances. Ana's life would be in Adelaide rather than in Darwin, and Rhette opportunity for love and stability was to follow Harry.

Life was going to be interesting, and not as planned, when they all sorted themselves out.


# End...

# ABOUT THE AUTHOR

*Rendezvous on the Opal Fields* is the 'follow up' novel to my first book, *Rendezvous at Lock 6,* which was set in Port Lincoln then on the Murray River out of Renmark, South Australia.

Both mystery thrillers are 'stand alone' books that are not essential to be read in a continuum. However some of the characters do continue from one book to the next ... and as I have suggested this is because the characters were not 'finished' with me or their stories. I'm not sure if this is an example of poor plotting or that as characters develop in my head they gain a momentum and a fascination.

After many years of writing poetry, short stories and film scripts in many genres - including Sci-Fi - retirement finally gave me the time to follow my inclination and to write that first complete novel. Like many before me I had un-named and unfinished piles of writings that, in film parlance, ended up on my editing floor. They would never see the light of any day given their limitations.

However sometimes a little success came my way with competition wins, being read on ABC National Radio and an added thrill of a short animated film, *The Long Beach,* which I wrote was made and shown in film festivals all over the world.

My previous working and general life experiences include a degree in Social Work; work in the prison system, the Criminal Court, housing, domestic violence and general counseling areas. On the medical side I've been a nurse, a St John Ambulance officer 'on the cars' and as an Air Attendant, instructed with the Royal Life Saving Society, and taught children to swim over many years. Study in diverse areas included archaeology and history have coupled with travel and life as a wife and mother have all given me arenas to stretch my writing wings. I write about places I know - except in Sci-Fi where the Universe is hardly enough in space and time - and the Australian landscape, flora and fauna, is where I belong.

I am very appreciative of comments I have received from readers of my work, especially those who have read *Rendezvous at Lock 6,* and welcome more - praise naturally, but constructive critiques are welcome.

My email address is: helenvr@southernphone.com.au

For better or worse more, and two or more characters, have knocked at my keyboard as I wrote *Rendezvous on the Opal Fields* telling me that they are not done and they may get their future chance.